A VETERAN'S QUEST FOR JUSTICE

A VETERAN'S QUEST FOR JUSTICE

GEOFFREY HUDSWELL

Rev. date: 03/23/2020

GIFT

To order additional copies of this book, contact:
Xlibris
800-056-3182
www.Xlibrispublishing.co.uk
Orders@Xlibrispublishing.co.uk
810892

DEDICATION

For Rob taken from us too soon.
And for all serving and retired members of HM Armed
Services, especially those who made the ultimate sacrifice,
and those maimed both physically and mentally.

AUTHORS NOTE

This is the revised edition of the book, which I originally published under the title "Veterans Justice".

The characters are entirely fictious, as are the organizations: Balkan War Investigation Team (BWIT) and Valhalla Investigations (VI).

The West Mercian Fusiliers is a fictious English County Infantry Regiment.

The Norfolk Constabulary does exist, but the officers portrayed in this story are my invention.

The Corps of Royal Engineers is a real life sabre arm of the British Army.

I have had the privilege of serving in both of the above entities.

CHAPTER 1

T he rain was lashing down and with the high winds was being driven almost at the horizontal, or that was the impression that Pegg got when he looked out of the constable's report room window. The pools of water on the rear car park erupted into miniature waves, with each gust of wind, causing spray to fly across the shining asphalt surface. A cat sheltering under one of the cars looked a picture of abject misery.

"Sunday night shifts," muttered Pegg, "don't you just love 'em?" He returned to the crime file he was working on. It related a case of shoplifting from one of the town's supermarkets. The thief was young man; Pegg had arrested him and taken him down to the Police Investigation Centre at Wymondham. He was a persistent offender, and hence the decision to hold him there in the cells overnight, before putting him before Norwich Magistrates' Court in the morning. Pegg needed to complete the file, before getting out of the station. He went back to his paperwork.

Archie Pegg was a constable in the Norfolk Constabulary, stationed at East Dereham. He was a large, proportionately built man, six feet two inches tall and fifty-four years of age; he had not been a policeman for all his working life. He had been born in Norwich; his father had worked at one of the city's breweries, and his mother had been employed in a shoe factory. His parents were not married, his father abandoned Archie and his mother when Archie was four years old. His mother tried her best to bring up the young boy. She suffered bouts of depression, after turning to alcohol her health went downhill, and she died at the age of thirty-two. This resulted in the young Pegg having to be put into care. He was twelve years old at the time. In spite of the trauma of losing his mother at such a young age, Pegg did well at school. He excelled in mathematics and science, physics being his favourite subject. Unfortunately, out of school he mixed with the wrong crowd. This course of behaviour resulted in his coming to the attention of the police. At the age of fifteen he appeared before the youth court. He was given the option of approved school or of joining the Army. He chose to enlist. His skills in maths and science were recognised by an astute recruiter, who recommended him to be signed up in the Royal Engineers apprentice tradesman programme. He attended the army apprentice college at Chepstow as a junior sapper and after three years he qualified as an electrician. At the age of eighteen he became an adult soldier. He went on to complete field engineer training.

He was posted to a Royal Engineers field squadron. His subsequent service took him to BAOR, UK, South Atlantic, and Canada. He had operational tours in Northern Ireland and the Falklands. After completing twenty-two years' service, he left the Army with the rank of staff sergeant. He could have gone a lot further but various incidents in his early career, had caused his regimental conduct sheet to be an interesting read. These subsequent misdemeanors affected his career advancement. Many of his peers within the Royal Engineers, who were with him at the army apprentice college were majors, and in a couple of cases, lieutenant colonels. Pegg was never a man to hold a grudge. He still kept in contact with them through The Royal Engineers Association and its various sapper reunions and of course the annual Waterbeach weekend. An event which is attended by sapper veterans of all ranks, where old comrades got together and reminisced, socialized, renewed friendships, and consumed enough beer to sink a battleship.

Pegg completed the crime file and faxed it through to the Wymondham Police Investigation Centre (WPIC), after which he left the hard copy in the WPIC's internal mail pigeonhole. He made himself a cup of coffee and returned to the report room. He finished his coffee, and gathered his equipment, in preparation to going out on patrol. The phone rang, and he picked it up,

"Constable's report room PC Pegg."

"Archie, Inspector Grimes, come down to my office, before you go out."

"Sure Guvnor, I'm on my way."

Pegg collected his CS canister, and torch, gathered up some papers and his packed meal and flask and walked to the Inspector's office. Bill Grimes was the duty inspector for the whole of the Mid Norfolk Division. Grimes was a career policeman, having joined the Force from university. At twenty-six he was relatively young for an inspector. He had a good relationship with Pegg, unlike many other senior officers, who said that Pegg was "difficult to deal with".

Pegg tapped on the open door of Grimes' office.

"Come in take a seat, Archie".

Pegg entered the office and sat down.

"What can I do for you, Guvnor?"

"You are less than six months from your retirement date, have you considered continuing after the age of fifty-five?"

"I've given the matter some thought, but I have not come to a definitive decision yet".

"I know that things have been difficult for you, these past eight months, but the Norfolk Constabulary would like to keep you on. I personally regard you as a good, hardworking officer, and I consider you to be a valuable member of my team, Archie. I appreciate losing Cath was a terrible blow for you, and I hope that we continue to be a source of support".

Pegg thought of Cath's death in the road accident, the result of a drunken driver colliding head-on with her car. She had been on the way home from visiting her daughter, who had given birth to Cath's first grandchild, a little girl, just two months old. Pegg had married Cath four years ago. She was a divorcee, and she had married Pegg, after meeting him at a village fete, which Pegg had attended in his role as the local beat officer. Pegg himself had never been married before. He always jested that he was far too young to get hitched!

The loss of Cath had hit Pegg very hard. After her death, Pegg immersed himself in his work. He volunteered for extra shifts, and stayed on after the end of his shifts, without claiming overtime. At times he had to be ordered to go home. Fortunately, Pegg had forged a good relationship with Cath's children, her son and her daughter. He in turn had found comfort in having them around.

"Thanks for your kind thoughts, Guv. It means a lot to me," said Pegg.

"Well you are off on leave for three weeks tomorrow. Give it some thought and let me know how you feel when you get back. Are you going anywhere?"

"I have decided to go off to the Peak District and do some walking; there are a couple of old army mates I'd like to look up. I'll be taking the caravan and pitching up in one of the small camp sites. Some are open all year, and the 'van has good heating".

"Well enjoy yourself, Archie. I'll bid you farewell, as I've got to go to Wymondham to do a couple of prisoner reviews, I'll not be coming back to Dereham tonight." Grimes got up and shook Pegg's hand.

With that, Pegg left his office and went to the back door of the station. It was still raining; the wind was strong and some of the gusts were quite powerful. He walked over to where a Land Rover Defender was parked and put his kit into the vehicle. He walked to the staff car park and to his own vehicle, which was also a Defender, but instead of a blue and yellow Battenberg paint job, this was dark green. He unlocked the car and a dark shape softly whined, a wet nose nudged Pegg's right cheek.

"Shh, boy. We don't want folk knowing I've brought you in to work," Pegg hissed.

The animal was a black miniature poodle, called Fred. He had been Cath's dog, and he was a year old when Pegg first met her. Fred had become very attached to Pegg, and when Cath died, Pegg did not have the heart to give him up. Like all poodles, Fred was a highly intelligent animal, and since Pegg had lost Cath, he become Pegg's inseparable companion.

"Come on then. Let's go and do some patrolling, boy". And with that, Fred followed Pegg to the other Land Rover.

Pegg opened the passenger door, and Fred jumped in and sat himself on the blanket, which Pegg had previously placed on the seat. Pegg went to the driver's side and got in. He switched on the radio and the other equipment. He was pleased to see that the fuel gauge showed a nearly full tank. He called the force control room.

"Delta Romeo four two, VK, show me ten-two in the four two area".

"VK, Delta Romeo four two, all received. VK standing by," the call taker in the control room answered.

Pegg reversed the vehicle out of its slot and drove out of the station. The exit barrier lifted, and Pegg turned left into Commercial Road, through onto the High Street, and into

Market Place. The rain had eased somewhat. There were very few people about. It was nine o'clock so Pegg did not expect to see much else, given the state of the weather. He continued past the George Hotel, and saw that the bar and restaurant were devoid of any clientele. He drove down the hill on Swaffham Road and continued west towards Scarning and Wendling. By now the rain had stopped.

Traffic was very light, all the way to the A47 at Fransham, Pegg crossed the A47 and continued north towards Beeston, passing the old airfield, which was now given over to turkey sheds. As he neared the village, the radio crackled to life.

"VK, Delta Romeo four two, I have a job for you."

"Four two send details, over", replied Pegg.

"VK, are you anywhere near to Whissonsett, over?"

"Four two, currently in Beeston, about twenty minutes away."

"VK, you are the nearest I've got. There has been a report of vehicles at a vacant unit on the industrial estate outside the village. Can you give it a look, I am getting some back-up for you from North Walsham, they are about finished with an RTC, on the A149, should be there in about thirty minutes?"

"That's fine show me attending", answered Pegg.

Pegg made his way out of Beeston and headed north to Mileham, and then through Tittleshall and on to Whissonsett. Norfolk is a county which is crisscrossed by countless lanes especially through the rural areas. These are referred to by the DoT as C roads. Some of these are almost the same as B roads, whilst others are narrow with passing places. Being a Sunday evening, it was fortunate for Pegg that there was very little traffic, and as a result he was able to make good progress. He slowed down, as he approached the village of Whissonsett. The small industrial estate was to the west of the village and off the main approach road to the village. The entrance road to the industrial estate was off to the right. Pegg switched the vehicles headlights off, and parked up in a small lay-by, about twenty metres into the estate. He decided to leave Fred in the vehicle, the dog would start to yap if Pegg found anyone in the vicinity.

"Stay here, boy, and be a brave dog and guard the car", whispered Pegg.

He got out of the Defender, secured the doors, and started to walk into the estate. The estate consisted of about twenty units. The units were accommodated in two long blocks, each being hundred metres long, and housing ten units. The two blocks faced each other. Between the two blocks was a concrete apron, which was a hundred and twenty metres long, and fifty metres wide. The area was illuminated by a solitary streetlight which stood at the far end of the right-hand block. It was not raining, and the wind had dropped as well.

In front of the end unit of the left-hand block Pegg saw a box van parked beside the unit's open door. The van appeared unattended, the back of the van and both the cab doors were l open as well. He saw that the key was in the ignition; he took it out and pocketed it. Pegg wondered what was going on, Sunday evening, a vacant unit; it all seemed moody. He crept round to the doorway. The first thing that hit him was the pungent odour emanating from the interior of the unit. It was a smell with which he was all too familiar. Cannabis. Voices came from the inside of the unit. There were two men inside the unit. It appeared they were setting up some sort of cannabis farm. He returned to his vehicle and told the control room what he had found. The control room informed Pegg that the other call signs were five minutes away, and that he should take no further action until they joined him.

"I'll not argue with that," Pegg said to himself. He got back into the vehicle. The poodle gave a soft whine; Pegg fondled one of the dog's ears, "Shh, boy, settle down", he whispered. At the same time, two patrol vehicles turned up. The leading vehicle pulled in behind Pegg's Land Rover, and the second one behind that.

Pegg got out of his vehicle and met the four officers. He briefed the new arrivals as to what he had found. He explained that the box van was not going anywhere, showing the officers the van's keys before putting them back in his pocket. He briefed them as to what he had found. They returned to their respective cars and drove to the front of the unit and surrounded the box van.

Pegg exited his vehicle and ran through the open door of the unit, followed by the other four officers. The source of the pungent odour was a mass of potted plants each being about 18 inches high. Electric cables and lamps were laying around the plant pots, none of them appeared to be connected or assembled. The interior of the unit was illuminated by strip lighting. Opened cardboard boxes were strewn over the concrete floor. Amongst all this paraphernalia were a couple of frightened looking men. Their ethnicity seemed to be either near eastern or south European. One of them tried to run away, but he was quickly apprehended by one of the officers.

Pegg informed the control room that about the two suspects apprehended, and what had been found in the unit. Neither of the two detainees seemed to speak English, nor did they indicate what nationality they were. Nevertheless, both were informed that they were under arrest on suspicion of being in possession of an unlawful substance. A search of the two men revealed that they were both carrying a large quantity of cash; one had a UK Driving licence, in the name of Enver Haji, born in Albania, and resident at a London address.

Pegg offered to remain at the scene whilst the other officers conveyed the two prisoners off to custody. It would require a full team to process the van and the contents of the unit.

"VK Delta Romeo four two, you are scheduled to finish at 0700, stay on site until 0600, by which time we'll get somebody out to you?".

"Four two understood I'll remain until relieved, four two out."

Pegg was relieved that he was not going to be involved any further. All he had to do was to write a statement, and that was an end to it. He returned to his patrol vehicle and let Fred out. The dog left the vehicle and for about 2 minutes trotted about with his nose to the ground, Pegg let the animal have free range, until he started to approach the van and the entrance to the unit.

"Fred, no, come here", the dog immediately returned to where Pegg was standing, "Come on, boy let's have a wander, and a play."

The dog looked at Pegg, cocked his head to one side, wagged his tail, and gave a quiet "woof". Pegg reached into the vehicle a retrieved a very soiled tennis ball. The dog jumped up, and sat down, staring intensely at the hand in which Pegg held the ball. His tongue was hanging out. Pegg threw the ball along the concrete apron which separated the two blocks of units. The poodle raced after the ball and retrieved it. He then raced around carrying the ball, occasionally jerking his head, releasing the ball, and catching it again. He trotted back to Pegg, shaking his head, terrier fashion, and growling softly. He dropped the ball at Pegg's feet and sat down.

"Again?" The dog gave a yap, and Pegg picked up the ball, and threw it again, the dog repeated his actions as before. After ten more minutes of play, Pegg returned to the vehicle, the dog followed him with the tennis ball in his mouth. Pegg opened the passenger door and reached inside for a bowl and a bottle of water, he poured some water into the bowl, and put it down. The dog dropped the ball, and proceeded to lap up the water, the dog paused, when the bowl was nearly empty. Pegg retrieved the ball and the bowl, and placed them along with the bottle, back in the vehicle.

"Up", said Pegg, and the dog, jumped into the vehicle, and settled down on the blanket. Pegg went to the back of the vehicle and retrieved some forms from the stationery box, after which he sat in the driver's seat. He took a clip board, and fastened one of the forms, a witness statement front sheet, and proceeded to write, he continued adding two more pages to the document.

The weather had cleared completely, and a half-moon had appeared. After about forty minutes Pegg had finished the statement. He read through it twice, and then filled in the back of the front sheet. After signing the bottom of each sheet, he returned to the back of the vehicle, and placed the statement in his briefcase. He would fax a copy of it to where the officer dealing with the suspects was located. The original will go into the internal mail.

After this Pegg got out his police notebook and started to update it. When he had finished ate his packed meal. He had balanced the top of his thermos on the dashboard and poured some coffee from the flask. He gave Fred a small piece of his cheese and pickle sandwich.

When he had finished his eatingl, he got out and brushed himself down, Fred was already sniffing around the driver's seat, and licking up the few crumbs which Pegg had dropped. Pegg glanced at his watch, it was three thirty. He got Fred's lead; the dog whined and jumped over the driver's seat, landing at Pegg's feet. He sat at stared at Pegg, his body quivering, as Pegg bent down to fix the lead to Fred's collar, the dog gave an excited yap. Pegg locked the vehicle and walked around the inside of the estate, always keeping the open unit in sight. As he walked round, the reason for the dog being on its lead was apparent. Several rabbits were grazing on the grassed area which surrounded the periphery of the estate. Like all dogs, Fred had a penchant for chasing these long-eared creatures, and once he was on the scent, he would be gone for ages. Pegg had tried hard to control the canine's natural hunting instincts. On this occasion he did not want to have to waste time getting the dog to come back again.

As he was walking round, his thoughts were directed to the things he wanted to do at the end of the shift. Before going back home, he would call on Angie, Cath's daughter. Her husband Ross was away in France on business. There was a problem with her washing machine, Pegg had got the replacement part, a relay switch, once this was fitted the problem with the appliance resolved. Angie could have got an engineer out, but when Pegg found out about the problem, he would not hear of it. He would see if there was any shopping that he could do for her. Then there was the job of getting his stuff together for his trip out to the Peak district. He would try and get everything ready, in order to leave early on Wednesday morning.

He walked around for another hour, before returning to vehicle. He put Fred back on his blanket and sat there for another 10 minutes, before seeing the headlights of a vehicle, which was proceeding quite slowly towards his location. When it finally came into view, he saw the blue and yellow Battenberg markings. He glanced at his watch it was five forty-five. It was his relief, early for a change, he thought. The car parked beside Pegg's vehicle. He got out and saw the vehicle was double crewed.

"Archie, what you say, my man?" said one of the officers. Pegg knew him, Dave "Splash" Waters. He was, like Pegg, an authorised firearms officer. They had spent many years on Royalty Protection duties at various Royal residences in West Norfolk.

"Bearing up, Splash, I'll be glad of a spot of leave after this shift. Booked off for three weeks, I have to use up time off in lieu of overtime," replied Pegg. "What's the score with this job?"

"Drugs Squad are taking it on, apparently there are a lot of these hydroponic installations being set up throughout the county; they reckon it's down to a gang from London. Anyway, we are staying up here until a team comes up from Yarmouth. So, it's PUFO for you Archie," said Waters.

Pegg said his farewells and drove off. By this time, it had got lighter, and Pegg took his time driving back to Dereham. He arrived back at 6-30 am, by which time it was broad daylight. He parked up and took the dog to his own vehicle and left the animal on the front passenger seat. He returned to his patrol vehicle and took his kit out. He informed the control room he was back at Dereham. He faxed the statement he that had written to the custody suite where the suspects were being held, the original he placed in the Drug Squad's pigeonhole which was located the CID office. At 7 o'clock he left the building and got into his Land Rover. Fred went and sat on his lap.

"Come you daft dog, get over to your side", Fred looked up at him, with pleading eyes. "Do it now". The dog reluctantly went over to the passenger side and sat down on his blanket. Pegg picked up his phone and phoned Angie his stepdaughter.

CHAPTER 2

The call was answered almost immediately.

"Angie, it's Archie, I hope I have not called too early."

"No, it's fine Archie, I was up anyway, the baby needed seeing to", said Angie.

"I've got the bit for your washing machine, and I thought I would come around on the way home and fit it for you. I expect the laundry basket is overflowing."

"Archie you're my knight in shining armour, yes please do come, the sooner the better, I'm am running out of stuff for the baby," said Angie.

"See you in about twenty minutes, by the way is there any shopping you want, I am going past Tesco," said Pegg.

"Great", said Angie, "Fancy having your breakfast with us?".

"Love to, what about a shopping list?", said Pegg.

"No worries I'll email one to you. Can you receive email on your phone; I've got your e-address."

"Angie, I may be a bit of a dinosaur, but I do have a smart phone! Just send the list", said Pegg.

Pegg ended the call and drove out of the station and headed to the Tesco supermarket located at the south of the town. He parked in the store's vast car park, after which he checked this phone and saw that Angie had sent her shopping list. I was quite large; she had indicated she would give him the money when he got to hers. Pegg entered the store and spent the next twenty minutes or so collecting the items Angie wanted. He also got some items for himself, after which he went to the check outs, which at this time of day were not busy at all. He went through the nearest one and paid for the items. On the way out he selected a couple of cardboard boxes from a pile near to the exit. These he placed in the trolley, before making his way to the cash machine, where he withdrew £300. He made his way back to the Landrover and placed Angie's groceries into the larger of the two boxes and placed his purchases in the other one. After securing the boxes in the back of Land Rover he left the car park.

Pegg drove onto the by-pass, to head west on the A47 to Swaffham. Angie lived in small close off the Mundford Road, to the south of the town centre. The house was a detached property, with 3 bedrooms. She and Ross, her husband, had bought the house 4 years ago. It had been a struggle to get the financing sorted out, but they had managed. They had been together for four years, the latter two as a married couple. The baby, Catherine Rose, was now 10 months old. She was Cath's first grandchild, and she doted on the baby girl. Now Cath had been taken from her family. Life is not fair thought Pegg as he drove the 10 miles to Swaffham. The bastard who killed her would be back with his own family in 3 years' time. The judge gave him 6 years, but he would be out after completing half his sentence. Pegg told himself not to dwell on this and try and move on. But he knew he could not.

"Oh Cath, I miss you so much", he said to himself, "but I promise I will always be there for Angie and the baby."

Pegg turned off the A47, and into Swaffham, three minutes later he pulled up outside Angie's house. He picked up the larger of groceries, and walked up the front path, before he got to the front door, it was opened by a slim blonde-haired woman, in her mid-twenties. Pegg thought to himself she was a younger version of her mother; the resemblance was uncanny. She was wearing a sweatshirt and blue jeans; her shoulder length hair was tied up in a ponytail. She threw her arms round Pegg's neck, nearly causing him to drop the box.

"Hey, steady on, Tesco's finest produce will be decorating the front path if you don't watch it, my girl", chided Pegg. He put the box down at his feet and looked at Angie. Her eyes were red, and there were tears in her eyes.

"Come on, my love, let's get this stuff inside, I'll get the part for your washing machine and my tools from the 'Rover. Is it all right if I bring Fred in, he's been well exercised, so he won't be his usual boisterous self", said Pegg?

"Of course, I'll leave the back door open and he can sniff around the garden", replied Angie.

Pegg carried the groceries through to the kitchen, he placed them on the table, and poked his head around the corner of the living room door, Catherine Rose was in her play pen, sitting on her bottom, gurgling away and examining a rattle. She turned around and looked at Pegg, before letting out a squeal of delight. She got up and toddled to the edge of the playpen.

"How's Miss Pretty today", said Pegg, going over and plucking her out of the pen. The baby gurgled with delight and placed a wet hand on Pegg's nose. Pegg swung her gently and the child squealed with pleasure.

"Archie, how much do I owe you for the groceries?" said Angie.

"Don't worry about it, some other time," replied Pegg.

"Here I've got some cash, I went to the bank yesterday", said Angie.

"Okay, the receipt's in the box", Pegg said, before continuing, "I'll just fetch Fred and my tools."

Pegg placed the baby back in her playpen; the child gave a short cry of dissent, before continuing to play with the rattle. He went out to the Land Rover, retrieved his toolbox, and let the poodle out of the front passenger seat. The dog trotted up the front path and into the house. Pegg secured the vehicle. When he got in he put his toolbox in the hallway and joined Angie in the kitchen. Angie gave Pegg the money for the groceries.

He could hear the baby in the living room, squealing away, he glanced in, and saw Fred with his muzzle poking through the bars of the playpen, and trying to lick the baby's hand. Like all dogs, he associated infants and small children, with the chance of obtaining morsels of discarded food.

"Fred", hissed Pegg. The dog looked round at Pegg.

"Oh, leave them be, she loves to see him, and he is such a big softy with her", said Angie.

"Right", she continued, "what would you like for breakfast, Catherine has had hers, and I've been waiting for you before I have mine. I can do eggs and bacon if you like, now you've got me some groceries in."

"I'll just have some cereals and toast please, I'll not have anything too substantial. Whilst you sort that out, I'll get the washing machine going again." Pegg said.

"Great", said Angie, "I have about two loads to do today. The weather looks as if it will stay dry; it'll make a change to get stuff out on the line."

Pegg went out to the utility room, and pulled out the washing machine, he unplugged it and took off the top to access the back of the controls; he took out the relay board, and replaced it with the new one, after which he replaced the panel. Before switching it on again he checked the connections for continuity with a multi meter. The lights illuminated on the control panel. He briefly ran through a quick programme, before switching it to spin. He pushed the machine back into position again.

"There you go, Angie, all working again. Do you want me to put a load on for you?"

"Thanks, but no; we'll have our breakfast first, I'll put a wash on after that."

Pegg packed his tools away, came into the kitchen and washed his hands. He sat down at the table, and helped himself to a bowl of cereal, and took a sip of coffee. Angie sat opposite him and helped herself to cereals. After a while Pegg asked,

"How's it going, I can see you have been crying, is the baby being difficult?"

"She's such an easy child, no, it's not having Mum around, I really miss her, and with Ross being away this past week, it has got on top of me, I really should get a grip of myself", she said.

Pegg reached across the table and placed his hand on hers, "Look", he said, "We both miss her, and I think of her all the time, but we have got to keep it together, and for her sake, we have to carry on. I do not have any family that I know of, so when you and your mum came into my life, I gained the family I never had. You all mean everything to me, and I want you to know I will always be there for you."

"Oh Archie, you are the real dad I never really had. I am so glad you had those years with Mum."

Pegg, released her hand and continued with his meal, he buttered a slice of toast, "When's Ross due back?"

"He's got a flight from Amsterdam to Norwich this afternoon; he should land at 5-30 pm. He is flying from Toulouse to Charles de Gaulle, and a connecting flight from there to Schiphol. It's great really as he avoids going to Stanstead or Gatwick."

Ross was an engineer, who worked for Rolls Royce; he was down at Airbus's factory in France, with a team sorting out some modifications to the current engines for the new A350 airliner. He would normally be based at Norwich airport, but due to a shortage of personnel, the company had asked him to stand in.

"Does he require picking up", said Pegg.

"No, he's getting met by his brother, but thanks for the offer."

Pegg finished and put his plate in the sink.

"When are you off to the Peaks?" asked Angie.

"Wednesday morning, I think. I'll spend the day tomorrow getting the 'van ready, and I should leave after eight the following morning"

"Would you like to come over for some supper tomorrow evening?" asked Angie

Pegg thought before answering, he did not want to encroach on her time with Ross. He had a good relationship with Angie and Ross, and he wanted it to continue. After being separated, they needed their own space.

"Thank you so much, but I need to get a good night's rest, having done a week of nights, my body clock needs to be realigned", Pegg replied. "Give us a quick call tomorrow, to let me know Ross has got home okay. If there are any problems regarding Ross's lift, let us know."

He went into the living room, Fred was fast asleep on the floor beside the playpen, the baby had put her hand through the bars of the 'pen and was stroking one of his ears. Pegg went and reached into the 'pen and picked the baby up. Catherine Rose gurgled, and clung to Pegg, with her arms round his neck.

"Goodbye, sweetie, he whispered into her ear," he put her back down, and she grabbed her rattle, tottering to the far side of her playpen.

He retrieved his toolbox and went to the front door; he put the money Angie had given him for the groceries on top of the table in the hallway, next to the phone. He took his leave.

"How much do we owe you for the washing machine repair", asked Angie?

"Oh, I'm not sure, I got it from the wholesale supplier, I'll have to check my account, I'll let you know", replied Pegg, knowing only too well that he had no intention of taking any money from her.

He gave her a peck on the cheek, and left the house, with Fred trotting behind him. Pegg unlocked the vehicle and opened the passenger door, and the poodle jumped in, after placing the toolbox in the back, he climbed into the driver's seat. He gave a wave to Angie, who was still standing on the doorstep, and drove off.

Twenty-five minutes later he was back at his house in the village of Gressenhall, just to the north of Dereham. The house was just on Litcham Road. It was a detached four-bedroom property, which Pegg had purchased after he left the Army. He had been a member of the Armed Forces Savings Scheme since he started as a Junior Soldier, and after 24 years the saving plan had accrued enough money for him to have bought the house outright. The house had benefited from a woman's touch after Cath had moved in with him. Although Pegg had installed an efficient heating system, and had installed a new kitchen and bathroom, as well as decorating it throughout, the house was sparsely furnished. Its contents were functional and rather bland. Cath had transformed it, and whilst not replacing any of the fitted items in either the kitchen or the bathroom, she had enhanced it with the addition of new curtains and blinds. She had also got Pegg to assist her in sorting the front and back gardens. Prior to this both these spaces had been grassed, which Pegg had kept mown. There were no flower beds in front of the house, and none to the back either. At the right-hand side of the house Pegg had constructed a hard standing with enough space to accommodate two vehicles and a touring caravan. It consisted of both cast reinforced concrete and paving slabs. apron.

Cath had got him to make flower beds around the grassed areas both at the front and at the back and the beds had been planted out with shrubs and perennials. The house also had detached brick and tile garage. The garage had long ceased to be used for its original purpose. Pegg now utilized it for a variety of purposes such as storing tools and equipment, and a fridge freezer amongst other things. He had installed electric lighting and 13-amp power sockets.

He parked the Land Rover at the side of the garage and let Fred out. The dog went into the garden and started to investigate the residue of spoors which had accumulated overnight. Nose to the ground, the poodle commenced his patrol. Pegg unlocked the side door to the house and returned to the vehicle where he retrieved the groceries and the cut flowers. He secured The Land Rover and went through the side door and into the kitchen. The alarm control panel started to bleep, Pegg went over to it and disarmed the system. He then unpacked and stowed away the groceries. The flowers were placed in a bucket, which he filled up with water taken from the butt at the side of the garage. He put the bucket and flowers in the garage and returned to the house.

He went upstairs, undressed, and had a shower. When he had finished he went downstairs again and let Fred in. The dog got into his basket, looked up at Pegg, and promptly went to sleep. Pegg went upstairs again and got into bed. He almost immediately went into a deep and dreamless sleep.

CHAPTER 3

P egg woke up with a start, he looked at his watch, it was 2-00 pm, and the house phone was ringing. He got up, put on his dressing gown, and went downstairs. He walked into the sitting room and picked up the handset from its stand, "Hello", he said, making his way into the kitchen.

"Archie Pegg, its Tony Spratt," the voice on the other end of the phone said."

"Tony, it's been almost two years since we last had a couple of scoops together, at the Sapperfest, how are tricks?"

"Not good I'm afraid, in fact things are pretty crap."

Tony Spratt was another ex-sapper, he and Pegg had served together many times. He had not been in the Royal Engineers as long as Pegg He left the army after serving for twelve years. Tony Spratt had been a sapper in Pegg's troop, Pegg being a sergeant at the time, when their unit was serving in the Germany. Spratt had left his native Belfast, when he enlisted in the Army, and had never returned to live there. He had been back for family visits, but when he'd left the army, he had started up as a self-employed carpenter and joiner. He had settled in Derbyshire, residing in a small village outside Buxton. He had married a local girl, and they had three children, all of whom had left home. He had built up his business, and now employed three people. The enterprise had branched out to fitting kitchens and bathrooms. His main clients were customers of the big stores like B & Q, and Homebase; Spratt's company was contracted to fit the kitchens and bathrooms which had been ordered by the stores' customers.

Pegg walked to the back door and let Fred out, before coming into the living room, and sitting down:

"Shit, Tony, the business is not going down the tubes, is it?"

"No work is fine, actually we are run off our feet, and I may have to take on some more staff. No, it's not that, it's something else, Archie. I don't know where to turn; I don't really know who to go for help. I remember you saying if there were any problems regarding police type stuff, just get in touch," continued Tony.

"Well why not tell me about it, I may not be able to give an answer right away, but I may be able to get in contact people who can," said Pegg, as he retrieved a pen and a pad from the sideboard, before sitting down again, he continued:

"Now Tony, shoot."

Spratt spoke, and after talking for about 10 minutes, Pegg interrupted him.

"Stop right there, Tony," he said. He paused and said nothing.

"Are you still there Archie."

"I'm here Tony. I don't know if this is Providence, but I have some leave, and I am heading up your way on Wednesday. So, give me your email address, and I will send you a brief list of info I require. Can you do this as soon as you can?"

"Sure," replied Spratt, he gave it and Pegg wrote it down.

"Now Tony, this is important, I need you to respond to the email I send you. I can start to make a few inquiries from my end, before I come up. Are you near a computer?"

"Sure, I have my tablet with me, I have to look at a job, but I will be home in an hour, so just send me your list", said Spratt.

"I'll phone again on Wednesday, after I am at the site I'm booked into. Keep your chin up, my man", said Pegg.

"Cheers, Archie, you're a real pal".

"No worries, sappers must stick together", replied Pegg, before ending the call.

He went into the kitchen, Fred was scrabbling at the door; after letting the dog in he went back upstairs, washed, shaved and got dressed. He returned to the kitchen and made himself a cup of tea, after which he fetched his laptop, and sat down at the kitchen table.

"Right Fred, we've got some work to do, Tony is in deep shit, and needs our help", he said.

The poodle looked at him, his head cocked to one side. Pegg looked at the notes he had taken whilst speaking with Spratt.

Tony had told him that he was under investigation by the Balkan War Investigation Team (BWIT), regarding the murder and mistreatment of Kosovan refugees in the '90s. Tony said that he had been attached with his section, to a company of the second battalion West Mercian Fusiliers (2 WMF). The unit had been engaged in peacekeeping duties outside Pristina, the capital of Kosovo. It had been a difficult time, trying to keep the ethnic Albanians (Kosovars) and the local Serbian population from fighting each other. Tony told him his section was carrying out mine clearance operations, and as far as he was concerned was not involved in any policing type jobs.

Pegg looked up the British Army web site and clicked on the link to the West Mercian Fusiliers. He read through the regiment's recent history. 2 WMF had indeed been deployed to Kosovo, but its operations were confined to the securing and maintaining a refugee camp in the south of the province which had been set up for Kosovars. Meanwhile a company of the battalion had been detached to the northern part of Pristina to protect the Serb minority. After the Kosovan war, there was a toxic atmosphere between the Kosovar majority and the indigenous Serbs, half of whom had fled to Serbia. He could not find any details of 2 WMF operating in the southern part of the city. He looked up the BWIT website and viewed its remit. He found that its UK investigators worked for a private agency called Valhalla Investigations, which had been contracted by BWIT to gather evidence of possible criminal activity involving members of the armed services.

He looked up Valhalla Investigations. The company's head office was based in Berlin, and it had subsidiaries in most EU countries including the UK. The UK branch of the company took on work for firms of solicitors and insurance companies. It had recently been granted a contract to carry out work for the Services Prosecution Authority (SPA).

Valhalla Investigations (UK), had amongst its staff a number former police officers, these people were carrying out a lot of the investigation work. At the same time these investigators were also employed in looking into allegations of misconduct by the Armed Services in Iraq and Afghanistan. Pegg thought to himself, I hope none of these investigators are former members of the armed forces.

"Now who was making these complaints", Pegg said to himself. He entered into his browser *"solicitors/Balkans/allegations."* There were not too many hits, but one stood out, Lawyers for Personal Justice. Pegg brought the firm's home page up. *"We take on cases where the complainant has been the victim of mistreatment and abuse by members of the armed forces or other government agencies. We also deal with claims for negligence* and injury *as a result of work or traffic accidents"* He saw that this enterprise operated out of an address in Nottingham. Pegg noted its name and contact details. He reviewed the list he had made. He composed an email to Tony Spratt, after checking what he had written, sent it.

Pegg cleared up the kitchen and the bedroom. After this he went to the garage and packed some secateurs and the flowers, as well as a small folding stool. Except for the flowers he packed all the items in the rucksack. He collected Fred's leash; the dog yelped and jumped up and down, as he always did when Pegg had the leash to hand. He donned the rucksack and put the leash, the dog almost thrust his neck into the collar. Pegg took the flowers and locked the back door.

"Come on boy, let's check on Cath." He left the house and walked the mile and a half to St Mary the Virgin church. Cath was interred in the churchyard. Pegg had just had a headstone erected. He visited the grave at least once a week. After fifteen minutes of walking they reached the churchyard. He kept Fred on his lead. The dog sensed that this was a special place and he never cocked his leg, whilst he was in the confines of the churchyard. People were used to seeing them both in the churchyard's cemetery

The church was special to Pegg; it was where their marriage had been blessed. Pegg and Cath attended the church services on an occasional basis, more at Cath's urging than Pegg's. Now that Cath had died, Pegg felt closer to her here than any other place.

He put his rucksack down. Cath's grave was in a corner of the churchyard under the shade of an oak. Acorns were starting to fall, and a few covered the newly laid turf he had laid, after the headstone had been installed. It had taken some months for the ground to settle before the stone could be erected. The stone was of polished granite and inscribed on it read, *"In loving Memory of a dear Wife and Mother Catherine Pegg, died 21 April 2010 aged 48 years."* Pegg took the existing flowers out of the vase at the base of the headstone, he emptied it out and replaced it with water from a bottle he had in the rucksack. He took the secateurs and trimmed the stems of the flowers he had brought with him, before placing the trimmed blooms back in the vase. Next, he took out the stool and placed it next to the headstone and sat down. Fred sat next to Pegg who picked the dog up and placed him on his lap.

"Well Cath, we've just finished a week of nights and I have got a few weeks leave. These are made up of a culmination of annual leave and time off in lieu of overtime," he said, before continuing, "We're off to that site outside Buxton you liked so much. We're booked in for a week for starters, I can see us extending that. On another note, I have been offered the option of carrying on in the Job, after fifty-five, I can't decide what I want. I wish you were still here, my darling, to advise me. Still after this holiday I may have an inkling of what I want."

Pegg remained there for another 20 minutes, by which time the poodle had dozed off. Pegg gently lifted the dog off his lap and put him down. The dog whined softly and stretched. He went to the headstone and sniffed it, before looking up at Pegg.

"I know, boy, we both miss her." He picked up a few more acorns and packed his things up in the rucksack again. He retrieved the end of the leash and with a kiss on the top of the headstone, left the churchyard, dropping the old flowers and other detritus into the wheelie bin at the entrance to the churchyard.

He walked back to the village, calling at the Post Office Stores. He purchased a couple of pints of milk, a loaf of bread, a book of First-Class postage stamps, and a packet of envelopes. He tried to support the village shop as best he could. "Use it or lose it", was a frequent refrain in rural communities, the same applied to the village pub.

He had got to the shop shortly before it closed. By the time he got back to the house, it was 5-30 pm. He put the bottle and secateurs back in the garage and put away the items purchased from the village shop. Fred went over to his water bowl and lapped noisily. He looked up at Pegg, water dripping from his muzzle.

"Yes, I know, boy, I'll get your feed going in a minute." Pegg went to the draining board at the kitchen sink. He took out dog bowl and went over to a cupboard where the dried food was stored. After filling up the bowl, he placed it down next to Fred's water bowl. The dog immediately gulped and snuffled his way through the food.

Pegg went over to his laptop, which was where he had left it on the kitchen table. Tony Spratt had replied to the e-mail Pegg had sent him. Pegg went to the sitting room and switched on the wireless printer, before returning to the laptop, where he printed off Spratt's e-mail. After which he took a file folder and placed the e-mail in it together with the pad, on which he had been making notes.

He fetched the caravan sites handbook and looked up the telephone number of Oak Tree Farm Camping Park. The park was a family run site, which Pegg and Cath had visited before. He called the number; his call was answered almost immediately. Pegg asked if there was a pitch available with electric hook up for a touring caravan. The call taker said that the site was nearly empty, and that there were several pitches available. Pegg asked for a pitch for 7 days initially, with an option for another week. He said he will be there on Wednesday. The call taker advised that he should not arrive before midday. Pegg ended the call and went into the kitchen. Fred was licking his muzzle and standing by his food bowl. He looked longingly at Pegg.

"Sorry boy, but that's all you're getting." He picked up the food bowl and placed it on the draining board. He made himself something to eat and poured himself a glass of beer. He ate his food and drank his beer. Afterwards he washed up and put away the cutlery and crockery.

He returned to the laptop, taking the folder with him. He typed into his browser *"Lawyers for Personal Justice"*.

He brought up the company's home page. The firm was in the Arnold district of the City of Nottingham, off the Mansfield Road.

He printed off the firm's contact details; then he went into their staff page and noted the names of the partners and paralegals. He looked at their history. The firm was set up by the senior partners, Mehmet Ali and James Smithson, in 1999. The firm was registered with the Law Society; as well as the run of the mill work, such as house conveyancing, and criminal law work, there was a large emphasis on litigation work. Industrial accidents, motor injury claims, and claims against the British Government for alleged mistreatment by members of the Armed Forces.

He went into the history of the senior partners. Mehmet Ali came to the UK with his family as a child, the family had escaped from the Communist regime of Enver Hoxha in Albania in 1975. His father was a doctor and was granted asylum for himself and his family. His father was accepted as a qualified clinician and had worked as GP in East London. Ali was an only child, his father put him through university, and he obtained a two-one law degree. After taking the Law Society exam he qualified as a solicitor in 1989. He initially worked as a junior partner in a practice in East London. He took on criminal law work, before moving onto civil law, and litigation work. He kept up his Albanian roots, by mixing with the Albanian emigre population in London and elsewhere in the country.

He met up with James Smithson in 1995 and went to work with him in Nottingham. There they worked together for a small firm which dealt in "No Win no Fee" cases, which were basically incidents where the claimants had been injured, or had property damaged, as the result of alleged carelessness by an individual or organisation. The advantage of the "No Win no Fee" system, was the claimant did not have to pay any money up front. The solicitors funded the case, and if they won, they would claim their expenses on top of the compensation they obtained, which they would give to their client whilst the solicitors would pocket the rest. If they lost, they would claim their expenses from a one-off insurance policy, which they had taken out on behalf of the claimant. The system had led to a great deal of abuse, and the government was looking to do something about it.

Pegg did some research on Smithson. He had qualified as a solicitor around the same time as Ali. He had acted as legal adviser to many legitimate groups on the left of the political spectrum, such as anti-blood sports, animal rights, and green issues; very laudable, thought Pegg. But as he read on, he saw that Smithson had gone on to specialise in negligence claims. He had been quite successful in winning claims for industrial injuries and for medical negligence. It did not seem he was involved in the claims against military personnel. It would appear the Lawyers for Personnel Justice had two sides to its business. Ali dealt with the war crimes and refugee asylum claims, Smithson dealt with the accident side.

Pegg looked at his watch it was now 9-00 pm. He read through what he had written on the pad and placed it in the folder. He switched off the laptop and put it away together with the folder. He went into the living room and phoned Angie. The phone was almost immediately answered by a male voice.

"Ross, it's Archie, welcome back home, my man, how did it go?"

"Archie great to hear your voice, thanks for looking out for Angie and the baby, and fixing the washing machine," said Ross.

"No worries."

"Yeah, we sorted the glitches out in France, and now it's back to the day job at Norwich, until the next time! Angie said you forgot to pick up the money for the groceries, and the cost of the part for the washing machine."

"Look", said Pegg, "You are my family, can't a dad, even a step-dad, do something for his kids? I do not want anything for them."

"Thanks, we really appreciate what you do for us."

"I am off to Derbyshire on Wednesday, so I will be dropping by on the way, will you be in?" said Pegg.

"I won't but Angie will, what time?"

"About 8o'clock, too early?"

"I don't think so, I'll ask Angie, she's in the bath."

"No, don't disturb her, she can call me tomorrow, any time, I'll be getting the 'van ready, so I'll not be going anywhere," replied Pegg, "Catch you later, Ross, have a good week."

"You too, Archie, many thanks again."

"My pleasure, bye," said Pegg, and ended the call.

Pegg went and sat down to watch a bit of television, he flicked through the channels before selecting a nature programme, wildlife in Patagonia. At ten he let Fred out into the garden, whilst he got ready for bed. He undressed and had a quick wash. He donned his dressing gown on, went downstairs, and let Fred in. The dog got into his basket, and with a sigh, went to sleep. Pegg checked his water bowl, before turning out the kitchen light and closing the door. He went upstairs and got into bed. He went to sleep immediately.

CHAPTER 4

I t was after eight the following morning, when Pegg awoke. He heard the dog scrabbling at the kitchen door. Pegg slipped on his dressing gown and went downstairs. He heard Fred whimpering, "Hold on, boy," he said. He opened the outside door of the kitchen and the poodle ran out into the garden. Pegg looked at the thermometer on the wall outside the kitchen door,

"Umm, 12 degrees, looks like it might be a good day", he said to himself.

He glanced into the garden, and saw that Fred was doing his business. He thought to himself, that he needs to clear up the lawn and remove the deposits left there over the past few days. He left the outside door open and closed the kitchen door to the lounge and went upstairs. He washed, shaved and dressed in a pair of old jeans and sweatshirt. By the time he got downstairs again, Fred was in, and lying in his basket. The dog went over to Pegg and sat in front of him. Pegg bent down and tickled the poodle's ears.

"We've a lot to do today, boy, so the sooner we start the better."

He made himself some breakfast, cereal, boiled egg, toast and a cafetiere of coffee. He sat down poured himself a mug of the coffee and ate his breakfast. Having eaten he cleared up and finished upstairs. He spent the next five minutes clearing up the lawn of the deposits left by Fred.

Next it was to the garage, where from the roof space he retrieved the equipment he required for the caravan. Water containers, wastewater tank, awning and poles, camp chairs and table, as well as a host of other stuff. He laid these items out on the floor of the building.

After this he went to where the caravan was parked. It was a two-berth trailer which Pegg had bought the previous year. He and Cath had used it a few times; the longest was a two-week tour of Scotland, stopping at various sites in the Highlands. They had planned to go to France this year. He and Cath had previously been out in it for a couple of weekends in the Spring. Pegg had debated whether to sell the 'van, but had second thoughts, and decided to hang onto it for the time being. He unlocked it. It was dry inside and needed very little doing to it apart from giving it a hoovering and wiping down the cupboards and floor.

He went into the house and got together some cleaning materials and a bucket of water, and then proceeded to clean the interior of the 'van. After completing this task, he connected up the garden hose and washed the exterior of the 'van down. By the time he had completed all cleaning it was getting on for midday. He packed away the stuff he'd used for cleaning and went into the house and made himself a sandwich and a cup of tea.

After a brief rest, he went out, taking Fred for a walk, he was out for about an hour. His route took him along Bilney Road towards Bittering. In his head he went through the things he had to do before he contacted Tony Spratt tomorrow. A "to do" list had already been compiled. There were several agencies he would need to research, and in some cases make contact. He also needed a copy of 2 WMF war diaries whilst they were in Kosovo. This would show where the various sections of this battalion were located at the time of the alleged incidents of mistreatment and abuse.

He carried on with his thoughts until he got back to the house again.

After writing out a shopping list, he drove into Dereham, where he parked up, and left Fred in the Landrover. He purchased some more stationery, as well as a small wireless portable printer from the small computer shop which he had always patronised. He returned to the vehicle, where Fred reluctantly gave up his place on the driver's seat and moved back onto his blanket. Pegg drove to the Morrison store and filled the Land Rover up with diesel, when he'd done this, he called in at the Police Station, and went to the constables' report room. The station appeared deserted except for the public enquiry clerk in the front office. He made a note of some addresses and telephone numbers from the report rooms copy of the Police Almanac. This publication held all the contact details for all the police forces in the United Kingdom, as well as the Garda Siochana, the police force of the Republic of Ireland. He checked his pigeonhole in the constables' report room. There was nothing there that could not wait.

He left the station and drove back home. It was now getting on for six o'clock. He gave the caravan one final check and went inside the house. He unpacked the portable printer and set it up and printed a couple of test pieces from his laptop, after which fed Fred and prepared something to eat for himself. Whilst waiting for his meal to cook, he phoned North Walsham police station. The call taker gave him "Splash" Waters home number, he phoned and managed to get hold of him.

"Splash it's Archie, here, I am off to the Peak District tomorrow, as I may need to contact you, may I have your email address? I do not want to use your job email."

"Sure," said Waters, "what are you going to be doing to warrant needing it?"

"At this moment I may not need to contact you at all, but I am just covering all bases."

Pegg went on to explain what had happened to Tony Spratt, and what Pegg intended to do in order to help Tony. Waters being an ex-serviceman himself (Royal Marines), had complete empathy with Pegg and Spratt. He gave his private email to Pegg, who sent him a test email in order that Waters would recognise that the emails were from Pegg when they arrived in Waters' inbox. Pegg put the phone down and saw to his meal. He got a bottle of beer from the fridge, poured it into a glass, sat down, and ate the meal.

After finishing he cleared up and went about selecting the clothing that he would need for the forthcoming trip. He laid the chosen items out in the spare bedroom. These he would load up in the morning, together with the groceries and items he had purchased earlier. He then went and watched some television. The weather forecast for the following day would be sunny and mild throughout East Anglia and the East Midlands.

"Looks like it's going to be nice for our trip up to Derbyshire tomorrow, Fred", said Pegg to the poodle, who was gently snoring on Pegg's lap. Pegg switched the television off and sat deep in thought. He came back to thinking of Cath, and the times they had been out in the 'van. The current trailer was the second one they had. The first was a used Bailey, which they had got for a song. It needed a bit of attention, but Pegg and Cath had worked hard to get it up to an acceptable standard of repair. They had decided to see if they liked caravanning, before spending a deal of money. The Bailey was traded in for a new Swift, and thanks to the work they had done on the Bailey, they had got a good trade in price. Cath had chosen the 'van, it had been a real success. And Pegg was looking forward to spending many years of touring with her. He put the thoughts away.

"Come on, boy, time for bed", he said as the poodle reluctantly gave up his warm place on Pegg's lap and jumped onto the carpet. Pegg got up, and went to the kitchen outside door, the dog followed, having a good stretch before trotting out into the back garden. It was a clear night, with a slight chill in the air. Pegg waited until Fred had finished in the garden, before locking up for the night. He watched the dog climb into his basket.

"Good night, boy, it's an early start in the morning", said Pegg before turning out the kitchen light and going upstairs to bed.

CHAPTER 5

P egg slept fitfully, he got up at half past five and after washing
and dressing, went downstairs to the kitchen. The dog was
still in his basket; he yawned and gave a slight whine, before
lying down again. Pegg left him be and got himself some breakfast
and a mug of tea. After he'd finished, he made some sandwiches
and a flask of coffee. He went outside and unlocked the caravan
and spent the next half hour stowing away the clothing, food and
stationery items plus his laptop and the portable printer. He removed
the trailer's wheel and hitch locks and went to the garage, where
he collected the items he had placed on the floor the previous day.
When he had loaded the items up, he unplugged the hook-up cable
and stowed it away in the front locker of the 'van. He checked the
two propane gas bottles, they were both full.

He went into the house again, grabbed his gilet, his cap, and the
keys to the Landrover. He reversed the vehicle up to the caravan and
hitched the 'van up to the Landrover, after that he connected the
trailer light cable, and tested the lights.

He went back into the house again and set the heating at
"holiday" and armed the burglar alarm.

After locking the house up, he opened the drive-way gates. The
poodle had already jumped into the front of the Landrover and was
sitting behind the steering wheel. "Move over, Fred", said Pegg
before getting into the driving seat. He eased the outfit onto the road
and switched on the four-way flashers. After closing the driveway
gate, he drove off.

He arrived at Angie's at a little before eight o'clock and parked the outfit outside facing the way he had come in. It was a bit of a squeeze maneuvering the outfit around at the end of the close.

Angie had opened the front door before he got to it. He went in and gave her the spare keys to his house and the code for the alarm.

"I've left the heating at a low setting, there's plenty of oil. I shall be away for at least two weeks and I have also left a note on the door giving your number as the key holder. I do not expect any problems."

"Don't worry; I'll check the house occasionally. Is there anything special that needs doing?" she said.

"No, I think that is all bases covered", Pegg said. He went on to explain what he was intending to do. He continued, "Angie would you mind if I call upon your expertise regarding IT issues when I'm up there in Derbyshire?"

"Of course, what sort of stuff are you talking about?"

Pegg went on to explain if he needed to get into the "dark web", questions about systems.

"Ooh, Archie this all sounds very exciting!" she exclaimed.

"I do not know what I will need, but it's good that I have an expert to fall back on. I have written down the address of the site I'll be staying at." He gave her a piece of paper with the details.

He went into the kitchen, where Catherine Rose was in her high-chair, having finished her food, at least that's what it seemed as her face was clean and the tray to the high chair was devoid of the detritus that accompanies a baby's mealtime. The child squealed when she saw Pegg and demanded to be picked up.

"Come on, Poppet, "he said as he lifted her up. Angie smiled.

"You two!" she said.

"I hope you don't mind; I can't help myself sometimes."

"No, we've finished, I shall get her dressed and we will go out to my friends down the road," she said.

She said that Ross will be home early today, he is due a few days off, as a result of the extra work he had to do in Toulouse. Pegg gave the child back to her mother and kissed them both before taking his leave.

The drive to Derbyshire was uneventful. He arrived at the site at about half past one. He booked in and paid for a week's stay, with the option of another week. The receptionist said it was not a problem, as the site was not even quarter full. He was directed to a pitch, with a hard standing and an electric hook up. Pegg drove the outfit round to the pitch and proceeded to set up the 'van and awning; by three o'clock he was finished. He decided to stretch his legs and took himself and Fred off for a stroll around the area. Whilst he was out, he called Tony Spratt.

"Hi, Tony, Archie here, I'm all set up now, I'm at Oak Tree Farm Camping Site, about a couple of miles outside Buxton, do you know it?"

"Yes, you are not too far from me; I am in Fairfield just to the east of Buxton itself." He gave the address in Waterswallows Road.

"I've got that Tony, right."

"How about coming up this evening for a bite to eat, I've got some more stuff through the post from these Valhalla people. It does not look good for me, Archie, I am really worried."

"Look Tony, I am here now, we'll sort this out. I'll be round at about seven that okay?"

"Look forward to that, Archie, see you then." Tony then ended the call.

Pegg returned to the site and let himself into the 'van. He left Fred in the 'van whilst he went to the shower block. He returned to the van, got changed and fed Fred.

It took about twenty minutes to get to Tony's address. It was about ten to seven when he knocked at Tony's door. Tony was a short wiry man of about forty; he spoke with a soft mid Ulster brogue. He had short cropped dark hair, and blue eyes. They went into the living room, Tony gave Pegg a beer. His wife was out at her daughters and would not be back for a couple of hours.

"Right where do you stand at the moment regarding these allegations?" said Pegg.

Tony showed him a letter he had received that morning.

"According to this investigators are coming to visit me. I must call the number to arrange a time during the day for them to see me. I have not done anything yet; I was waiting for you to come and give me some advice," he said.

Pegg read through the contents of the letter, he re-read it, and said:

"Right Tony, it looks as if they are coming to see you to get a general idea of what your side of the story is. From my experience this is not at all acceptable. I see they have not mentioned anything about you having some form of legal advice prior to them seeing you, or during the interview, they say it will just be "an informal chat". In my view this is a load of bollocks. Here's what I suggest you do."

Pegg went on to explain that Tony should arrange a time to see these investigators, but that Pegg should be there as well. He asked Tony when the best time of day for this would be. Tony said that he had a lot of jobs to do, and he worked all day, not only doing some of the fitting jobs himself, but also to visit other sites where his workers were installing kitchens and bathrooms. His men were good hardworking people, but some were new to this line of work, and Tony was training them up. He could really do without taking time off.

"Right", said Pegg, "have you got an office or somewhere else apart from home. I don't feel these people should come here. Your misses could do without it."

"Well, there is an office up at our workshop; it's about a mile away from here, on a small industrial estate."

"Perfect," said Pegg, "what I want you to do is to call the number given in the letter and maintain that you are unable to be interviewed during the day, it will have to be after hours, as you are too busy with work. They will have to come at your convenience, and the venue will show that you are not bullshitting. Now when you have fixed a time and date, in my view the sooner the better, let me know immediately, if you can't get through to me, send me an email."

"Sure thing, what if they say they want to see me during the day?"

"Tell them that it is not possible. Tell them you are willing to see them, but at your convenience. If things are getting a bit heated, hang up, and contact me. I can come any time for the next couple of weeks, after that I'll have to re-arrange things", replied Pegg.

Tony went into the kitchen and sorted out some food. He had a couple of pies heating up in the oven, and he had prepared a small salad. He laid up a couple of places at the kitchen table.

"Come on Archie, time for some scran, want another beer?"

Pegg joined him in the kitchen, and Tony refilled his glass. The two men sat down and ate. During the meal, Pegg explained to Tony, that he will be able to assist him. Some of the stuff he would be telling Tony would appear strange, but it was essential that Tony do as Pegg instructed.

"When you call these people, do not say anything regarding the allegations; just give them the date, time and venue. Use your mobile and not the house phone, if they require a land line number; give the number of your office. These people will record anything you say on the phone, so just keep the conversation to making the appointment," explained Pegg. "I will be with you when they speak to you, some of the stuff I say will be seem to be totally strange but believe you me it will become clear to you."

Pegg went over his notes he had made prior to this meeting. He asked Tony if he can recall his time in Kosovo. Tony explained he had been sent with his squadron as part of the British Army's deployment to the then Serbian province. The deployment was part of the NATO operation, endorsed by the UN, to bring peace and ensure the safety and security, of the majority Kosovar population from the forces of the government of Belgrade. After the initial conflict, many of the Serbs fled to Serbia itself. The remaining Serb population were deemed vulnerable to intimidation, or worse from the Kosovars. After years of persecution by the Serbian government there were many members of the Kosovar population who were out to settle old scores. In July 1999, he explained that he, with his section of combat engineers, were attached to a rifle company of 2 WMF. He further explained that their role was to clear any unexploded ordnance and suspected booby traps. A lot of the 245,000 population of Serbs had fled the city, and the remaining population were at risk from the vengeful Kosovars. He said that he had not encountered the majority population, and at the end of August his section was withdrawn. He was not sure when the rifle company of 2 WMF was withdrawn.

Pegg said that he would do a bit more research when he got back to the site, and he would be in touch in the morning. He advised Tony to make the call to the investigators first thing and give them his works number. Pegg would phone him at about ten the following morning.

Pegg bade Tony farewell, and went to his vehicle. Fred was still asleep, on the passenger seat, snuggled into the blanket. It was a clear night with a slight hint of a frost in the air. Pegg got back to the site at ten o'clock. He parked up beside the 'van, took Fred's lead, and went for a twenty-minute walk. The night sky was spectacular, no light pollution, resulting in such clarity, with the constellations shining brightly. The site was near to the southern edge of the Peaks National Park. He hardly needed the torch he was carrying, as the starlight was ample illumination. It was very quiet; there was the occasional hoot of an owl, and distant bark of a dog.

He thought about what Tony had told him concerning the allegations. It was plain to him that Tony was not even in the area of where the alleged assaults took place. He had never been involved in dealing with prisoners. So where were these allegations coming from, who was making them, and how did Tony Spratt's name come up. It just did not make sense.

Pegg went back to the 'van. He had already made up his bed, before he'd gone to Tony's. He left the heater on the low setting, he got Fred's basket from the awning, and put it down on the floor of the 'van. He undressed and got into bed. He fell asleep almost immediately.

CHAPTER 6

Fred had jumped onto Pegg's bed, and had woken him up, putting a cold wet nose in his ear.

"Bloody heck, you daft bugger, get off", Pegg exclaimed. He glanced at his watch it was half past seven. The dog was whining; he jumped off the bed and sat at the door of the 'van.

"OK boy, just give me a second."

He slipped on a pair of jogging bottoms, and a fleece, grabbed the dog's lead and went out, picking up a couple of poop bags and slipping them into his pocket on the way. He walked the dog for about fifteen minutes, picking up Fred's morning offerings, and put the poop bag into the receptacle which was located at the site entrance. By the time he got back to the site, the site office was open. He purchased a weeks' worth of Wi-Fi and went back to the 'van. Fred went over to the water bowl in the awning and lapped the contents dry. He sat down licking his dripping muzzle, and he looked at Pegg.

"Okay boy, I'll fix you a bit of grub," with that Pegg fetched the dog's food bowl poured out some dried food and placed it in front of the dog. Fred was not a faddy animal and ate anything that was placed before him. Sometimes Pegg thought he was a Labrador inside a poodle's body. The bowl was soon empty.

"That's all you're getting for now," said Pegg. He went into the 'van and made himself some coffee and breakfast. The dog settled in his basket. After he had finished eating, Pegg cleared up the breakfast things, and remade the bed. He locked up the 'van and went to the shower block, taking the breakfast washing up with him as well. He washed and shaved, and then took the bucket containing the items to be washed up to the vegetable preparation and dish washing facility. After washing and rinsing the breakfast items, he returned to the van and stowed away the cup and plates as well as his washing gear. Fred did not bother to move out of his basket. Pegg dressed in slacks and a sports jacket. He took his file and laptop out and sat at the table at the front of the 'van. Fred jumped onto the seat beside Pegg and lay down.

Pegg switched on the laptop and logged on. He looked at the Valhalla Investigations website and noted the details of the contract the company had with the Services Prosecution Authority. He then looked at the company's UK personnel list. He found that there were several its investigators who were former police officers. There were about twenty names. The print-out he made was two pages long and displayed the names, and brief resume of each investigator. He then went onto the website of Lawyers for Personal Justice. There were a couple of pages, mainly giving contact details of the company, and its solicitors and paralegals. He printed these off and put these together with the other sheets he had printed off into his growing file.

"Right Fred let's go for a walk", he said. Fred immediately lifted his head and a gave a small yap. He almost thrust his head into the collar Pegg had in his hand. Pegg put on a jacket and a cap. He attached the leash to the dog's collar, and after locking the 'van and zipping up the awning and headed towards the site entrance. It was a fine day, and the weather was quite mild. There was a public footpath opposite the site entrance. Once on the footpath he let Fred off the lead. The dog trotted on ahead of Pegg, nose to the ground, and occasionally glancing back to see where Pegg was. The path continued downhill into a wooded area. The trees were still in leaf, although some of the leaves were turning brown. Pegg doubted he would get a signal here, but he was quite relaxed that he had no calls on his phone. He could never understand why people could not relax and leave their phones to ring if they were not able to answer, after all each phone provider supplied its customers with an answering facility on their devices.

Pegg walked for a further hour, before turning back and retracing his route. He got back to the 'van and gave the dog a drink and some more food. He made himself some coffee, and as he was doing so his phone rang. It was Tony Spratt.

"Archie, I've arranged for the investigator guys to see me tomorrow at seven in the evening at my office. It suits me fine as I am staying on after my lads have gone home to do some paperwork."

"Great ", said Pegg," did you say I would be there?"

"No, I thought it better they didn't know."

"Well done my man, I'll be down at around six, and we can talk tactics. Just remind where your yard is."

Spratt told him, and after writing the details down, Pegg hung up.

He did a bit more research online, concentrating on the events in Pristina, involving the units who were in Kosovo at the time of the allegations against British service personnel. He managed to read the war diaries of the second battalion the West Midlands Fusiliers, the only unit in the in Pristina was the Battalion's D Company and they were operating entirely in the Serb sector of the city. Units from other NATO nations were operating in the Kosovar sector of Pristina. He noted these facts and put what he had written into his folder.

It was now early afternoon; he decided to get something to eat. He took the dog's leash, and put on his coat and cap,

"Come on boy, let's go to the pub." The pub was not far from the site. It took them about five minutes to reach the hostelry. There were a few cars parked in the car park to the side of the premises. A notice beside the front entrance proclaimed: WELL BEHAVED PETS WELCOME.

"Fred you see what that says, don't show me up." The dog looked at Pegg and wagged his tail.

They went inside, Pegg ordered a ploughman's and a pint of bitter. He took a seat near to the fire. There were several people sitting at the bar, and more in the restaurant section. Fred immediately settled down in front of the fire. One of the customers, a woman in her fifties went over to where Fred was. The dog clearly enjoyed the attention and closed his eyes when she caressed his ears. The woman explained that she loved the breed and had recently lost her own dog. By the time she had finished stroking the dog, Pegg's order arrived. The woman went back to the bar. Pegg took a sip of his beer and started on his food.

"Fred, you're a tart", he said. The dog looked at him and settled down in front of the fire again.

After he had finished his meal Pegg returned to the site. Once he had got back to the 'van, he got his laptop out again and looked up the website of Lawyers for Personal Justice. He phoned Angie.

"Hi Archie, how's it going?"

"We're fine, how are you and Ross, and my little poppet?"

"All in order, Ross as you know, has some time off. He's taken the baby out to do a bit of shopping for us."

"Great, well give him my regards. Here, it is turning into a bit of a busman's holiday, I will not go into details now, but an old army mate of mine is in a bit of a muddle. I just wonder if you can work your magic on the IT. I am going to ask you to do something which may be a bit naughty, but it is in a noble cause; if you can't do it, or you are unwilling, no worries."

"Oooh! Archie, this sounds exciting, what is it you want me to do?"

"I do not want to give too much over the phone or by email, I'll put it in a letter, you should get it tomorrow."

The rest of the call was taken up with small talk, and after a couple of minutes, he hung up.

Pegg got a sheet of printing paper and proceeded to write Angie a letter. Angie was a very skilled computer programmer. She had the skills to use the Dark Web, she had shown Pegg how criminals can access this system for their nefarious activities, everyone from murderers, thieves, drug peddlers and sex offenders. She showed how it was possible to access remote servers abroad, and in doing so, to hack into almost any company's or organisation's IT systems. Pegg was enthralled by her skills with the mouse and keypad.

He finished the letter, sealed it up, and affixed a stamp to the envelope. He looked at his watch, half past four, he had noticed that the last collection time on the post box outside the site was five o'clock. He took a walk with the dog to the site entrance and posted the letter to Angie. All being well she should get it in the morning. After posting the letter he went for a stroll for twenty minutes before returning to the 'van.

Pegg realised that what he was asking Angie to do was on the peripheries of legality, and he was conscious of the care needed not to leave evidence of this on emails. He had been educated in all aspects of IT security by the various courses he had done with the police. But he needed to wander into the darker side of IT in order to assist Tony Spratt in his hour of need. The thought of those retired police officers working for Valhalla Investigators and through them the BWIT, enraged him. In common with all army veterans, he had a fierce sense of loyalty to serving and retired comrades, and the fact that the establishment was seeking to hang brave men and women who had served their country with honour, out to dry, really stuck in his craw.

He decided to go on his laptop again and visited the web site of the BWIT. Although it had been in existence for some years, no members of the British Armed Forces had ever been charged with any offences. It really left a bad taste in his mouth, that the government would invest resources into investigating its own armed forces, whilst cutting back on what he considered on critical funding for equipment and recruiting. We must be the only country in the world whose politicians are eager to defame the good reputation of its service personnel, he thought. There was very little on ongoing cases, just a few lines saying that investigations were current, it did not even say how many people were being investigated. He decided to re-visit the Valhalla Investigators website. He clicked onto the UK division, and scrolled onto staff. He was surprised to find that names were given, together with a brief resume of each person's career and qualifications. He clicked onto "Investigation Personnel". About twenty names came up; there were no photographs just the names, of which he had already made a list Pegg decided to give Spratt a call.

"Tony", he said, "Archie here, can we speak?"

"Go ahead Archie, I am in the yard helping the lads to load up for a couple of jobs in the morning."

"Great, can you tell me the names of the guys who are coming tomorrow evening?"

"Hang about, I'll just pop into the office."

Pegg waited and after about a minute Spratt came back on the line.

"Richard Hoskins and Raymond Walker, is there anything else you need?"

"No thanks Tony, I'll let you get on. I'll see you at around six pm tomorrow."

"Cheers mate see you then," with that, Spratt terminated the call.

Pegg went back to his laptop. Richard Hoskins, that name rings a bell. He wracked his brains. He decided to go onto Facebook and searched for "Richard Hoskins". It was a long shot, but it never ceased to amaze him how people seemed to put everything about themselves on social media. His search came up with several names of "Richard Hoskins". But none of the names came up as working in the Investigation Industry. He went into his Linked In page, and again entered the name "Richard Hoskins". "Gotcha!" He said to himself. Richard Hoskins, he viewed his profile. "Former police officer with the Norfolk Police." That's where I know you from, thought Pegg, used to be a DS in Professional Standards. I can't recall what happened to him. On an impulse he phoned Splash Waters. To his surprise the phone was answered almost immediately.

"Splash, it's Archie here."

"Archie what do you say, my man."

"Splash can you speak?"

"Sure, I'm on my break, what can I do for you me ole bewty."

"Do you recall a DS in Professional Standards, Richard Hoskins?"

"That bent bastard, yeah, he tried to stick me on for an arrest I made, where the prisoner claimed I planted the drugs I found on him. Transpired Hoskins was knocking off the scrote's sister. He investigated me after the prisoner made a complaint. It was all kicked into the long grass and the incident was NFA'd."

"Can you remember what happened to Hoskins?"

"Not long after the case against me was dropped, there was another incident involving Hoskins, where he was supposed to have tipped off a dealer, whose house was about to be raided by the Drugs Squad. Nothing was proved against him. After that he took early retirement."

"Well I never. His names come up as one of the investigators who are putting ex-squaddies through the mill regarding alleged war crimes."

"It does not surprise me; he always was a piece of shit." Pegg heard the radio which must have been Waters', "Sorry Archie I've got a call to go to a shout, take care my man", with that he ended the call.

Pegg put his mobile down and glanced again at the screen of the laptop. Well Mr Hoskins what a bastard you are. You want to harass my former comrades, well bring it on, he thought. He could not find anything on social media for Hoskins' partner, Raymond Walker. The only information he had about him, was that on VI's web page. That he had been an investigator and loss adjuster in the insurance industry.

Pegg looked at his watch; it was getting on for seven. He made himself a sandwich and a mug of tea. He listened to the radio as he ate, the weather was going to be a mixed batch tomorrow, with showers and sunny periods.

"Right, Fred I think we'll take a trip to Nottingham tomorrow, fancy that boy?" The dog looked up at Pegg from where he was lying on the bench, licked his muzzle and wagged his tail. Pegg finished his sandwich and drank the tea. He rang Angie. He told her he had sent the letter and she should get it first thing tomorrow, could she get her responses back asap. She would inform him as soon as she had it, and she would get to work with her responses. Her answers would be with him on Saturday. He confirmed that she had the postal address of the site.

He then reviewed what he had gleaned over the past two days. He needed to find out more about Lawyers for Personal Justice. He would pay them a visit and find out more about the partners, Mehmet Ali and James Smithson.

He settled down and put a CD in the radio and listened to some music. Pegg enjoyed a large range of music, pop, jazz, heavy metal and classical. The album was a compilation of clarinet music by Mozart. Whilst listening he made a list of what he wanted to do in the morning. He would leave after nine and should be in Nottingham by half past ten, thus avoiding the mornings rush hour.

He decided to turn in early. He took the dog out for the last time that day. It was dark and he kept within the environs of the site. He used his torch to guide him around the area. After returning to the 'van, he left Fred and went over to the washrooms, where he had a shower. He made up his bed and put some fresh water down for the dog and went to bed. Fred jumped onto the foot of the bed. Pegg was too tired to put him on the floor again.

"If you fall off because I have turned in the night, that's your fault," he muttered. With that he fell asleep.

CHAPTER 7

Pegg awoke after a good night's sleep. The dog was still at the foot of the bed. He got up and went to the shower room, after which he put on a pair of jogging bottoms and a sweatshirt. Fred was already waiting at the door, Pegg put the lead on the dog, it was drizzling so he put on his waterproof jacket, and after securing the 'van, went off for a twenty

minute walk When he got back, he toweled Fred down, and made some breakfast. After clearing up, he got dressed, selecting shirt and tie, slacks and a sports jacket, and on his feet he wore brown brogues. He decided to take the waterproof jacket he'd been wearing. He packed the laptop in its case along with the file he'd been producing. He also took some dried food and water for the dog.

He put the case in the front of the Defender, between the passenger and driving seat. He let Fred into the passenger side, the dog laid down on the blanket, which had been spread over the seat. After securing the 'van and awning, he drove off.

The drive to Nottingham was uneventful, and he arrived in the city at about ten-thirty. Mansfield Road in the north-eastern part of the city. He arrived there twenty minutes later. He found Coronation Buildings; the condominium was a parade of shops and offices built in 1937, typical of the architecture of the period. He pulled in and parked up in one of the bays in front of the parade. He left the front passenger side window a quarter open for the dog.

"I'm just going to have a look round, you be a brave dog and watch the Lanny for me, Fred", Pegg said. The poodle lifted his head up, looked at Pegg, and laid down again.

Pegg walked along the front of the shops and between a convenience store and a betting shop, he saw a door and screwed to the doors centre was a brass plaque on which was inscribed, "LAWYERS FOR PERSONAL JUSTICE." Pegg opened the door, and entered a small lobby, a flight of stairs lead out of the lobby. He climbed the stairs and found himself on a landing. There was a window in front of him which overlooked Mansfield Road, and to the left was a half-glazed door with frosted glass, a small notice on the door invited visitors to ring the door-bell, and an arrow pointed to a button switch on the right side of the door. Pegg glanced out of the window, he could see the Landrover, it was a bit further on to the left from where he was looking. He went up to the door, he could see through the frosted glass that the lights in the offices were on. He rang the bell. After a short while the door was opened by a young woman, she asked him to come in. The office was a large open plan affair, with about a dozen people of both genders, sitting at desks in front of monitor screens and speaking on telephones, whilst others were going through papers. A counter ran the whole width of the office and a hinged top at the end gave access to the main office area. Pegg noticed that the waiting area behind the counter was covered by a CCTV camera mounted on the wall to the left. The whole set up was bigger than it appeared when it was viewed from street level. The length of the office clearly stretched further than frontage of the two the shops on the ground floor. Beyond the main office area there were what appeared to be a corridor which Pegg assumed led to either individual offices or storerooms. The counter was set back about 6 feet from the door, and to the left of the door there was a small cubicle, with a couple of chairs and a small table.

"Good morning, sir, how can we help", said the woman.

"I'm looking for a bit of advice", Pegg replied, "You see I have a friend who is in a bit of a muddle regarding his mortgage repayments."

"Let me stop you there, sir, we do not do any property work here, I can give you the details of our affiliated department which may possibly help you out," she said.

"Okay, but what sort of stuff do you do here?"

"Nothing to do with what your friend will be requiring, I'll fetch you the details of our affiliated department," she said, and with that she went back into the main office area. She came back a couple of minutes later and gave Pegg some leaflets. She then ushered him to the door which he had originally entered.

"Hold on said Pegg, before I go, I might need your services."

"In what way, are you the victim of some sort of accident or something like that?"

"Well it could be what can you do for me."

"Our clients tend to be either people who have suffered injury as the result of motor or industrial accident and medical negligence, or victims of incidents as a result of British Government policy."

"Gosh that seems quite serious stuff. What sort of incidents."

"Who did you say you were Mr...?"

"I didn't."

"Well in that case I've nothing more to say to you."

She bade him farewell and with that she closed the door behind him. Well, that was short and sweet Pegg thought. It was almost as if they did not want outsiders to know what they are up to. Why would this be? What have they got to hide? Pegg realised he would have to do more research into LPJ. He made his way down the stairs again and onto the street.

As he was thinking about it, his attention was drawn to a scream which came from where he had parked the Defender. A youth wearing a hoody, had right his arm through the vehicle's front passenger window. It would seem his arm was stuck. Pegg ran to the vehicle, as the youth was getting a screwdriver out of the pocket of his jeans with his free hand. Pegg grabbed the hand with the screwdriver and twisted it so the youth dropped it.

"Aaah me 'and that fucking dog has bit it."

"Serves you right you thieving little shit", said Pegg. He could see that Fred had his jaws firmly around the youth's right hand, and was shaking his head and growling, the laptop was lying next to the dog. It would appear the youth had been attempting to steal it but had not seen that Fred was lying next to it. There were hardly any people about, which was probably why the youth was taking his chances and stealing from the vehicle without being noticed. Pegg placed the youth's left arm in a lock. The youth was white, about 15, skinny and quite smelly. Pegg shouted to the dog, "Leave", Fred reluctantly let go of the youth's hand, the youth immediately withdrew it from the inside of the vehicle.

Pegg tightened the armlock and felt in the youth's jeans, he withdrew some paperwork from the pockets. Among the items was a police bail notice, dated that day.

"Now listen to me, you slag, I see you are already on bail for burglary, I don't think it will look too good if I get you nicked again, offending on bail, that will mean remanded in custody. You want that?"

"Please don't mister; I am in enough shit as it is."

Pegg couldn't be bothered with the hassle of getting the youth arrested, making a statement, he had other things to do.

"Right, I'll tell you what I'm going to do. I'm going to let you go, I suggest you get that hand cleaned up. I now know your name and where you live. Carry on as you are, and you will regret it, I know some nasty people who owe me a favour, who are quite happy to give you a hiding on my say so. Get my drift?"

The youth was trembling and there was a look of abject terror on his face,

"I understand" he stammered.

"I'm pleased to hear that. Now fuck off, before I change my mind."

Pegg released the youth, who scampered away holding his bleeding right hand. Pegg picked up the screwdriver dropped by the thief. He saw that it was sharpened to a point which could have caused Fred serious injury or worse, if the youth had the chance to use it.

"Good boy, that taught the bastard not to mess with us," he said to the dog.

Fred was looking immensely pleased with himself. Pegg went around to the driver's side, unlocked the door and got in. The dog came across and onto his lap. Pegg ruffled the poodles top knot and lifted him gently back onto the passenger seat.

"Settle down now you've been the brave dog I knew you were, now we will find a nice spot for a bit of lunch and a walk."

Three quarters of an hour later they came across a pub on the road back to Buxton. Pegg gave Fred some water before walking into the main bar. The bar-staff were quite happy for the dog to come in. Pegg ordered a pint of bitter and a round of corn beef sandwiches. After he had finished his drink and food, he took Fred for a walk, returning to the Defender about half an hour later. He gave the dog another drink. A short hour later he was back at the site.

CHAPTER 8

At half past five he left the site and drove to Tony Spratt's yard. It was starting to get dark when he finally pulled into the front apron of the premises. Spratt's yard was located in the middle of a small business estate about half a mile from his house. It was not a yard in the literal meaning of the word, there was a concrete apron outside a unit. The unit was a brick and steel building, with a large roller door giving vehicular access, and a side door. The lights were on in the office. On the access door there was a sign which read "AS Baths and Kitchens". Pegg parked the Defender in front of the large door. He locked the vehicle, leaving Fred sitting on the front passenger seat, and walked through the side door. The doorway gave access to the main part of the unit. There was a white Ford Transit panel van parked inside, around the edge of the unit there were a series of metal shelves onto which were stacked boxes and power tools. On the opposite side there was another set of doors, one of which would be the office and the other was the WC and washroom.

The office door opened, and Tony Spratt came out,

"Come on in Archie, where's the wee dog?"

"I left him in the Lanny, you don't want him in, he'll start yapping at your visitors, it's best he stays where he is".

"Okay come on in, do you want a cup of tea?"

"I'll pass on that, thanks."

They both went into the office. Tony had already set two chairs in front of the desk, as well as putting an extra chair beside his own.

The office was quite tidy and clean. Pegg did dare ask if it was always kept in this state of cleanliness and order.

"I thought that it would be best to have you beside me and have a distance between us and the visitors", said Tony.

"I could not have organised it better myself, we want to give the impression these people are visitors here, and this is your space."

Tony picked up some papers he had been working on, and took them over to a filing cabinet, and placed them in a tray on top.

"Right Tony, let's have a look at the letter you got from the BWIT."

"It's here on the desk," he said giving it to Pegg.

Pegg read through it. He looked at his notes he had made over the past few days.

"OK, let's go quickly through what you and your troop were doing in northern Pristina. What was the aim of the mission?"

"As I remember it after the NATO invasion and the air strikes, the Serb army withdrew back into Serbia proper, leaving Kosovo. On the way a lot of bad stuff happened. A lot of it by the Serbs but the Kosovars in some instances were just as bad. Our job was to clear mines and unexploded ordnance.

The Serbs had laid mines very haphazardly, there were no marked minefields. The first instance we had of mines was when some poor civilian had set one off. We would identify mined areas and mark them and if possible, fence them off. If we had time later, we would clear them."

"What about dealing with detained persons?"

"We never had anything to do with that side of things. Fucking hell, Archie, we were working full time clearing mines, booby traps and God knows what else. I really don't know how my name came to be on the list of this BWIT thing."

"Yeah, that's the key to it, where these bastards got the names from."

"I really hope something is sorted out, because this is doing my head in. My Misses is in bits, am I going to jail for something I did not do?"

"Don't go there Tony, this is why I'm here, we'll get you out of this, I'm not going to let them stitch you up."

"Do I need a lawyer?"

"It may come to that but leave it to me, I'll have a look on the web, because I'm sure the BWIT has a few more British squaddies on their list. If this is the case there may well be a firm of solicitors who are already involved in defending soldiers both serving and retired, from these allegations."

Pegg read and re-read the letter. He paused and made a few notes on the pad he had with him.

"Right Tony, here's what I think we should do. I strongly suspect these two investigators do not have any powers to detain you. So, you should answer the questions they put to you. I will be acting as your adviser; are you happy for me to do this for you?"

"I'm in your hands Archie; I will be guided by your advice."

"Great, now what I want to find out is what the allegations against you are. If we are lucky, we might get the name or names of the persons making these accusations. My gut feeling this is all a load of bollocks, and I aim to show what a pack of lies this affair is."

As they were talking, they heard the sound of a car pulling up outside the unit. Pegg went over to the office window.

"Looks like they're here," he said. Outside a blue Ford Focus had parked outside the main door next to Pegg's Defender. The two occupants sat in the car for a bit, talking to each other. They eventually got out of the vehicle and made their way to the access door. Tony Spratt was clearly beginning to feel agitated.

"Archie, I don't know if I can keep it together."

"Yes, you can, come on where's that tough little Irishman, who was such a pain in the arse? I need him now, understand?"

"Sorry Archie, I'll get a hold of myself," said Spratt smiling weakly

He let out a big sigh, made his way to the door and let them in. Pegg remained in the office. The taller of the two men introduced himself.

"I assume you are Mr Anthony Spratt", he said.

"I am and you are?"

"I am Richard Hoskins, and this is Raymond Walker. We are working for the Balkan War Investigation Team also known by its acronym, BWIT."

Hoskins was about six feet tall, aged about forty, slim build with short cropped dark hair and piercing blue eyes. He was dressed in a charcoal coloured suit, white shirt and red tie, on his feet he was wearing a pair of highly polished black shoes, he was carrying a black messenger bag. Walker was much shorter in stature, about fifty years old, and was slightly overweight with thinning sandy hair. He was dressed in a navy-blue blazer, grey slacks and brown shoes, he wore a light blue shirt and red and blue striped tie, and he was also carrying a black messenger bag.

"Come this way guys", said Tony leading them into the office.

On seeing Pegg, Hoskins stopped. "Who's this, I thought you said you'd be alone."

Tony had pulled himself together and now exuded an air of confidence. Pegg was relieved, it was the old Tony he knew, combative awkward

"This is a friend of mine, Mr Archie Pegg. He is an old army pal, and he's here to advise me in answering any questions you have for me. When I said I'd be by myself, I made it clear to you when we spoke on the phone that my employees would not be here. There was no mention of me not having anyone to sit with me."

Good on you Tony thought Pegg, get these arseholes on the back foot.

"Right before we start", said Pegg, "let's see some ID."

Hoskins was clearly uneasy; he had not expected this.

"I have explained to Mr Spratt that we are working for the BWIT."

"Not good enough, you could be anybody, and as part of your introduction it is normal to show any interviewee your credentials, so show us them, please." Hoskins and Walker reached into their jackets and produced their ID cards. Spratt and Pegg scrutinized the proffered documents.

"It says here that you are employed by Valhalla Investigators, nothing about BWIT."

Hoskins looked flustered, "Sorry about that", he said, he opened the messenger bag and produced an A4 sheet of paper, and gave it to Spratt, he read it and passed it on to Pegg. Pegg read it and passed it back to Hoskins, who put it back in the bag.

"So, Valhalla Investigators are authorised to carry out inquiries on behalf of BWIT. I notice that you have no powers other than to interview people, and take statements," said Pegg.

"Look I don't know who you are, but this is between us and Mr Spratt," Hoskins snarled, "so you'd better leave us."

"Mr Pegg stays, or the pair of you fuck off, do you understand? This is my office and you have been invited here, as Archie says you are not policemen, just ordinary civvies like us," Tony said.

Hoskins thought for a minute, it was clear he was not used to being challenged, he appeared to change tack.

"I'm sorry we have obviously got off on the wrong foot, we just want to ask a few questions," he said. He put a small recording device on the table.

"As you have said this is just a case of asking a few questions," said Pegg, "This is not a formal interview, right?"

"Correct", sneered Hoskins.

"In which case as this is an informal interview it would have no evidential value, so you can pack that up and put that thing away, "said Pegg, indicating the recording device.

"Are you Mr Spratt's brief?" asked Hoskins.

"No, he's an old army pal of mine. As I have said before, he stays or you two go," Tony said, before Pegg could reply to the question.

Hoskins glared at Pegg, there was no sign of recognition, this did not surprise Pegg, because during the time Hoskins was with the Norfolk Constabulary, Pegg had only completed about 4 years' service, and had not had any dealings with the Force's Professional Standards department. Pegg decided not to enlighten him as to what his current status was.

"So now we have got that cleared up, perhaps you could let us know what the nature of the allegations against my friend is, and who is making them?" asked Pegg.

"It is about ill treatment, and abuse of civilians who were detained by British military personnel during the occupation of Pristina in Kosovo, during 1999," said Hoskins, before continuing, "We have reason to believe that you, Mr Spratt, were involved in the processing of alleged suspects, arrested for terrorism, and like offences."

"Who is making these allegations," asked Spratt.

"We are not able to tell you at this time," replied Hoskins.

"Well you can tell me where and which unit I was serving with at the time," said Spratt, who was clearly growing in confidence with Pegg at his side.

"What was your regiment in the Army".

"You're the investigator you tell me," replied Tony.

"Come on gentlemen, this is getting us nowhere," interrupted Raymond Walker, who was clearly getting exasperated with the way the conversation was developing.

"Mr Spratt we are not trying to pull a fast one on you, we are trying to establish some facts and thus get to the truth", Walker said frowning at Hoskins, "I understand you were a regular soldier in the Royal Engineers in 1999."

"Correct."

"Where were you in Pristina at the time?" he asked.

"I was on detachment in the northern section of the city. We were involved in clearing up munitions, mines and booby traps. There was a section of us sappers, and some assault pioneers from the infantry unit we were attached to. The retreating Serb army and their special police units had left a lot of stuff behind; some of the local kids had been killed and maimed as a result of playing around with stuff they had found lying around. Initially we identified the danger areas and marked them off. Afterwards we went about clearing up the items as best we could."

"Who was in charge of this operation?"

"I suppose I was because I was the section commander, but ultimately it would have been the battalion commander of the infantry unit we were attached to."

"Who was that,"

"Second Battalion the West Midland Fusiliers, the commanding officer would have been a lieutenant colonel. But it was a company of the battalion that my section was attached to. The rest of my squadron was based in Macedonia assisting in the construction of refugee camps. Our immediate boss in Pristina was the company commander of 2 WMF's detached company."

"What was the company commander's name?"

"For fucks sake I was just a corporal, I didn't know personalities. We identified unexploded ordnance, mines booby traps and cleared them as best we could."

"Right", said Pegg, "where are these allegations coming from, who is making them, are the complainants Kosovars or Serbs?"

"It is Albanian speaking Kosovans who are making the allegations," said Walker.

"Well that rules me out and the other sappers, we were not involved in the detention and interrogation, of any people. Our lot were involved in clearing up the shit that the Serb military left behind. This conversation is over as far as I am concerned," said Tony Spratt.

"Now the question I'd like to ask is where you got Mr Spratt's name from. Someone must have given it to you?" asked Pegg.

Hoskins and Walker looked at each other, Walker was clearly uneasy. There was a long pause. Spratt was already on his feet.

"Well we can't tell you at this time," Walker said, "suffice to stay it would seem that your name came from a credible source."

"Well if that's the case, the next time you want to speak to Mr Spratt, he will have the appropriate legal representation, now as Mr Spratt has told you this meeting is at an end," said Pegg.

"You'll be hearing from us, I'll tell you that," said Hoskins, who was clearly rattled at Tony's newfound belligerence.

"Look forward to that, and next time, have a better attitude; now do us all a favour and clear off, said Tony.

Hoskins and Walker gathered up their things and left. Outside Walker started to berate Hoskins. A shouting match ensued outside on the car park, Walker got into their car, and started up the vehicle, Hoskins was still standing there as Walker put the vehicle into reverse and started to move backward. Hoskins rushed round and got into the passenger side of the vehicle. The car drove off.

"Well", said Spratt, "that seems to have lit a thunderflash under their arses. I love it when the opposition has a falling out with one another."

"Yes, it is satisfying, but I have a few concerns. It appears that Hoskins seems to be a loose cannon, and he needs to be watched. Tony I'll just pop out and get the dog, that okay?"

"Sure, bring him in."

Pegg went out to the Landrover and let Fred out. The poodle leapt out and with his nose to the ground did a quick circuit of the parking area, before stopping and lifting his back leg against a lamp standard. He followed Pegg back into the office again. Fred gave the office a quick once over with his ever-inquisitive nose before going to introduce himself to Spratt, who promptly tickled the dog's ears.

"Well you're a friendly wee feller, so you are," he said.

"Right that's enough, boy, come here and settle down," said Pegg. The dog went and lay down by the filing cabinet.

"Okay Tony, what I need to do is to get you covered legally, in case there are more visits by the BWIT's agents. What I am going to do is a bit of research and see if there are any law firms looking after the interests of serving and retired service personnel. The one thing I want you to keep in mind is that you never be interviewed again without some form of legal representation."

"I understand completely, Archie. You can be sure that I'll not fall for any stuff about "little chats" again. I know that during my time in Kosovo, I have not done anything wrong, and to the best of my knowledge, neither had any of the guys I was serving with at the time."

"Good", said Pegg, "now I'm going back to the site, I've got some research to do. Is there anything more you want to ask before I go?"

"No, I think that it's all clear to me."

"Right I'll be off. What's the best way of contacting you?"

"Mobile would be best, as I can't guarantee I'll be in the office. I have a couple of jobs on the go at the moment and some more in the pipeline."

"I'll just take your contact details, including home and emails, have you got a Facebook or Twitter account, or other suchlike social media stuff?"

"I'm on Facebook."

"Good, I'll send you a friend request. After I've done that, keep monitoring it, I take it is not linked to your business?"

"No, the company has its own account."

"OK I'll be off then. Don't let this business get in the way of your day to day life, I am here for you Tony, and I'll not let you be thrown under a bus, take care my man. I'll contact you in the morning."

With that Pegg took his leave, and with the poodle trotting behind him, he left the unit. During the drive back to the site, Pegg was seething. How could the system allow decent people like Tony Spratt to have their lives thrown into disarray by what are clearly very dubious allegations about events that occurred such a long time ago. He arrived at the site at about Nine o'clock. He parked up at his pitch, unlocked and went inside the caravan. After switching on the lights, he sat down. Fred settled down next to him on the bench. Pegg tickled the animal's ears and said:.

"It's a rum old do, boy, and that's for sure. We've got a lot to do in the morning," he said.

The dog looked at him cocking his head. I'm sure he understands everything I say, thought Pegg.

He got his file and taking a fresh sheet of paper, wrote up the rough notes he had taken during the interview the agents from the BWIT had with Tony Spratt. When he had finished, he reviewed what he had written. He took out his rough notebook again and wrote on a new page. *"Sat 9/10/10 Things to do"*. Underneath the heading he jotted down notes with bullet points.

- *Collect any mail from site office.*
- *Research Balkan War Diary 2 WMF.*
- *Research firms of solicitors acting for veterans of Balkan Operations.*
- *Get details of a brief to Tony Spratt.*

Pegg put his file away and made himself a sandwich. After finishing it he tidied up and grabbed Fred's leash.

"Let's do a quick turn around the block, boy, and then we're off to bed."

The dog almost thrust he neck at Pegg to get the leash attached to his collar. Pegg took a torch and made his way from the caravan towards the site entrance. It was a clear night, and the stars were bright. There was an orange glow coming from the direction of

Buxton. Pegg kept Fred on his lead, he had previous for straying off into the night, and being very deaf when called.

He thought a great deal about what had occurred at Tony's office. There does not seem to be any substance to the allegations that the claimants are making against Tony and the other veterans. He returned to the 'van, he avoided the temptation to work on the information he had so far. He needed to get a good-nights rest, and with that he went to bed.

CHAPTER 9

By eight-thirty Pegg had showered, dressed, walked Fred and breakfasted. He walked over to the site office and purchased some more milk; the site manager had some mail for him. There was just the one item, an A4 brown manila envelope. It was the information he had asked Angie to gather. He returned to the 'van and made a quick call to Angie, acknowledging receipt of the mail. He did not speak much more, saying he would get a letter off to her over the weekend. He opened the letter, which contained several sheets of paper, printed on both sides. Pegg started to read. Angie had used a server located in one of the Baltic states and had managed to covertly hack into the emails of Lawyers for Personal Justice (LPJ), and also those of Mehmet Ali and James Smithson. "You have done well, my girl," thought Pegg as he read through the papers. "Bloody hell", he muttered, "you devious little bastard!" One of the emails to Mehmet Ali was from Richard Hoskins.

The email informed Ali that Hoskins had been investigating allegations of misconduct by the British army in the Balkans, but there was no evidence of any offences being committed. This could be that nobody had made any complaints. The email went on further to ask if the firm had the names of any victims of mistreatment, or people who would be prepared to make allegations of mistreatment. Pegg was puzzled, why would investigators for the BWIT be contacting LPJ, surely it should be the other way around. He continued to read, a bit later he came across names of clients. The names were not English sounding, at first Pegg thought nothing of it, after all there were many citizens of these islands whose families came from ethnic origins. But some of the names jumped out at him, they are all Albanian he thought. Well Kosovars were ethnic Albanians, thought Pegg. One name rang a bell, Enver Haji. "I know you my friend, I nicked you last Sunday in Whissonsett," he said to himself. Pegg read further, Angie had obtained his date of birth and his address in London. Pegg noted them down. He picked up his phone and called Splash Waters.

"Archie you old warhorse, what do you say?"

"Splash can you do me a quick favour, remember that chap I nicked last Sunday for the cannabis thing in Whissonsett? His name is Enver Haji, can you tell me what happened to him?"

"Hang you on, my man, just need to look at my pocketbook", there was a slight pause before Waters spoke again, "right Enver Haji, born 11/12/1980 Tirana, Albania, his address is 14 Somerville Road, Camden, London. He was remanded in custody by Yarmouth magistrates to appear at Norwich Crown Court. Do you want the details of the other chap, he was another Albanian, Hirsi Meci?"

"Yeah I better take them."

"This chap was also born in Tirana and his date of birth is 14/6/1978, he resides in Barking, 28 Manston Avenue, he was also remanded to appear at Norwich Crown Court. Is there anything else before I go? I've got a file I need to get finished before lunch, so I have to love you and leave you Archie." Pegg made a note of Meci's details.

"No that's it for now, cheers for what you have done so far, Splash."

"It's always a pleasure never a chore, bye."

Pegg finished reading through the papers Angie had sent him. He then wrote her a letter, he informed her that there was a goldmine of useful information, and from it he would be able to go a long way to help refute the allegations made against Tony Spratt, and possibly any other veterans being investigated by BWIT. He would keep her in the loop regarding what he had done so far. He urged her not to mention anything about her findings to anyone. He knew she was very alert to cyber security, and that her hacking activities were nearly impossible to detect, as they were made through a server remote in the realms of the dark web. If at any time she wanted out, that was fine with him. He finished off the letter with a few queries regarding what they were doing over the weekend, and especially regards to Catherine Rose and Ross. He sealed up the letter, and taking Fred with him, walked to the post box outside the site entrance. He looked at the time, it was ten-thirty, the collection was due at eleven, he was pleased the day plate, it still said "SAT". He posted the letter and walked for a further twenty-five minutes before returning to the site.

On returning to the 'van he made some sandwiches and a thermos flask of coffee, these items he packed in his rucksack. He cleared away and got out the laptop. He first visited the West Midlands Fusiliers web page. He scrolled down and looked under the battalion's operations, clicking on the Former Republic of Yugoslavia (FRY). During the Kosovo crisis in 1999 The main body of the battalion was located in the Republic of Macedonia, where its soldiers were assisting in the administration and security of refugee camps for ethnic Albanians or Kosovars, who had fled Kosovo as a result of the ethnic cleansing by the Serbian army, and the Serb special police battalions. D company was on detachment to northern Pristina, assisting in securing the local area for local the Serb civilian population from the Kosovan Liberation Army (KLA). In addition, the retreating Serb military had left behind a lot of ordnance, stores and ammunition, as well unexploded bombs and shells (UXBs), which needed to be made safe and cleared. The unit and its attached personnel left the northern part of the city in December 1999, after being relieved by a Danish battalion.

There appeared no further involvement in the NATO Kosovan operation by West Midland Fusiliers, and the Battalion returned to its barracks in England. There were a number of awards to members of the unit, but there was no indication of any misconduct by its members. Not even any minor military offences, which would have been dealt with by company commanders or the commanding officer. This would be normal in an operational theatre, as soldiers tend to be too occupied to misbehave in such an environment. A bit different if the boys were back in barracks in some garrison town in the UK, thought Pegg.

Pegg noted his findings on a sheet of paper and added it to his file, he also noted the address of the unit's website. Next, he searched on the net for firms of solicitors, especially those who represented veterans and veteran groups. He scrolled through a number of law firms, before coming across a firm of solicitors based in Manchester, Open Justice Advocates. He got the firm's homepage up website and clicked onto the "About Us" tab. The firm was set up in 1990 and after a short while started to specialise in the defending sailors, soldiers and airmen at courts martial. They then moved into defence of police officers, fire fighters, and paramedics on behalf of the Police Federation, the Fire Brigades Union, and the public service trade union Unison. They had considerable success in defending their clients and getting them cleared of any wrongdoing. They had recently taken on cases where serving and retired members of the security services in Northern Ireland had faced allegations of ill treatment and in a couple of cases, murder, during the Troubles. Pegg read through and could plainly see this firm of solicitors fitted the bill.

He looked at the firms contact numbers and addresses. He was surprised to find that the office hours were 0900- 1600 on Saturdays. Pegg took the plunge he phoned the firms main number.

"Open Justice Advocates, Amiya speaking, how may I help?"

"Oh hello, my name's Archie Pegg and I'm calling on behalf of a friend who is under investigation by the Balkan War Investigation Team, it would appear that he has been wrongly accused of something he has not done."

"Okay, Mr Pegg" said the call taker, "I'll put you on hold for a minute, whilst I get somebody who can speak to you about this matter." The line seemed to go dead for a time before another female voice came back.

"Hello Mr Pegg, I'm Rachel Gluckstein's secretary, I'm afraid Rachel is away in Belfast at the moment, if you can give me brief details of what is at issue, and Rachel will get in touch as soon as she can, she may even call from Belfast."

Pegg gave his contact details and that of Tony. The secretary said she would email some forms to both Pegg and Spratt. There was a discussion about funding the case, but the secretary said that can be dealt with later. The first thing was to get as much information so that the solicitors could make a decision as whether they should take on the case. Pegg asked when the forms would be sent.

"Immediately I have finished this call", she said.

"Right thank you for your time, just one other thing, I am away from home at the moment, so anything you send through the post will not be dealt with for a week or so."

"Don't worry, Mr Pegg, we will keep in contact electronically or via your mobile number, I take it Mr Spratt, will not be away from his address for a bit?"

"No, he's staying in Buxton for the foreseeable future as far as I know," replied Pegg.

"Okay, Mr Pegg, we'll be in touch; we'll contact Mr Spratt on Monday on his mobile, Good Day to you."

Pegg phoned Tony and explained what he had done.

"Archie you're a star, perhaps you could come over tomorrow for some lunch, say about twelve-thirty, is that too early?"

"Sounds perfect, Tony, is it alright to bring the dog?"

"Of course, we have an old beagle, the misses is more of a dog person than me, she'll love to see him. We're having Sarah's mam and da over as well, they're a lovely old couple, he's an ex Grenadier Guardsman, she's a former nurse. Sarah was their only child, so they are very close. The misses does a mean roast beef and Yorkshire pud."

"Can't wait", said Pegg, "maybe we can look at some of the paperwork that the solicitors say they are going to send me, if it has arrived by the time I come to see you."

"Sounds like a great plan, see you tomorrow", replied Tony.

Right thought Pegg, that's the "to do" list complete. He went back to his laptop and on checking the emails, found that Rachel Gluckstein's secretary had fulfilled her promise, an email and some attachments were sitting in the inbox. Pegg printed off the attachments. There were three of them, one a resume of the company, the second was a three-page questionnaire, and the third was a two-page guide as to how the second form should be completed. It was obvious that Open Justice Advocates were not going to commit themselves until they knew where the case could be going. Pegg looked at his watch, it was eleven-fifteen.

"Right Fred, I think we shall go out and do a bit of Fell Walking, does that sound like a plan boy?" The poodle wagged his tail and gave a soft woof.

"I'll take that as a yes then. Right, I'll just put on some appropriate gear and we are on our way."

Pegg got out his rucksack again and packed some food and water for Fred. He carried the rucksack out to the awning, where he put on his jacket, walking boots and his tweed cap. After securing the 'van and awning he walked out of the site accompanied by Fred. He kept the dog on the leash, until they'd left the road and were on the footpath. It was a cold clear day, and the leaves on the trees were starting to turn, resulting in a kaleidoscope of differing shades. Autumn was Pegg's favourite time of year, such a pity that by the end of next month nearly all of the trees would have shed their leaves. It had been a couple of hours since Pegg had set out. He continued with the walk, thinking about of Cath, and how she would have loved being here, walking with him, and just taking in the beautiful Peaks. He missed her so much, his eyes welled up, and a couple of tears fell down his cheek. His thoughts were abruptly interrupted, by Fred barking. The dog was enthusiastically bounding around a German Shepherd, who in turn was whimpering and whining, and scampering about. The dogs started to chase each other, yapping like a pair of pups.

"Fred!" shouted Pegg, "come here boy."

"Oh, let them be, they're only playing," a female voice said from behind him." Pegg turned around, to see a woman on the path behind him.

"You were miles away," she continued. She was slim, wearing a pair of Craghoppers, walking boots and a red Berghaus jacket, she was also wearing a backpack. She had dark auburn hair, done up in ponytail and brown eyes, she was thirty-five to forty-five Pegg estimated, and spoke with a soft Yorkshire accent.

"Yes, I'm afraid my thoughts were elsewhere, I tend to think a lot whilst I'm out walking."

"The dogs certainly seem to be getting on don't they", she said.

"Fred seems to have that effect on other dogs. I think it is something about the breed, he is zany but intelligent," he replied.

"My Zena is a rescue dog, she is only 2 years old, her owner died, and the family were moving away, so they gave her up for re-homing. I got her from the Dogs Trust in Sheffield, she is a very gentle and affectionate animal, and just seems to love everyone and their dog!"

Meanwhile the dogs had stopped their playing and trotted over to Pegg and the woman. Pegg bent down and greeted Zena, she reciprocated by licking Pegg's hand. Fred watched the proceedings, before sniffing the woman's proffered hand, and allowing her to tickle his ears.

"By the way I'm Pat Warrington."

"Archie Pegg.

"Well Mr Pegg, do you mind if we walk along with you two for a bit?"

"Archie, please, yes of course, nice to have company for a change." They continued walking; the dogs went ahead of them.

"So, are you a regular visitor to the Peak District, Archie?"

"Not as often as I would like; I used to come here with my wife quite often."

"Is she not able to be with you?"

"I lost her about six months ago, she died in a car accident," he said before stopping, he could not help himself, he wiped his eyes with the back of his hand. Pat stopped and for a while she said nothing.

"Oh Archie, I'm so sorry, I did not mean to pry, sometimes I can't seem to help putting my foot in it," she put her hand on his forearm.

"It's fine, Pat, may I call you Pat; sometimes I stop and think about her, and there are the happy times and the sad times we had together, I never really had any counselling, maybe I should have. Look I'm sorry to unburden myself on you."

"It is no problem for me, I tell you what, why don't we stop and have a bite to eat, I've got some sandwiches in my backpack."

"Snap", said Archie, "I was thinking of taking a break soon anyway."

Up ahead was a small rocky outcrop, a sort of tor. They made their way to it and sat on one of the stones. They unpacked their food, and Pegg took out a couple of bowls, one of which he poured water into, and put it down for the poodle, the Shepherd promptly went and emptied it, whilst Fred looked on. She finished and licked her muzzle, Pegg refilled the bowl, and the poodle drank his fill.

"Zena I've got a drink for you, naughty girl, taking Fred's water!" Pat said. "I've got some food for her; let me get it out, before you feed Fred."

With that Pat took out a plastic container, with some form of mush in it, she removed the lid, and put it down for the waiting shepherd, who promptly started to wolf it down. Pegg meanwhile emptied the dried food into a bowl and placed it in front of Fred. Now that the animals had been fed, Pat and Pegg got their sandwiches, and ate.

"So, tell me about yourself, Pat, where are you from?" Pat welcomed the chance to steer away from what she considered her faux pas.

"I live in a village just outside Sheffield, called High Bradfield, it's just on the edge of the Peaks National Park. I live with my parents, lived there all my life."

"What do you do?"

"Well I actually work at the University; I'm a research assistant in with the Engineering faculty. I have been doing the job for about five years now."

"Are you a graduate?"

"No, I came in through the back door. I did an engineering apprenticeship with an agricultural machinery company after I left school. I went through night school and eventually got an HND. I worked in sales for a bit then this job at Sheffield University came up. What do you do Archie?" she asked.

"I am a policeman actually, I am with the Norfolk Constabulary, been doing the job for the past 15 years, before that I was in the Army, I enlisted as a junior soldier, and started adult service when I was 18, I did nearly 23 years."

"You have family?" she asked.

"My mother died when I was eight, and my father abandoned us shortly when I was four. I grew up in care. I met my wife whilst I was in the police. She has a daughter, Angie, and her husband Ross, they have a baby daughter. They are my family now. I have no kids of my own."

"I never married, I was engaged once, but we called it off. I have a good circle of friends at the University, and I have my interests, one of which is fell walking as you can see."

They finished eating and packed their things away, clearing up the detritus, placing it in bags and then into their respective rucksacks. Pegg looked at the time, it was getting on for three.

"Well I think I need to be getting back, it will start to be getting dark in a couple of hours or so."

"Me too", said Pat, "I've got one or two things to do in the morning."

"Where's your car parked?" Pegg asked.

"About a mile down the track," she said, indicating the direction they were both originally heading."

Pegg thought for a minute, and then plucked up the courage to ask:

" Pat, I am pitched up about eight miles away, on a site just to the north of Buxton, Oak Tree Farm Camping. Why not join us for a bite to eat, it'll take me and Fred an hour or so to get back, I'll show you on the map where it is."

"I've got a better idea than that," said Pat, "why don't you come with me and show me the way?"

"Great! let's do it!" Pegg replied.

They continued walking together, with the dogs trailing behind. After twenty minutes they came across a parking, area there were about four cars at this location. Pat got a set of keys out and pressed an ignition key, the indicator lights on a blue Nissan X-Trial lit up, as the vehicle was unlocked. She opened the tail gate, there was an old blanket on the floor of the luggage space, without any hesitation, Zena, the shepherd jumped up and sat down on the blanket. The poodle looked at Pegg,

"Go on boy, up!" Without any further ado, Fred joined Zena on the blanket. The shepherd proceeded to lick his muzzle.

"Those two have really hit it off," said Pat closing the tailgate. They went to the front of the vehicle and got in.

Pegg looked at his map, a 1/25000 Ordnance Survey of the local area. "Okay" he said, "turn right out of the parking area, and continue on the road for about a mile, until we get to a set of crossroads, take a left and follow the signs to Buxton, that will take us to the site."

Pat started up and put the X-Trail into gear and pulled out onto the road. A while later she was driving through the entrance to the site. Pegg indicated the site office, and she pulled up outside, whilst Pegg went into the building. Whilst she was waiting, she made a call to her parents saying that she would be home a bit later. Pegg returned to the vehicle shortly after this.

"Normally visitors have to park here, but as there are not too many caravans here, you can park your car next to mine," he said.

Pegg indicated where Pat should drive and two minutes later she had parked the X-Trail next to his Land Rover. Pegg unzipped the entrance to the awning, and got a couple of old towels, one of which he gave to Pat, the other he used on Fred's paws. Neither dog was too muddy, as the ground they had been over was reasonably dry, and there had been no stretches of water for the animals to jump in. After the dogs were dried, Pegg unlocked the 'van, reached inside and turned on the awning light.

"I think we can sit out here, are you okay with that?" he asked.

"That's fine by me, "she said before continuing. "May I use the bathroom?"

"Sure", said Pegg, "are you okay using mine or would you rather go to the shower block?".

"Yours would be fine, "she said.

Pegg took off his boots, and Pat did likewise, he entered the 'van and showed where the 'vans washroom was. He went back outside again. He got out the water bowl and poured the dogs some water. Zena went first and when she had drunk her fill, Pegg topped it up, and the poodle drank his fill as well. Pat joined them.

"What would you like to drink, tea, coffee, or something else," he asked.

"Tea would be fine, white 2 sugars."

"Coming right up, I've got some vegetable soup and some rolls, would that be okay?"

"Perfect", she said, "can I help at all?"

"Well I'll pass some things out to you, if you can put them on the table," he said indicating the folding camp table. He proceeded to rattle around the inside of the 'van, emerging with a tray, on which he had placed some plates, cutlery, butter, rolls and cheese slices. Pat placed them on the table. The dogs eyed the table but remained lying on the floor of the awning.

"I think it might be best if I stay out here, otherwise our supper may end up inside our dogs."

"Good thinking," said Pegg, "Fred's normally quite good like that, but even the best-behaved animal can't help itself! After we had ours I will feed Fred, what about Zena?"

"I think I'd rather wait until we go home, if you don't mind, Archie," she said.

"That's fine I'll wait until you've gone before I feed him, not fair on your girl, Fred having his scoff whilst she has to wait for hers," he said.

He came out again this time with two mugs of tea, which he placed on the table, before going back inside of the 'van. A short while later he emerged with 2 bowls of soup. They sat at the table and ate their food. They talked about themselves further, and about dogs. Pegg talked about his future with the police and the decision he must make as to whether he retire or continue his service. He explained the pros and cons about continuing and asked what her thoughts are. She asked if there was anything else he wanted to do, he said there was nothing that came to mind. He could go back to his old trade of electrician but would have to do some sort of refresher training if he was to work professionally.

They continued talking for a further 2 hours. Pat looked at her watch, it was nearly a quarter to eight.

" Well, Archie we need to be making tracks, I know it's Sunday tomorrow but I'm going out to lunch with some friends, and I've got some stuff to do first thing," said Pat.

"Yeah, me too, well it's been great having your company, sorry about the simplicity of the meal," he replied.

"It was sufficient for me," she paused before continuing.

"Look Archie, I'd like to meet again, if that's okay with you."

"I'd like that, I'll tell you what we can exchange email addresses and phone numbers?"

"Of course," she said.

Pegg went inside the 'van and returned with a pad and a pen, he wrote his details down, tore the sheet of the pad and gave it to her, she did the same on the pad's next sheet.

"Right come on Zena, it's time to go, say goodbye to Fred." She put her boots and jacket on.

Pegg fetched a torch lantern and accompanied Pat to her car, she put the shepherd in the back and went to the driver's door.

"Thanks for today, Archie, we'll speak very soon."

"Look forward to that, are you okay navigating your way out of here, turn right at the site entrance and that takes you to Buxton."

"I'll be fine, once I get to Buxton, I'll be home in about an hour," she said.

"Okay, to put my mind at rest give me a quick call when you get home."

"I'll do that," she gave Pegg a peck on the cheek, "thanks again", she got into the vehicle, started up and drove away.

Pegg went back to the 'van, he was feeling a bit lightheaded, that was an afternoon well spent he thought. He cleared away the table and placed the crockery and cutlery in a bucket, to be washed with the breakfast things in the morning. He fed Fred, and went inside the 'van, he poured himself a beer, and called Angie, he talked for about 10 minutes. He then got a book and read; Fred had decided that Pegg's lap was better than his basket in the awning. Whilst he continued to read the dog started to softly snore. His phone rang, it was Pat saying she was safely back home, they talked for 5 minutes. After they had finished Pegg thought about their afternoon. He would like to meet her again, but he was now feeling slightly reticent. He was still pining for Cath, and how would Angie feel that he was going to start a relationship with another person. We'll have to see how it pans out he thought. But he was realising that in the short time he had met Pat, how much he enjoyed her company.

He yawned, "I think it's time I turned in, boy. Let's go once round the block."

The poodle jumped off his lap and after having his leash put on, they went out for 5 minutes. Pegg returned to the van and got ready for bed. By the time he turned the lights out it was about eleven o'clock. He went to sleep.

CHAPTER 10

Pegg woke up with a start, he felt a weight on his chest, and it was not until he felt a cold damp nose in his ear, did he realise that Fred had jumped onto his bed. He looked at his watch, it was ten to eight.

"Come on boy, off," he said getting out of bed. He put on a pair of jogging bottoms and a sweatshirt, before going out into the awning and putting on the walking boots and jacket. He spent the next half hour walking the dog, before returning to the 'van. He put the poodle in the front of the Defender and then went to the shower block, where he showered and had a shave.

After returning to the 'van he let the dog out and both went back into the awning. He breakfasted on cereal, toast and boiled egg. He fed Fred and put him back in the Defender. After returning to the shower and washing the dirty crockery and utensils, he tidied up the 'van and the awning.

Then he set up his laptop and did a bit more online surfing. The knowledge he now had regarding criminals of Albanian origin, he decided to look into Albania's recent history. He saw that the Albanian people had suffered a great deal since being invaded by the Axis Powers during the Second World War. After the war, there was over fifty years of a brutal Stalinist dictatorship, under Enver Hoxha. Hoxha died in 1985, and the regime finally fell in 1992. Since its fall Albania has struggled to become a modern democracy, but the level of corruption and criminality has increased since the fall of the communists. The Albania mafia gangs have made the lives of this sad country's citizens a misery. Family feuds are rife, and many of the people escape the country because of this. Albanian mafia gangs are part of the criminal scene throughout Europe and Scandinavia. In the United Kingdom they are active in people trafficking, prostitution, and in the supply of illegal drugs. They launder the some of the proceeds of their nefarious activities through the numerous hand car wash facilities that are now located in cities and towns throughout the UK. Pegg already knew about the car wash money laundering as this was published in the Police Intelligence bulletins. He continued to search for more information about the Kosovo war, and NATO's involvement, after an hour. He packed his laptop away.

"Right, Fred, best we start to get ready to go to Tony's", he said. The dog lifted his head up from where he was lying on the bench, and cocked his head to one side, looking at Pegg. He then resumed the prone position he was in, sighed, and went back to sleep.

Pegg dressed in a pair of slacks, a shirt and tie, and a blue blazer. He decided on his regimental Sapper tie, the blazer had no Corps badge on the pocket. He put on a pair of black brogues. He put Fred's leash on and locked up the van. He had with him his file, and the newly printed email attachments. By the time he drove off the site it was a quarter to twelve. He decided to call in at a supermarket in Buxton. There he purchased some flowers, 2 bottles of wine and a box of chocolates. He then drove off to Tony's place, arriving there a few minutes after twelve-thirty.

Tony lived in a modest three bedroom detached house, built in the 1930s, there were two bay windows on the ground and upper floors, to the right of the house there was a detached brick built double garage, the house itself was set back from the road, which allowed for off street parking. A green Vauxhall Astra was parked in front of the house, there was still plenty of room for Pegg to park the Defender.

"Right you'll have to stay here for a bit, whilst I find out what's what," he said to the dog. Fred sighed and lay down again on his blanket.

Pegg went around to the back of the vehicle and took out the items he had purchased in the supermarket. He left the file and its diverse paperwork in the back. He walked to the front door, before he could ring the doorbell, the door was opened by Spratt.

"Archie, glad you could make it. Come on in and meet the family."

Archie entered the house and was ushered into the sitting room. There was an elderly couple sitting down in two of the three armchairs. The man got up, he was about 6 feet tall slim, and in spite of his years, still had a ramrod straight back. He had a good head of grey hair which was neatly trimmed. He was dressed in a pair of light brown trousers and a V necked pullover. It did not need the Guards tie he was wearing to tell Archie here was a former Guardsman.

"This is my father-in-law, Dick Winterton, and my mother-in-law Doris Winterton." Doris was clearly quite frail and did not get up. Pegg took Dick's proffered hand, the handshake was surprising strong. Pegg went over where Doris was sitting and gently took her hand. Doris was quite a small woman, in her eighties, with silver hair, and behind her glasses she had startlingly sapphire eyes.

"Pleased to meet the both of you, I expect Tony has told you, we were soldiers together," said Pegg. He did not mention anything about the BWIT business.

"Yes," said Dick, "Tony had mentioned you earlier. We were just talking about you before you came."

"I'll just go and get Marge, she's currently out the back," said Spratt, and with that he left the room.

"I understand you are a policeman," said Doris.

"Whereabouts do you come from, your accent appears to be East Anglian."

"Yes, well spotted Doris, I am from Norfolk, born in Norwich, spent all my early life there until I joined the army as a junior soldier. After I left the army, I joined the Norfolk Constabulary, and have been there ever since."

"Do you have family, children?" she asked.

"I have a stepson and stepdaughter, they are my wife's children. I was widowed about six months ago. I have no children of my own. I am very close to my stepdaughter, and she and her husband Ross have a baby girl, who is an absolute delight to us all."

"Oh Mr Pegg, I'm so sorry, I didn't mean to be so nosy"

"Archie, please Doris, no don't worry, I take no offence at all. What has happened has happened, it is part of my life now."

Tony came back and with him was tall slim woman in her forties, she had the build of her father, but her mother's vivid sapphire eyes. Her hair was light brown and tied in a bunck.

"Archie this is Marge," he said.

"Hello Archie," she said, "Tony has told me so much about you, I'm so pleased to meet you in the flesh." She glanced over her parents before continuing. Pegg could see there were tears starting to well up in her eyes. "This business about Tony's time in Kosovo, it is really getting to us."

"I'm here to sort something out, don't worry about it, we'll get it fixed for him. Here, these are for you." He said giving her the flowers and the box of chocolates.

"And these may need a few minutes in the chiller, "he said giving the wine to Tony.

"Thank you so much", said Marge and Tony in unison.

"I understand from Tony that you have your dog with you, Archie, can you fetch him in?" said Marge.

"Yes certainly, he's been briefed to be on his best behaviour. He'll just want to introduce himself and then he'll settle down."

"Fetch him, I can't wait to see him," Marge replied.

Pegg went out to where the Defender was parked, and opened the front passenger door, the poodle was already on his feet, standing on the seat. He collected his laptop and bag from the back of the vehicle as well.

"Come on boy, there are folk who want to see you, "said Pegg picking the dog up and placing him on the ground. Pegg walked towards the house, Fred followed, but not before he had lifted his leg up against the back wheel of the Defender. Pegg felt a bit easier now that had happened, no grounds now for the dog to disgrace himself. The dog trotted to the front door and followed Pegg inside the house.

Fred immediately made his way into the front room. Marge stooped down and put her hand out. After giving the proffered her hand a thorough examination with his nose, he licked it, and she reciprocated by stroking him and tickling his ears. Fred was in seventh heaven and went into "you're my best friend mode". He went over to Doris and Dick and gave the elderly couple a cursory greeting before going back to Marge.

"Come on Fred", she said, "let's go out the back and I'll introduce you to Max." With that she bustled out of the room, with Fred eagerly following her.

"Be careful, Archie, or you'll lose him, she has really taken a shine to him." said Spratt.

"I'm really glad he is such a sociable animal."

"Where did you get him?" said Doris.

"He belonged to my wife, he was a pup when I first met her, and he is about seven years old now. When Cath, my wife, died I decided to keep him. To tell the truth I just did not have the heart to part with him. He's good company now I live on my own. I manage to take him with me to work most of the time. When I can't Angie, my stepdaughter, looks after him. I shouldn't really have him with me, but he sits in my Landrover patrol vehicle, when I am out and about, and he's out of sight. I think the guvnors know about it, but they seem to turn a blind eye."

The small talk went on for a few minutes longer, before Spratt said:

"Right, drinks, what would you like Doris?"

"A small sweet sherry." She replied.

"Dick?"

"A glass of beer please, Tony."

"The same for me, thanks my man", said Pegg.

"Right coming up", said Tony, with that he left the room.

Pegg asked Dick what he did before he retired. The older man said that he worked as a carpenter after leaving the army. He said he originally did his National Service with the Grenadier Guards, before signing on for three years, in order to get the extra pay. He served for twenty-two years before leaving with the rank of colour sergeant. He served in Korea, Cyprus, Aden and Borneo. He'd met Doris whilst on sick leave, after having picked up a piece of shrapnel whilst fighting in Korea. They'd met at a local hop which was held in a village hall near to Buxton. She was a student nurse, at a teaching hospital in Derby. After recuperation Dick returned to Korea, and on returning home he continued to see Doris on various leaves between postings. When she qualified as a State Enrolled Nurse (SEN), she took up a post as a casualty ward nurse in Buxton. They married in 1954. Margaret was born in 1960. Dick left the army in 1970. He had trained as a carpenter and joiner after leaving school at fifteen, by the time he was called up in 1948, he was an indentured tradesman. He immediately found work in Buxton and worked for the same company until he retired from full time work in 1995, and after that he worked part time, he still did the odd job, but not too often now Doris was getting frail. Doris, who was four years younger than Dick, retired from the NHS in 1994, she continued to work part time at a GP's practice, until ill health forced her to give up work completely in 2004.

Spratt returned with a tray of drinks, after everyone had their respective tipple in their hands, the small talk continued until Marge came in and informed the party that lunch was on the table, she ushered everyone into the dining room. After they had all taken their places, Spratt said the Grace. This did not surprise Pegg, as Spratt came from church minded family, and he respected him for that. The meal was served up, and as Spratt had promised, Marge had prepared and served a marvellous feast.

"Where are the dogs," asked Pegg.

"Oh, don't worry about them. They are getting along fine, they're in the kitchen, and they've got something good to eat," Marge replied.

The conversation moved onto Spratt's involvement with the BWIT investigation, it was something Pegg did not really want to talk about, but in spite of his best efforts to steer the talk away from it, Marge was getting quite concerned, and Pegg decided to allay some of her and Tony's concerns.

"You hear about these veterans being investigated for events that happened in Northern Ireland and Iraq, where is it all going?" she said.

"Look, I've had a quick look at some of the stuff that is alleged to have happened in Kosovo, and it just does not add up", said Pegg before continuing, "it would appear that places times and dates are all out of sync. Where the allegations are coming from is a complete mystery, which we intend to get to the bottom of. I've brought some stuff with me, which I'll be going over with Tony later this afternoon. So, let's enjoy this delicious food, try not to worry too much. Things are not so bleak as they seem."

With that the meal continued without the conversation going back to Tony's involvement with the BWIT. A dessert of apple pie and cream followed. After they had all finished and the dishes were cleared, Spratt and Pegg went to the kitchen, to wash up, whilst Marge joined her parents in the living room. The dogs were in the garden, Fred had one of one of Max's toys in his mouth and Max was chasing him. Spratt rinsed the plates and placed these along with the cutlery in the dishwasher. The pans and the more fragile glassware were washed in the sink. Pegg dried the items after Tony had washed and rinsed them. It always amazed people how domesticated servicemen, both serving and retired, were. A lot is due to personal pride, and the fact that it was drilled into recruits the need for tidiness and cleanliness. Hours of mess hall fatigue duties, and barrack block conservancy, meant that the average veteran loathed to live in filth and squalor. As both men continued to clean the kitchen after the meal, Pegg informed Spratt of what he had done.

"The firm of solicitors have sent a load of stuff, which I'd like to go over with you; I've printed a lot of paperwork off. There are forms to fill in, and sign. I'd like to get it done whilst I'm down here, today if possible, is that okay with you?"

"That's fine with me. I've sort of cleared it with Marge," replied Tony.

"What about your children?"

"Oh, don't worry about Jane, she's on shift, at the hospital, she's works as a nurse in A&E. Anyway, she lives the other side of town, I've not told her about this yet. Bryan is at university in Birmingham, he'll not be home until Christmas."

"It is my intention to get all the forms filled in and posted off this evening, are you up for that?"

"That sounds like a plan to me Archie. When we've done here, we'll take the hounds for a wee bit of exercise, and then we can get started, we'll use the dining room."

After they had finished in the kitchen, Spratt went to the living room and informed Marge what they were going to do. They then took the dogs and left the house. There was a small park nearby and there they let the dogs off their leashes, the animals promptly went into play mode and proceeded to chase each other. Pegg explained to Spratt that he believes there is no case for him to answer, but having said that, it was wise to get solicitors to take on the case. After about thirty minutes they returned to the house. When they got in, the dogs went to the kitchen and took it in turns to nearly drink Max's water bowl dry. Then with wet muzzles they retired to Max's basket, and after managing to squeeze themselves in, went to sleep.

Marge who was in the kitchen, making some coffee said,

"What have you done with these boys Tony?"

"They've been chasing each other ragged all around the park, behaving like a pair of pups, they really have become the best of buddies."

"Well at least Max's bed is big enough for them both, but they can't be comfortable, look at them!"

Fred lifted his head a bit and then went back to sleep; Max was gently snoring.

"Archie and I will have our coffee in the dining room, are you okay if we go through some papers from the solicitors?

"Just get it done, all this business is worrying me sick, mum and dad are fine with it, like me they just want it sorted out."

"We'll take our coffee to the dining room." "Wait I got some pastries, take them in and then you and Archie can help yourselves."

Tony put the cafetiere on the tray along with cups, saucers and cream. Marge loaded up another tray with side plates and a plate of Danish pastries. They proceeded to the living room, where Pegg was in deep conversation with Dick and Doris. Marge poured them their coffees and where appropriate added cream. Pegg and Tony retired to the dining room, each with a cup of coffee and a side plate with a pastry on it. Pegg retrieved his laptop and folder from the bag in the hallway. He checked in the kitchen, and on seeing both animals deep in slumber, joined Tony in the dining room. For the next hour Tony, under Pegg's guidance read through and filled out the various forms. There was a little concern from Tony as to how he was going to fund the cost of the solicitors in contesting the allegations against him. It would appear that the forms included something about legal aid. Another form asked for details of any insurance policies. Pegg explained some household and commercial policies contain legal expenses clauses. Solicitors will look to these to see if a client may be covered. Pegg also said that if the client wins their case, then the solicitors will claim back legal expenses on the clients behalf. Once all the forms were completed, Pegg sealed them up in the addressed Freepost envelope provided by Open Justice Advocates.

"I'll speak to OJA in the morning, and if I deem it appropriate I'll email Rachel Gluckstein and let her know what I've found out, you don't have a problem with that do you?" said Pegg.

"No, Archie, you just do what you think is necessary." "Another thing, Tony, if you get arrested, and this may not happen, but if you do, before they interview you, you'll be asked if you want a solicitor, make sure you do not say anything in interview until you have spoken to a solicitor, or got a solicitor present."

"Why I've got nothing to hide, I should be okay." "Tony you are an innocent! Take it from me the type of person who'll be interviewing you will be after tripping you up and getting you to say things you did not mean, do as I advise, honestly it's in your best interest," replied Pegg.

"Okay, I'll be guided by what you tell me," replied Tony, who was clearly starting to feel uneasy and stressed out.

Pegg could clearly see how upset his friend was getting. "Look, my man, you are not alone in this, I am with you all the way. We'll get through this, and then some bastard is going to pay for make these false accusations against you. Now I'm going to spend the rest of my time here in Derbyshire, making inquiries and getting things up and running. What I want you to do is to carry on with your work and home life. We'll meet up in a weeks' time. Remember, I am at the end of the phone, call me any time. Now I'm going to take my leave of you good people; I'll let you spend the rest of the day with the misses and the outlaws."

They returned to the living room and joined Marge and her parents. Pegg said farewell to Dick and Doris. Marge and Tony walked Pegg to the front door. "Thank you so much for the meal, it was a delight to meet your parents, Marge," Pegg said.

"The pleasure's all mine, Archie," she replied.

"Right where's that hound of mine? Fred come on boy!" With that he heard a scuffling from the kitchen and the poodle came trotting to the door, closely followed by the spaniel. "Oh can't, you leave him behind?" asked Marge, half-jokingly.

"Be careful what you wish for," said Pegg laughing.

With that they said their farewells and Pegg went to the Defender, followed by the dog. He opened the passenger door, and the animal jumped in. Pegg entered the driver's side, started the vehicle up, waved at the Spratts, and drove off. As he drove onto the road and away from the house, he did not notice the black Vauxhall Astra that was parked just down the road from the driveway. The car pulled out and followed the Defender. The driver of the Astra kept a good distance from Pegg's vehicle. The journey back to the site was uneventful, there was a bit of traffic on the road, which meant that the presence of the Astra did not seem out of the ordinary, as he turned into the site, the Astra drove past without slowing, seemingly just another car driving past the site.

Pegg drove to his pitch, parked up, and both he and the dog entered the caravan. The driver of the Astra pulled up a short distance from the site, turned Around, and drove past the site entrance again. He stopped in a small lay-by about a hundred metres from the site's entrance. It was now nearly dark. The driver got out, he was dressed in dark clothing, and wearing a woolen "Beanie" hat. He made his way towards the site and stole past the entrance. There were only a dozen or so caravans, plus a couple of motorhomes parked up. The man saw the Defender, and the caravan. He noted where it was and left the way he came. A few minutes later the Astra drove off.

Pegg meanwhile phoned Angie and spoke to her for about ten minutes. He told her about his afternoon with the Spratts, without mentioning the paperwork he and Tony had completed for OJA. He ended the call, saying he would be in touch tomorrow evening. He took Fred out for a final walk and returned to the 'van. He got ready for bed, and by ten-thirty pm he was asleep.

CHAPTER 11

T he following morning, Pegg was up and dressed by seven-thirty. He went out for an hour with the dog, walking to the local shop where he purchased a paper. He returned, made some breakfast, and read the paper. After clearing up and tidying the inside of the 'van, he switched on his laptop. He visited the BWIT website, bringing up the "Contact Us" page. There were several telephone numbers and email addresses. He decided on "General Enquiries". After dialing the number, an automated answering system invited the caller to select a number of options, Pegg did what he always did when dealing with these systems. He waited for his call to be put through to an operator.

"Balkan War Investigation Team General Enquiries, my name is Kevin, how may I help?"

"I'm Archie, I'd like to speak to someone about some serious concerns I have regarding allegations being made, about serious mistreatment of civilians in Kosovo."

"Hold the line whilst I try to put you through to someone who can assist you with your query."

The line switched to some inane music, after waiting for a minute, another voice came on the line.

"Hello, I understand you have some information regarding mistreatment of civilians in Kosovo."

"I'm sorry but I want to find out who is making these allegations."

"Are you representing someone who has been subject to mistreatment by members the British Army?"

Pegg was getting increasingly annoyed; he kept his feelings to himself. He thought for a minute, he wanted to tease some more information out of the call taker, before he continued.

"No, but I have been in contact with a guy, who claims members of his family were, and I'd like to be pointed towards someone or an organisation which might be able to help him."

"I see, well the Balkan War Investigation Team has its own investigators, so If you could let me have some details. Where in the Balkans does this person come from?"

"Do you arrange for people to go to see these people in their country of origin?"

"If necessary yes but there are a lot of them who are refugees in this country, so our investigating teams work within the UK as well."

Pegg thought he had said enough, without arousing any suspicions, it was time to end this telephone call.

"That's brilliant, I've got your details from the web page, and I'll pass these on."

Pegg ended the call. He made some more notes. It would seem that the BWIT does not actively go out to find out about war crimes but relies on complaints being made and then these are investigated. So how did they come to investigate Tony Spratt? Where did the information come from? He decided to contact OJA.

"Rachel Gluckstein's secretary, how can I help, Mr Pegg," she said.

"I'm just wondering how the BWIT obtains the information regarding complaints against members of the armed forces?"

"From our experience it would appear that BWIT does do some sort of canvassing. They put announcements in the press both at home and abroad, such as Albanian language publications in the UK and obviously the local press in Kosovo. Of course, the firms of solicitors who act on behalf of alleged victims, would also do their own type of canvassing. By for example leaving adverts in community centres, on Albanian language TV and radio programmes"

"But how do they get the names of the soldiers, and the units in which they were serving at the time?"

"That, Mr Pegg, we are not sure about. Maybe it's the MoD which does this. I believe this is the case with the Iraq Historic Allegations Team enquiries."

"Well thank you for your time. By the way Mr Spratt has completed the paperwork you sent him; you should be getting it soon. Thank you again."

"You're welcome Mr Pegg; if you have any more information for Rachel, it would be most welcome. Goodbye Mr Pegg."

Well I can see how Lawyers for Personal Justice obtain names of potential complainants, but where do the names come from, thought Pegg. Some department within the Ministry of Defence has this information, and once a complaint has been received by the BWIT this department then furnishes the details of the unit and personnel. Okay, he continued with his thoughts, then the Lawyers for Personal Justice lodge a complaint on behalf of their clients to the BWIT, and they then investigate the case. Seems straight forward enough, but one would have thought that the investigators would look at the facts first before embarking on interviewing any British Armed Forces personnel regarding allegations of misconduct. One complaint for certain was bogus, Enver Haji was Albanian and not a Kosovar. If this is the case how many others are making bogus claims? He decided to send an email to Rachel Gluckstein, voicing his suspicions regarding the allegations being made to the BWIT, but not yet mentioning this specific complainant. He made some more notes and added the pieces of paper to his growing file.

It would seem that Tony Spratt's name had been put forward only because he was in Kosovo, and especially in Pristina at the time of the alleged incidents. What a bastard system, he mused. Pegg, thinking like a policeman, at the start of an investigation one would like to think all the evidence of wrongdoing would be looked at before people started knocking on doors. Surely the veracity of the complainants should be ascertained first. Maybe I am being a bit too simplistic he thought. It is time to take the bull by the horns and confront Lawyers for Personal Justice.

"Come on Fred; let's take another trip to Nottingham."

The dog pricked up his ears and waited eagerly by the 'vans door. Pegg gathered his file and dog leash and made his way to the

Landrover. He secured the 'van, and placed Fred and his papers in the front. He drove out of the site and headed towards Buxton, where he took the route to Nottingham. He arrived in Mansfield Road around midday, parking off Mansfield Road he walked to Coronation Buildings. He'd left the dog, but this time he had the driver's side window open. The vehicle was in the shade and although the weather was dry, it was overcast. Pegg made his way to LPJ's offices.

This time he found that the office door on the first floor was open, so Pegg walked in and waited at the counter. This time a different person got up from his desk and came over to where Pegg was standing. The man was in his 30s, well built with shoulder length brown hair and grey eyes.

He did not seem too friendly, but he did not recognise Pegg from his previous visit, "What do you want?" he asked.

"Well, I could be a potential client, there's no need to sound so hostile."

The man's English, whilst reasonably fluent was heavily accented. "I'm sorry if I give that impression, we are here to help, so sir, I ask again what can I do for you?"

"I understand your firm does act for victims of mistreatment as a result of the Balkan operations involving NATO Forces."

"That's correct, how do you know this?"

"From the internet, there are a lot of firms dealing with claims from victims of mistreatment from the British Armed Forces in Iraq, Afghanistan, Northern Ireland and the Balkans, I found the name of your firm, and you deal with complaints regarding the Balkans, especially Kosovo. How do you get the information regarding potential victims, the reason I ask is that I know of someone who thinks he may have a claim, but he is anxious not to give me anything other than his name, as he does not want to get involved with the authorities."

"How do you come across a guy, who does not want to give his name?"

"Well he works at a hand car wash, which I regularly take my car to, I see him quite often and I got talking to him, He mentioned his time in Pristina, before he managed to get out."

"I see just wait there a minute." With that the man left the counter, and went away, he went to one of the offices at the end of the large.

Pegg waited some ten minutes before the same man came back to him. He was frowning and he came up to Pegg. "I think it's time for you to leave, we've got nothing to say to you," he said.

"Hey steady on, I'm here to try and help a chap. What on earth is the problem?"

The man came around to Pegg's side of the counter and opened the outer door which led to the landing and stairs

"Leave now," he said

Pegg did not want to argue and decided that discretion being the better part of valour, left the building. Someone must have recognised me from the previous visit he thought. He looked at the CCTV camera that covered the waiting area. He walked through the door, which was slammed shut behind him. He heard the door being locked. Pegg made his way down the stairs. He checked the entrance lobby and saw no further CCTV cameras; he noticed a keypad on the wall next to the street door, which must have been for arming and disarming the burglar alarm. He took his phone out and surreptitiously took a photo of the keypad. He opened the street door and could see that there were sensors around the door frame. He walked out into the street and looked at the outside door and the wall around it. The brickwork was devoid of any sign of CCTV equipment. Pegg walked away and returned to the Landrover. This time there had been no attempt at breaking into the car. He went to the driver's side and unlocked the door. Fred got up from the passenger seat and went over to the driver's side.

"Good lad, thanks for looking after our stuff", he said. He tickled the dog's ears and gently pushed him back to the driver's seat. Right he thought time for some serious action. LPJ is obviously an organisation that sails very close to the wind, and it would appear a degree of its day to day workings are clearly illegal. It really needs bringing to account. He pondered as to how he was to get the evidence of this and pass it on to a person or organisation that will expose LPJ's nefarious activities. Pegg was under no illusions that he could obtain such evidence openly; he would have to work covertly. The next thing he considered in obtaining such evidence, could he do this legally. He put away his thoughts and started up the Landrover and pulled out of his parking slot.

He made his way out of the city and headed back to Buxton. Before he left Nottingham he stopped at a Superstore and purchased a couple of USB memory sticks. On the way to Buxton, he pulled into a lay-by cum rest area. There were a couple of articulated lorries parked up near to a trailer snack bar. The back of the lay-by gave way to a small wooded area. Pegg got out and put Fred on his leash. He walked to the wooded area; the close proximity of the main road precluded Pegg letting Fred off the leash. He wandered about for about ten minutes, before returning to the Landrover, where gave the dog some water, after which he put the animal back in the Landrover. He wandered over to the snack bar and bought an egg and bacon roll. By the side of the snack bar there were some plastic chairs and a table. Pegg joined a pair of men who must have been the drivers of the artics. Pegg chatted with them whilst he ate his roll. He continued to make small talk until both drivers got up, one of them saying that his rest period was nearly up. Pegg bade them farewell and made his way back to the Landrover. He glanced at his watch it was half past two.

He decided to give Angie a call on her mobile. The call was picked up almost immediately.

"Hi Archie, how's it going? I hope that you are doing nothing and just chilling!" she said.

"Oh in between various visits I'm doing just fine. Just a bit of advice regarding IT stuff. How would I get around a pass-word on a computer?" he asked.

"Well there are ways and means, where are we going with this Archie?"

"Well in a hypothetical situation, a friend needs to get into a PC or laptop, and he has forgotten his password, what could be done?"

"Well Archie the obvious way would be to locate the password. Many of us are told the password should be in our heads. But the fact of the matter is most people can't remember them, especially if they have not been on their computer for a period of time. The result is that they write the password down, and keep it on them, or in a desk. In the office would you believe I've seen people write it down and stick to the PC's screen. So really I would advise your friend to have a look round and see if he has written it down somewhere. Nowadays people have so many passwords to remember it is inevitable that some passwords would be recorded somewhere which is near to hand."

"If I am unable to locate a password, what can be done then?"

"There are things you could do, but they would require a great deal of expertise. I am sometimes required to do it on an official basis in connection with my work. I am available to various companies, who are our clients, and I assist staff to unlock PC's and reset passwords."

"How can you do that without actually visiting your clients' premises, I mean you work from home don't you?"

"Yes, I can do this remotely, you see if the client's employee is at their PC, there is a method that I can take them through it over the phone."

"You can't do this without them being there?"

"Not really, any other way without their permission is stretching the bounds of legality."

Pegg went on to ask how things are with them all. Angie assured him everything was fine, and that they were going to Banham Zoo in the morning. They would make a day of it. Pegg wished her a good visit. He said he'd ring again tomorrow evening, hung up and went back to his laptop.

He took the memory card out of his phone and uploaded the image of the alarm keypad. He enlarged it so that it filled the whole of the laptop's screen. It is a fact that unless the keys of the keypad are cleaned, regular contact with uncovered fingers will cause the keys to be marked. As the code to an alarm is normally four digits, then only four of the ten keys would be pressed. The numbered keys went from '9' to '0', similar to the keys on a calculator. The keys were on four rows, numbered from the top and going from left to right the numbers read '7', '8', '9', and '4', '5', '6', and '1', '2', '3', and finally '0' in the centre of the bottom row, with the "alarm set" key to the left of the '0' and the "alarm disarmed" key to the right of the '0'. The four keys that were slightly discoloured compared with the rest of the keys on the keypad were **'2'**, **'4'**, **'6'**, and **'8'**. These keys were in the pattern of the points of the compass; **'8'** being north, **'2'** being south, **'4'** being east and **'6'** being west. Thinking logically, the code"**2468**" would seem too obvious. The points of the compass are normally read in the order north, south, east, and west. So, the alarm code would read **"8246"**.

Pegg pondered his findings. He thought of the entry codes to keypads at work. He realised that many were in a pattern, and when one entered the numbers on a keypad, one pressed the keys in a pattern rather than entering individual numbers. There was method in this madness, as a number of people would be needing to enter premises, and making the combinations too complicated, can lead to alarms being set off accidentally. This system is fine providing the access codes are changed on a regular_basis. It appeared that LPJ is neglecting to do this at its office in Coronation Buildings.

Pegg realised that if he was going to get the information he needed to assist in putting the BWCC's case against Tony Spratt to bed, he needed to obtain it by unofficial means. He'd need to have a good look around LPJ's office.

"Right, Fred, time to go back to the site, we've got stuff to do."

The drive back to Buxton and the camp site was uneventful, he arrived back on site at about a quarter to four. He noticed a black Vauxhall Astra parked in the layby prior to the site; the driver appeared to be making a phone call. Pegg thought nothing of it and continued onto his pitch. Pegg was unaware that the phone call the driver was making concerned Pegg himself.

"He's back now," the driver of the Astra said to the person to whom he was making the call.

"Okay", the voice at the other end of the phone said, "wait until he goes out again, and when it's dark, go and do what we agreed."

"But supposing he does not go out, I can't go snooping round, that dog will alert him."

"Wait until midnight, if he has not gone out by then, leave and come back tomorrow."

"I don't like this, it's just not right. What you want me to do is wrong. You asked me just to find out where this guy was," complained the driver of the Astra in accented English.

"Stop whingeing and do as you're told, you know what will happen if you don't. "said the English voice. The Astra's driver sighed and terminated the call; he continued his vigil.

Meanwhile Pegg made preparations to make a nighttime trip to Nottingham and re-visit LPJ's office. He realised the risk involved, and if an undetected entry into the premises could not be affected, he would immediately abort the operation, and get as far and as quickly away from the area. He would park the Landrover at or near to the place he had left it earlier that day. He would dress in some clothing he had not worn on his previous visits. He had a box of disposable gloves with the 'van, as it was his habit to wear these when carrying out maintenance and waste disposal jobs pertaining to the day to day operation of a caravan whilst on site. He packed them away in a small rucksack, together with a roll of tools and a LED head torch and also the USB sticks he had purchased earlier. During his career in the army, and latterly with the police, Pegg had accrued a lot of knowledge into the mechanics of locks. This had proved invaluable in getting into houses in the case of emergencies, especially elderly people who had collapsed at home and were unable to get to the door. Gaining entry to such premises, without causing damage saved on insurance claims and saved the police budget.

Pegg contemplated the possibility he would be committing the offence of "going equipped" if he was caught. However, he had thought that on the balance of probabilities the chance of this happening was minimal. In his mind he saw that a corrupt system was persecuting innocent soldiers, who had done nothing more than their job in very difficult and harrowing circumstances. The attitude of politicians in allowing this to happen was beneath contempt. He believed the end justifies the means.

He took Fred for another walk. If he had walked past the lay-by he would have seen the black Astra still parked; but he didn't, he continued out of the camp site in the opposite direction. He walked for about forty minutes before returning to the 'van.

At five o'clock he made up a packed meal, sandwiches and a flask of coffee. He put these in the rucksack. He changed into a pair of jeans and a sweatshirt, putting on a hoody over the sweatshirt; on his feet he wore an old pair of trainers, this footwear he intended to throw away once he returned from his trip to Nottingham. By the time he had made his preparations it was six and getting dark.

At forty-five minutes later he left the camp site. He passed the lay-by, the driver of the Astra ducked down in his seat as Pegg drove past. He waited until the taillights of Pegg's vehicle disappeared before he got out of the car. He went to the back of the car, opened the tail gate and removed a small bag. He closed the tail gate and locked the car, before making his way towards the camp site.

CHAPTER 12

Pegg continued onto Nottingham, the weather had turned cold and it had started to rain. The road was not too busy.

"The weather should be a bonus to us tonight, Fred", Pegg said to the poodle, who was lying on the passenger seat, "not too many folk about on a night like this."

The dog sat up and Pegg tickled the dog's ear with his left hand. He continued to Nottingham, arriving at the city's outskirts at around nine. About thirty minutes later he was parked up in a position which was very near to where he had parked earlier that day. He reached down to his rucksack and took out the flask and the sandwiches; he placed these behind the driver's seat, away from where Fred could reach them. He took the tool roll, USB sticks and the head torch out of the ruck sack and placed these items in the pockets of his jacket.

"Okay boy, time for me to leave you for a bit. You are to be a guard dog for me and do your stuff if anybody tries to get into our car, good lad," he said as the dog nuzzled his head into Pegg's arm.

Pegg got out of the vehicle and locked it. He made his way towards Mansfield Road. It was still raining as he crossed the road and approached Coronation Buildings. The windows of LPJ's office were in complete darkness. There was moderately light traffic on Mansfield Road, but there were hardly any pedestrians about. Pegg had the hood of his jacket up as he made his way towards the street door of LPJ's office. He put a pair of disposable gloves and he took out the tool roll before selecting a ring with a series of different sized picks attached to it. He quickly knelt beside the door and started to manipulate the Yale type lock.

Thirty seconds later he felt the lock give, he turned the handle, and gently pushed the door open. There was a pause before the keypad started to bleep. Pegg made his way to the keypad and entered **"8246"** and pressed the "alarm disarm button"; he held his breath, ready to make a rapid exit should he have failed to have entered the correct code. The keypad emitted a short bleep and then fell silent. Pegg heaved a sigh of relief. He secured the street door by engaging the Yale latch button. He waited to see if anyone had noticed anything. After five minutes he slowly made his way up the stairs. He bowed his head and kept it down as he climbed the stairs to the upper landing.

He approached the office door and knelt down and took out the picks again and started to manipulate the mortice lock. He had the door open a short while later and went into the main office space. All the blinds were closed, and the only illumination was from the outside streetlamps. He saw that none of the desk top monitors were on. He glanced at one of the desks. It was clear of any paperwork. He continued and he made his way towards the two small offices at the end. They were both open. Unlike the main office space, both the desk top monitors appeared to be on standby. As with the rest of the office space, the blinds on the windows were also closed. Pegg put the head torch on and entered the office to the left. He tapped the "enter" button on the desktop's keyboard. The screen invited him to enter a password. Pegg had a quick look round the top of desk. He could find no clues as to a password, he tried the drawers at the side of the desk; he found that these were locked. Pegg continued his search by entering the office on the right; the layout was similar to the other office.

He could see a calendar on the wall next to the desk. The days of the week were in a foreign language, and the picture for the current month appeared to be a view of a coastal town, in what appeared to be a Mediterranean setting. At the top of the picture he recognised the word "Shqiperise" and "Durres." Of course, he thought the first word is Albania in that country's language and Durres was a city on the country's coast. Pegg came to the conclusion he was in the office of the Albanian born partner of LPJ, Mehmet Ali, and the other office must be that of James Smithson, the firms other partner.

Pegg was startled when the phone on the desk rang. He could see that the phone was part of an answering machine; there was a short pause and the machine clicked and another pause before a male voice came on speaking in a foreign language. Pegg thought to himself, I bet the caller is speaking Albanian, and that he was leaving a message for Ali; more than likely a bit of trade for LPJ. After a couple of minutes, the machine went quiet again. Pegg continued with his search. He could see that the desktop was on. He pressed the "enter" key on the keyboard. This time the screens desktop appeared.

"Good grief no password, what are you like my man!" Pegg exclaimed to himself. He clicked onto the documents icon, and the screen was filled with file icons, which fortunately all had their titles written in English. One said "Recent Clients" Pegg opened it and immediately saw the name Enver Haji. Pegg closed the icon and took a USB memory stick out of his pocket. He put this in a USB port he clicked onto the Recent Clients file icon and sent the contents to the memory stick, it took 10 seconds to do this. He looked at other file icons and clicked on "BWIT". There were quite a number of files; without further ado Pegg sent the contents of "BWIT" the memory stick, this time it took twenty seconds to download.

Pegg could not see anything else of immediate interest on the list of files. He removed the USB stick and replaced it with another one. He then opened up the email icon and clicked onto the inbox. He did not open any of them, instead pressed "save as" the all files column appeared, and he sent the entire email contents to the USB memory stick. Pegg removed the second memory stick and put it in his pocket. The telephone on the desk rang again. This time the voice leaving a message was male speaking English.

"Just to let you know I have just been informed that our difficulty has been resolved." The machine went silent again. Pegg froze. The voice was that of Richard Hoskins. Pegg glanced at the clock on the answering machine; it was now eleven-thirty. He took the handset off its cradle and saw that the call had been made from a mobile number taking a post-it from the pad beside the phone and he scribbled down the number and put the post-it in his trouser pocket. He went over to the window, and pulled the blinds back slightly, it was still raining, and except for the occasional passing car Mansfield Road was quiet. He decided that he had seen enough, and that enough information had been obtained for the time being. He gathered up all his stuff and removed the head torch. He checked the offices again and left the desks and the computers as he had found them.

He put the hood of his jacket over his head again and moved to the main office door, going through it, he locked it again and made his way down the stairs. He took the Yale off its latch, and he opened the door slightly and glanced outside. The street was clear of any pedestrians. He went over the alarm keypad and entered **"8246"** and pressed the "alarm set" button and went out of the street door and closed it again. He heard the alarm go "bleep" "bleep" and then went silent. Pegg tried the door to make sure it was locked, before he made his way back to the Landrover. He removed the gloves and placed them in his pocket. He got back to the vehicle without any incident. Fred was all over him when he got into the vehicle.

"Good lad, we'll just have a drink and a sandwich and then we'll go back," he said.

Twenty minutes later they set off back to Buxton.

CHAPTER 13

Pegg arrived back on site. It had stopped raining and it had turned cold. It was one-thirty in the morning by the time he had got inside the 'van and settled in. He was very tired. Fred had appeared quite unsettled when they had entered the awning, he was sniffing about the immediate vicinity of the 'van, he had his nose to the ground and was concentrating his attention around the area of the side opposite to the awning. Pegg thought it must have been some nocturnal animal, maybe a fox or a badger.

"Come on boy I'm tired, you can do your sniffing in the morning." The dog reluctantly gave up his searching and joined Pegg inside the 'van. It was quite cold so Pegg decided to turn on the heater. He used the gas setting on the heater over the electric option. The gas was more efficient and heated up the space faster than the electric. He set it to "high" for a bit whilst he got ready for bed. He unpacked the rucksack and placed the 2 USB sticks inside his laptops bag, he undressed and finished in the washroom; he turned the heater down to "medium". He got into bed and after turning the light out fell asleep almost immediately.

*   *   *

He was woken up by the howling of an alarm. It took a moment for Pegg to gather himself together. His immediate thought was it was the smoke alarm and there was a fire. He glanced up with horror to see the Carbon Monoxide (CO) monitor flashing.

"Fucking hell", he shouted. He turned the lights on and turned the gas heater off. He opened the door of the van as well as all the windows. Fred was still asleep; or seemed so. Pegg grabbed him and went outside into the awning.

"Oh no, no, don't do this boy." Pegg felt the animal's chest, he could feel his heart, and he was also snorting slightly, next the dog opened his eyes and gently licked Pegg's hand.

"Thank goodness for that, what on earth happened to us?" He glanced at his watch; it was half past two. Pegg carried Fred in his arms, whilst he made a quick assessment of the situation. There must be a fault with the gas heater, but he had the whole system checked out a month ago when the 'van was serviced. He removed the CO monitor and left it in the awning to vent it. He removed the batteries and the howling stopped. He put Fred down; the dog was a bit unsteady on his feet but wandered out of the awning and started to retch. He vomited, and then went inside again and emptied his water bowl.

Pegg put on a jacket, took a lamp, and proceeded to carry out an external examination of the 'van. He checked the area which Fred had been a great deal of interest. He found a partially used roll of "Kim Wipes"; these were blue heavy-duty paper towels and are the preferred choice of mechanics and engineering workshops. He glanced up and shone the lamp on the gas vent pipe at the top of the 'van. He could clearly see that there was something blue sticking out of the pipe. He shone his torch at the area around the right wheel of the 'van. He could see two small indentations in the ground. They were about 12 inches apart. It would seem that they could have been made by a ladder. There were no marks on the top of the 'van where the top of the ladder would have been positioned. If the upper part of the ladder had been placed against the awning rail then, no marks would have been left behind.

Pegg went back into the 'van again. Fred seemed to have recovered somewhat. He decided to keep the door of the van open and one of the windows opposite the door open as well. This would vent the 'van completely and blow away any remaining CO.

CO is a colourless and odourless gas, which unlike carbon dioxide (CO_2) is slightly lighter than air. The gas is lethal if inhaled over a period of time. It is produced by any form of combustion. All gas appliances have flues which vent the exhaust fumes. Should the flues be faulty or blocked the fumes which will contain CO will enter the space where the heater is situated and subsequently poison any person or animal in the vicinity. There have been many incidents of campers being killed due to them placing barbecues or open fires within the tent area with the result of them being asphyxiated by the CO fumes emitted from these sources of heat.

Pegg got some plastic sheeting and went outside again; he put the sheeting over the area where the ladder had been placed. Although it had stopped raining, he wanted to examine the area in more detail in daylight. He decided that there was little more he could do now, and that the best thing was to try and get some more sleep. The inside of the 'van was very cold now; the door and the window were left open. Pegg put some extra clothing over his pajamas and got another blanket which he put over his duvet. He got into bed again, before doing so he lifted Fred up onto the bed. The dog settled at the bottom of the bed, and Pegg finally got off to sleep again.

CHAPTER 14

After a surprisingly good sleep, Pegg woke up to a clear sunny morning. It was coming up for eight o'clock. He checked Fred who was lying at the foot of the bed. The dog was still asleep, and his breathing was regular.

"I'll get you checked out this morning boy", Peg said to himself. Pegg got up; he turned the electric heating on and closed the door and windows. Although it was sunny it felt very cold in the 'van. Pegg went over to the washrooms and had a shower and a shave. The headache and drowsiness he had when he woke up had largely dissipated by the time he got back to the 'van.

He dressed and got some breakfast. Fred was still asleep. Pegg finished his breakfast and placed the used cutlery and dishes in a bucket which he placed in the awning. He then went over to the site office, where he asked if anyone had been on site after seven yesterday evening. The manager sad that he was unaware of any visitors coming onto the site. Pegg asked the manager if he could borrow a ladder. The manager and Pegg went over to the store shed, where Pegg was given a light folding ladder.

He walked back to the 'van and placed the ladder against the side of the 'van. He then went around to the awning went into it. Fred who was still on the bed, stirred and sat up; he gave a yawn and jumped off. Pegg picked him up, the dog licked Pegg's face.

"We're going to the vets this morning and get you checked out, boy," he said.

He got Fred's leash and took him for a short walk at the site's dog exercise area. The dog did his business, and Pegg cleared up, the waste appeared to be normal. He placed the waste bag in the waste receptacle and made his way back to the 'van. He put Fred in the front of the Landrover, after which he then climbed the ladder and looked at the end of the flue pipe and pulled out the paper wipes. The flue was not completely blocked; if it had been, the CO alarm would have sounded very shortly after the gas heater had been turned on. By partially blocking the flue, the build-up of the poisonous gas would have been gradual, and the alarm would have sounded sometime later. The gas would have built up and entered the 'van at the level of the heater, and being slightly lighter than air, would have risen to the roof of the inside of the 'van where the CO alarm was located.

He had thought of reporting this incident to the police, but he knew that any investigating officer worth is salt would want to know why Pegg's 'van was selected for this attack, and not any other of caravans on the site. One thing would lead to another and he just did not want the aggravation at this time. He realised that his involvement in Spratt's predicament had touched a nerve somewhere, and he had seriously pissed someone off. Instead of scaring him, it spurred him on to find out more about the way the alleged war crimes in the Balkans were being investigated. Still first things first, it was time to get Fred checked out. He took the paper wipes that he had removed from the flue, came down the ladder, took it down, and returned the ladder to the site office. He found out the address of the nearest veterinary surgeon from information board. He took a note of the address; *High Peak Veterinary Practice, 8 Market Place Buxton.*

He drove into Buxton and found a place to park in the Market Place car park. He put Fred on his lead and lifted him over to the driver's side of the vehicle. He got out and put the dog down. He looked around and saw where the veterinary practice was located and walked over to it. Fred at first trotted quite happily with Pegg. Pegg hoped that he could get the animal into the vets without further ado. Fred like many dogs has an aversion to veterinary premises, or at least to the practices in Dereham. "Fingers crossed", thought Pegg to himself as he entered the practice. He opened the door, Fred must have immediately picked up the smell of the practice and dug his claws into the pavement outside and refused to move. Pegg picked the trembling dog up and walked in. The reception area was devoid of anyone else except the young woman who was manning the reception desk. Pegg walked over to the desk.

"My dog has been poisoned by carbon monoxide, he seems a bit better this morning, but I would be happier if you could give him a check-up," he said.

"Yes of course, we are not too busy, and there is a vet free; can you let me have a few details about your dog, and then we'll get him looked at," the receptionist said.

Pegg gave her his name and where he was staying and continued to give her Fred's details. She took all these down on a form, and asked Pegg to sign it. Pegg quickly checked the paperwork, which included his permission for the vet to examine the animal. The receptionist asked Pegg to take a seat, whilst she went away with the completed paperwork. Pegg carried the quivering Fred and sat down. After a couple of minutes, a door at the side of the reception desk opened, and a tall woman wearing green scrubs stood holding the door open.

"Mr Pegg please come in," she said, ushering in Pegg, who got up and carried Fred through the door.

The door opened into a room with an examination table in its centre. On the walls were various diagrams of the anatomy of dogs and cats. In the corner there was a rack of shelving, on which were bottles of what Pegg assumed were medicines and chemicals and other paraphernalia appertaining to veterinary procedures. The woman indicated for Pegg to place the now terrified Fred on the table.

"Come on boy, this lady is one of the good guys," said Pegg. The dog settled down a bit.

"Now Mr Pegg what seems to be the problem with this chap?"

"I am camped out in my caravan on a site just outside Buxton; last night I it was quite cold, so I put the gas heating on, before I went to bed. Fred was on my bed. I went to sleep, and I was woken up by the CO alarm. I realised that the gas heater must have had a fault. I found out that Fred was very listless, and whilst we both got out of the caravan, I had a headache which I seem to have got over, poor Fred was much the worse for wear. He has been sick and does not seem to be interested in his food. I brought him in for you to check him out."

"Okay, Mr Pegg, I will do that, he seems to be a lot better than the condition you have described at the time of the incident. Have you had yourself checked out?"

"No, do you think I should, I feel alright, and anyway I don't want to clog up some busy A & E Department."

"No need for that we have an excellent Minor Injuries Department at Buxton Hospital, in London Road. I strongly recommend you go there."

"Right let's see how you are, boy," she said. She used the stethoscope around her neck and listened to the dog's heart. She took his temperature, and looked into his eyes, and lifted the lids of both eyes.

"Well, all his vital signs are okay, his heartbeat is strong, and he has not got a temperature. If there was any CO in his system it would appear to have gone. I'll give you some medication for him. It is in the form of a tablet; let him have one three times a day for three days. He should be fine now. Get that heater checked out."

Pegg thanked the vet and took Fred out to the reception area. After a couple of minutes, the vet came out again and gave Pegg a small envelope with some tablets inside and some instructions written on the outside. The receptionist made out a bill, which Pegg paid using a debit card. He left the veterinary surgery with a relieved dog pulling on his lease as if he couldn't wait to be out of the place. Pegg made his way to where the Landrover was parked. He put the dog in the passenger side of the vehicle and got into the driver's side.

He drove out of the Market Place and headed south to London Road. He found the entrance to the hospital, at the entrance the sign on the wall said: *Minor Injuries Unit Open Daily 8-00 am to 10-00pm.* Pegg was fortunate enough to find a parking space. He parked up and made his way to the Minor Injuries Unit. He reported into the reception. There were a few of people in there. One a young man in working clothes holding a bandaged hand sitting next to a similarly dressed older man, the other was an elderly woman sitting next to a man of the same age. She looked pale and very frail. Pegg quickly explained what had happened to him, and he was taking the advice of vet who had examined Fred. He was asked to take seat. A nursing sister wearing what appeared to be blue scrubs came out and invited the young man to come into one of the treatment rooms. He and his companion followed the sister. Five minutes later a male nurse similarly dressed came out of another treatment room. He called out Pegg's name; Pegg got up and entered the treatment room. After explaining what had happened, the nurse took Peg's temperature, and blood pressure as well as using a stethoscope to listen to his chest. He asked Pegg about any ailments and whether he smoked or not. He looked into Pegg's eyes and asked about any other instances where he may have had previous CO poisoning. Pegg told him that as far as he knew this was the first time. The medic pronounced that his blood pressure, temperature, heart rate and lungs all appeared normal, and the effects of the CO were only temporary. He advised that if he should start to feel unwell to seek medical attention as soon as possible.

"Oh, and one other thing before you go, Mr Pegg," he said.

"What's that?" asked Pegg.

"Forgive me if this sounds obvious, but get that heater checked out before anything else."

"I certainly will. Thank you so much for your time. Do I owe you anything?"

"No, you pay us through your taxes and your NI stamp."

Pegg shook the man's hand and left the Department. He walked to the Landrover and drove out of the hospital's grounds. Twenty minutes later he was back on the site. He let the dog out of the Landrover and went into the awning. The dog, after a short pause to lift his leg against a nearby bush, followed Pegg into the awning. It was now coming up for midday. Pegg got Fred a small amount of food. Before he put the food down in the awning, he got out one of the dog's tablets, and gave it to him by placing it on his tongue, holding his mouth shut and gently massaging the animal's throat. Fred swallowed a couple of times, and the tablet was on its way to his stomach. He put Fred down. The dog went into the awning, drank some water from his bowl, and then proceeded to eat his food. Pegg left him at it and went back into the 'van.

He got his laptop out and logged on. The first thing he entered in the browser was caravan servicing Buxton. He found the names of a couple of mobile service engineers. He selected one and dialed the number. He did not want to explain what had happened to the flue. He said it was just peace of mind that he wanted the gas heating system checked out. The engineer said he could be up in a couple of hours. Pegg gave him the location of the site, the engineer knew where it was. After agreeing to the engineer's conditions for attending he ended the call. Pegg really wanted to make sure that no damage had been done to the gas system and flue during the intruder's attempt to tamper with the flue. He made himself a cup of tea and a sandwich. After eating he cleared away and added the cutlery and crockery he had used to the growing pile in the bucket, which he had previously placed in the awning. Fred who had finished his food, started to nose about in the bucket. Before he could proceed to lick the plates, Pegg snatched the bucket a way and placed it on the picnic table.

"No, you wretched animal!" chided Pegg, "you're obviously back to your normal self, thank God; I'll give you a bit more food." He went back into the 'van and fetched some more of Fred's food, pouring it into his bowl. The dog returned to the bowl and ate.

Pegg went out to the awning and to where he had placed the ladder. He took up the plastic sheeting he had put down earlier. He fetched a pair of latex gloves from the front locker of the 'van and put them on and returned to where the sheeting had been. He gave the area a thorough examination. Although Pegg was not officially qualified as a crime scene examiner, he was experienced in thoroughly searching an area. He picked up the skills during his time as a Royal Engineers Search Adviser (RESA), and as a serving constable. He looked at the ground as well as the partially used roll of Kimwipes, which had also covered by the sheeting. There were a number of greasy marks on the inner cardboard roll on which the paper towels were wound, including what appeared to be a number of fingerprints; these were at both ends of the roll. Pegg looked further. There was a small pattern at the bottom of each of the indentations made by the intruder's ladder. Pegg got his phone out and took photos of each of them. Just by the inside the right wheel of the 'van, something caught Pegg's eye. It was a small crumpled manila envelope. He photographed the envelope where it was lying in situ. He then picked it up and saw that there was what appeared to be a sheet of paper inside.

He carried the roll of Kimwipes and the envelope back to the awning and went inside the van again. He placed the items on the table, and picking up the envelope, examined it. It was the standard buff coloured variety which drops onto the doormat of any number of homes on an almost daily basis, but there was no postage stamp. There was an address window, but the paper inside was folded in such a manner so as not to reveal the name of the addressee. Pegg teased the contents out of the envelope and found that it contained not one but two sheets of paper. It appeared to be an invoice. It was from a company which dealt in cleaning materials, and it was addressed to The Manager New Start Car Wash, and its address was given as Arnold Road Nottingham NG5.

Pegg mulled over what events of the last 12 hours or so. He had illegally entered the offices of LPJ solicitors, he had taken information from a computer. Technically the stuff from the computer was the property of LPJ, thus he had committed the crime of burglary. He could not therefore officially complain about the attempt on his life. He considered that he must have seriously rattled somebody's cage. It would seem the person who had tampered with the gas flue had a connection with the car wash. The perpetrator had stuffed the envelope into their pocket and dropped it whilst gaining access to the gas flue pipe. Pegg speculated as to how this might have happened. The perpetrator may have been in a hurry or had gone to retrieve another item in the pocket, perhaps a phone, and in pulling the phone or other item out, had caused the envelope to fall out. Anyway, it was a stroke of luck for Pegg.

Pegg thought back to the message he heard on the answering machine in Ali's office from Richard Hoskins, "…. our difficulty has been resolved." It all seems to fit, I am the "difficulty" and by permanently removing me, it leaves them free to continue their nefarious activities, he thought to himself. He needed to do some more digging.

He took the file he had begun, and wrote some more on a sheet of paper, including the address of New Start Car Wash. He then took out one of the USB sticks and placed in one of the laptops ports. It was the stick on which he had downloaded the emails. The emails went back a couple of months. Nothing had been encrypted, so they were easy enough to open and read. Pegg scrolled through the list on the inbox, opening the occasional email and examining its attachment. Most of the emails appeared to be in English, but there were a few in a foreign language, which he assumed to be Albanian. Many of the emails dealt with applications for Legal Aid, and other topics regarding the day to day running of the practice; however, some caught Pegg's eye. The sender in quite a few cases was rickhos666@gmail.com. Pegg opened one up and read the contents. There was an attachment. The main part was about the content of the attachment. It read:

"Mr Ali, please find attached more names of British Military Personnel. I hope you will find the information will assist you in your endeavours. Regards Richard Hoskins."

Pegg was appalled at the depth of treachery to which Hoskins had sunk. He opened the attachment. It contained the names of ten soldiers. They ranged in rank from captain to through to Fusilier. In all they were two officers, five NCO's and three Fusiliers, and the unit was B Company, the second battalion West Midlands Fusiliers. Pegg printed the email and its attachment. He opened another one from Hoskins. This was asking for an early settlement for the information he had previously given to Ali. Pegg now realised how LPJ were getting the names of soldiers, but where was Hoskins getting the names to feed to LPJ. There must be a source leaking names from the Ministry of Defence to Hoskins. Normally in any criminal case the victim makes a complaint. The investigator then takes details of the alleged crime, gathering evidence of an offence including a statement from the victim. The crime is logged into the system. Next witnesses are sought if there are any, and their evidence in the form of statements is taken. The investigators will then from the evidence they have obtained, seek to identify perpetrators to the crime(s). The alleged perpetrators are then interviewed. The evidence is then assessed, and a decision is made to either prosecute or take no further action. Finally, the defence team will have disclosure as to how the prosecution has built its case.

It would appear that the system currently operated by the BWIT, is that soldiers' names and units are found that fit the operational theatre profile. The next thing is to find incidents, either real or imagined, to link the soldiers or their units to these incidents. The final part of the system is to find "victims" and connect them to the incident. So, the system is the complete reverse of how an investigation should be conducted.

Pegg decided to let OJA know of his suspicions. He composed an email to Rachel Gluckstein. He said the he has enough proof, using the "Civil Procedures Rules" burden of proof "beyond the balance of probabilities", to seriously undermine the credibility of BWIT's portfolio of cases. He sent it off and packed away his laptop. About twenty minutes later a Ford panel van pulled up and parked beside Pegg's Landrover. The signage on the van indicated it was the caravan service engineer. Pegg went out to meet the driver.

"Hello Mr Pegg, you phoned me earlier, what is the problem," asked the man.

"I was woken up last night by the Carbon Monoxide alarm going off. I had the gas heater on, I've since turned it off. I would like you to check out the system to see if there are any CO leaks."

Pegg explained when the 'van was last serviced; he produced the service book to confirm the date. The service engineer spent the next 30 minutes examining the heater and the gas system. He turned the heater on and used a meter with a probe attached, he went outside and using a ladder examined the flue pipe, inserting the end of the probe into the pipe. There was a beep; the engineer climbed down and packed up the ladder. He tested the 'vans CO meter. After he had finished he packed up and joined Pegg again in the awning.

"Well I've checked the gas system including the heater; everything checks out. The flue is fine, and the gases coming out of the flue are in full flow. You may have heard my probe bleeping;

it showed that the CO was exiting through the flue as it should do. The only explanation I can see of the CO alarm going off was some leaves blowing into the end of the flue. There are a lot leaves on the ground from the Autumn fall; and a breeze could easily blow stuff onto the roof. The only other thing that comes to mind is a foreign object getting wedged inside the flue. These CO alarms are very sensitive, and so they should be."

Pegg was not going to tell the engineer the real reason for the alarm going off, "Well thank you so much for checking everything out. How much do I owe you?"

"Including my call out fee and VAT, and as I have not charged for any parts, that'll be £60 please," he said as he gave Pegg an invoice.

Pegg handed the cash to the engineer who endorsed the invoice "Paid with thanks" and gave it back to Pegg. The men said their farewells and the engineer left the site.

Pegg went inside the 'van again and got the laptop out again. Rachel Gluckstein had not responded to the email Pegg had sent her. He got the file out and checked the telephone numbers on the cards the investigators from Valhalla had left when they had the meeting with Pegg and Tony Spratt. Both of the investigators, Raymond Walker and Richard Hoskins had the telephone landline numbers of office and fax on their cards together with a mobile number. The office and fax numbers were common to both cards, but each had an individual mobile number. Pegg compared the mobile number on Hoskins' card and that of the number Hoskins had contacted Mehmet Ali's office phone. The numbers were different.

Pegg decided to go for a walk. He put his coat on and put Fred's leash on him. He left the campsite, and walked a bit on the road, before turning onto a footpath. He let Fred off his leash. The dog appeared to have completely recovered and was adopting his normal routine, nose to the ground and investigating the myriad of smells as they progressed along the path. Pegg was deep in thought. The first thing he needed to do was to follow up on the address shown on the invoice which he found under the caravan. New Start Car Wash was on Arnold Road Nottingham, but the address of the suppliers of the cleaning materials, which was across the bottom of the invoice, was near to Buxton. In fact, it was on a small industrial estate between the caravan site and Buxton. He would start by contacting the company. He may be lucky and get a name of the person in charge of the car wash, and from this maybe find out who tried to kill him. At this stage he did not want Rachel Gluckstein to know about the attempt on his life. He decided to visit both the company which supplied the cleaning materials and the car wash in the morning. It was getting on for four. He walked a further mile before returning to the campsite.

When got back to the 'van he fed the dog. Fred had seemed to have regained his appetite. He finished off the contents of his food bowl, and continued licking the bowl, pushing it round the floor of the awning in the process. Pegg took the bowl off him and gave him some more medication. Pegg then made himself something to eat. He opened a small tin of corned beef, and diced a coupled of small potatoes, which he microwaved until they were soft. He sliced up a large tomato, and half an onion; these together with the potatoes and corned beef, he placed in a bowl and mixed them together. He then placed the bowl in the microwave and cooked the mixture for five minutes. He laid the table, opened a bottle of beer and served up his meal. As he ate he pondered over what had occurred over the past twenty-four hours. The attempt on his life had hardened his resolve rather than put him off. Someone is going to regret what they have done to me, he thought. He felt completely justified in entering the premises of PJA and removing information from Mr Ali's computer. After he had finished his meal, he cleared up and put the washing up in the bucket.

"Right boy, it's time for me to wash all the stuff I've used today; you stay in the 'van, I shan't be long."

Pegg made his way to the shower block and the dish washing facility where he washed up the day's used pots, cutlery and crockery. He returned to the 'van and dried washed items, after which he stowed them away. He went on his laptop again and checked his emails. There were two new items. One was from Angie and the other was from Rachel Gluckstein. Angie's email was an update on what she and Ross had been up to. She asked if he had managed to help his friend with bypassing the password on the friend's laptop. Pegg sent a brief reply to Angie's email. He did not mention the attempt to poison him with CO neither did he say anything about his visit to PJA's offices. Next he opened Rachel's email. She had written that all her suspicions regarding the way PJA carries on its business seem to have been vindicated. She asked if they could meet in person.

Pegg decided to give her a ring, she may still be in the office. He dialed OJA's number, the call was answered immediately, and the call taker put Pegg through to Rachel's office.

"Hello Archie, thanks for getting back to me. We need to speak as soon as possible, where are you at the moment?"

"I'm on a caravan site just outside Buxton in Derbyshire."

"So, we are about 35 miles from you. Can I see you tomorrow morning? They'll be 2 of us. Shall we say about elevenish at the campsite?"

"Yes, that sounds good to me, do you know how to get to me?"

"Just let me have the post code."

Pegg gave her the post code and the address of the site before saying, "Give us a call when you are nearly here, and I'll go up and meet you."

"Great, Archie, let me have what you have got, when we see you."

"Who's coming with you?"

"One of my paralegals, she also does a bit of investigating for the firm. She is a safe pair of hands don't worry."

"Okay I'll see you then," said Pegg ending the call.

He decided against writing anything down, he would let Rachel know what he has found out, and she could decide what notes she needed.

He decided to give Spratt a call.

"Hello Tony, can we speak?"

"Go ahead Archie I was just watching a bit of telly, the misses is at our daughter's. By the way I've got some good news, that lawyer Rachel Gluckstein has been in touch. She phoned me this morning on my mobile, I was at work. She's got the paperwork and she is on my case."

"Oh, Tony I'm so pleased for you, "said Pegg, who decided not to let him know she was coming to see Pegg tomorrow. He continued, "The solicitors must think that you've got a good case for them to do that. Have they mentioned anything about funding?"

"No, they mentioned something about some of the legal insurance policies I've got, but they told me not to worry about it at this stage."

"So, I expect you are feeling a bit more positive now you know you are not on your own."

"You can say that again Archie!"

"Right Tony, I'll love you and leave you, speak soon my man."

"Cheers Archie 'bye now."

Pegg looked at his watch it was half past nine. He decided to have a shower and get ready for bed. He went up to the shower block again and showered and shaved. He returned to the 'van and took Fred up to the dog walk. After five minutes sniffing around, the dog did what he needed to do, they returned to the 'van. Pegg got ready for bed. He used the electric heating on a low setting. He was not quite confident to turn the gas heating on, in spite of the engineer's good efforts. He turned in and went to sleep almost immediate

CHAPTER 15

Pegg got out of bed at half past six, and after visiting the shower block, he got dressed and took Fred out for a thirty-minute walk. It was a bright crisp autumn morning, without a cloud in the sky. He returned to the 'van and had some breakfast. After tidying up, he prepared to drive out and visit the supplier of the materials ordered by New Start Car Wash. The address at the bottom of the invoice read Ashbourne Road Buxton. Pegg got out his laptop and brought up Google Street View, after inputting the post code of the suppliers he located the small industrial estate where the premises were situated. He printed the map off.

"Come on Fred, let's find out some more about these bastards who want to do us harm," he said, taking his jacket and the dog's leash of the hook by the 'van's door. He went to the Landrover and Fred jumped onto the driver's seat, before moving on to the passenger's side. After securing the 'van, Pegg got into the vehicle and drove out of the site and towards Buxton, a quarter of an hour later he entered the industrial estate, which was larger and busier than he thought. He parked the Landrover on the main drag within the estate, between two LGV's, one of which was a rigid and the other was articulated.

"GDF Supplies, now where are you?" Pegg said to himself. He looked at the main board near to the entrance of the estate and located the company's location on the diagram displayed on the board. Three minutes later he was walking into the customer entrance of GDF Supplies. The door opened up into a space which had a counter along its entire length, behind the counter there were two people seated at opposite ends on a large desk. The surface of the desk accommodated two computer screens, keyboards, telephones and paperwork. Both the people, a young man and a middle-aged woman, were speaking on the phone. The woman looked up as Pegg came in. She was the first to finish on the phone.

"Yes sir, how can I help", she said, getting up from her desk and walking up to the counter.

"I understand that you supply cleaning materials to hand car washes," aid Pegg

"Yes, we do amongst other firms. We also supply industrial cleaners, offices, you name the organisation we supply them," she replied.

"I was at a car wash in Nottingham, New Start Car Wash, and I wanted some details of how to obtain cleaning materials."

"Right sir, we supply a vast range of products, for the trade, unfortunately we do not do retail at these premises. Depending what you are looking for, you could go to someone like Halfords, B and Q, or a hardware shop."

"You misunderstand me, I am starting up a cleaning enterprise, and I was after suppliers, one of the guys at the car wash gave me this old invoice with your details on it," Pegg said showing her the invoice.

"Oh, I see I'm sorry. Yes, we do supply these people," she said, handing the invoice back to Pegg

"How does it work with you? I mean do your customers have accounts, and do you deliver?"

"We operate monthly accounts, which we expect to be settled by the second Monday of the following month. We do not deliver, our customers collect."

"So, the guys from New Start come here?"

"As it happens we have just had an order in, and they are due to collect it tomorrow morning."

"So, if I phone in an order, you can have it ready within twenty-four hours?"

"If the items are in stock we can do it immediately."

Pegg asked for details of the firm's contacts. She gave him a business card and a catalogue of the products they stock. Pegg bade her farewell and made his way back to the Landrover and returned to the site.

He made himself a cup of tea and opened up his emails. There was nothing new in his inbox. He looked at his watch it was 10-50 am. He put Fred in the front of the Landrover and made his way up to the campsite office and let the warden know of his visitors, asking him if it would be alright if his visitors could park their car at his pitch. As there were not many caravans on site the warden informed Pegg that would be okay, and that the car could park on the adjoining pitch's hard standing. Pegg thanked him and made his way to the site entrance, where he waited for Rachel and her assistant. He hadn't been there long when he spotted a blue Ford Galaxy approaching, the driver of the vehicle was a young woman with an older woman sitting in the front passenger seat. The car indicated right to turn into the site entrance.

Pegg waved at the car, which slowed and pulled up beside him. The driver unwound her window.

"Hello Archie, we meet at last!" the woman in the passenger seat said.

"Rachel I'm so pleased to see you, if you let me in the back I'll guide you to where I'm pitched up."

Pegg got into the back of the Galaxy and pointed out to the driver where to go. A couple of minutes later, the Galaxy parked up next to Pegg's pitch. They got out and introduced themselves to each other more formally. Rachel Gluckstein was a small woman in her fifties with shoulder length dark brown hair, and dark blue eyes, she spoke with a soft Mancunian accent. Her assistant was a slim woman of south Asian heritage, aged about twenty-four, with dark hair tied up in a ponytail, and again spoke in with a Mancunian accent, she introduced herself as Amiya Gurung, and confirmed she was the call taker when Pegg first contacted OJA. She said that her father had served in the British Army with the Ghurkas, sadly her family lost him in Afghanistan.

Pegg got out and opened up the awning and unlocked the 'van.

"I think we'll sit in the caravan rather than the awning, it's still a bit chilly," said Pegg.

"That's fine with us, have you got Wi-Fi, I could do with plugging in my laptop, it's not essential if not," said Rachel.

"I've bought a week's worth; I'll give you the details when we're settled in."

"Is that your dog," said Rachel, pointing at Fred who was watching them from the front of the Landrover.

"Yes, that's Fred, my poodle. He's very friendly, but I decided to leave him in the Lanny, as he'll be all over you like a rash. Considering all the stuff we've got to get through, I think it's for the best."

They made their way into the caravan, where Rachel and Amiya sat next to each other on the window which ran the width of the 'van.

"Right ladies, what would you like to drink, tea or coffee? If you need to use the bathroom, it's through the screen and the door at the end," said Pegg indicating towards the screen which he had drawn across the area which separated the sleeping compartment and the lounge and kitchen area. "If you've never used a 'vans loo before, I'll show you."

Rachel said, "I'm okay we have a motorhome, what about you Amiya?"

"I'm au fait with the mechanics of a caravan's bathroom," she said

They both asked for coffee and remained seated. Pegg set up a small collapsible table in front of the window seat, on which Rachel placed a small laptop and Amiya placed some papers and a notepad. Pegg produced the two memory sticks on which he had uploaded the information from Mehmet Ali's desktop computer.

Rachel switched on her laptop and searched for the Wi-Fi. Pegg gave her the details of the site's system and the password. A minute later the laptop was connected to the system. Pegg continued to busy himself with making the coffee. After asking how the women wanted their coffee, he poured it into their cups and added sugar and milk where appropriate.

"In view of what I have found out about these alleged war crimes committed in Kosovo by our soldiers; everything is a pack of lies. I know for a fact one of the claimants is an Albanian, born in

Tirana. The only British troops in Pristina were in the northern part of the city, where the majority of the population were Serb and not Kosovars," said Pegg, as he placed the mugs on the table in front of Rachel and Amiya.

"We suspect that this is the case. We have quite a few cases of allegations of mistreatment by members of the British Army. Many of them were found to be spurious and our clients have been cleared of any wrongdoing. In these cases, it was about incidents in Afghanistan and Iraq. This is the first instance of us being aware that the same thing is occurring regarding the Balkans. Now what we would like to do Archie is for you to let us have any information you have which will enable us to build our case against BWIT."

"Well I have some useful stuff which I have obtained which may be of some assistance. Please don't ask how I came by it. As you may probably know, Lawyers for Personal Justice is a firm owned by Mssrs Mehmet Ali and James Smithson. I have done a little bit of research on the internet, and it would appear that Mr Ali has a bit of a colourful past to say the least, it is said that he had been involved with some pretty unsavoury characters in the world of illegal drugs, money laundering and people smuggling. The Law Society had given him "words of advice" but no other action was taken against him. Mr Smithson's side of the business would seem to be more of what you'd expect of a solicitor. My gut feeling is that he is not involved in the things Mr Ali is up to.'

"I have found out that the person making an allegation against my friend Tony Spratt is called Enver Haji. Now I nicked a man of that name and same date of birth last Monday week for drugs offences. He is not a Kosovan, but an Albanian, born in Tirana. If you do more digging I think you will find that this guy has never been to Kosovo, let alone Pristina.'

"Further to that I'd like to mention the contents of these memory sticks. The first one is a list of Mehmet Ali's emails and the second is a number of files. The contents of these sticks were downloaded from Mr Ali's office desktop. They were obtained by covert means, and as such I assume the information obtained could not be used in its current form as evidence. You may take them away with you if they help."

"Well Archie let's have a look at what we have got", said Rachel.

"One thing that concerns me is that names of soldiers, their units and where they were serving are being fed to Mr Ali by someone working on behalf of the BWIT. Is this ethical, surely it's up to the complainants and their representatives to furnish this information", said Pegg.

"Well this is normally the case", replied Rachel.

"I'll let you browse through the contents of the sticks; I'll take the dog for a run around the block, for about thirty minutes you okay with that?"

"That's fine we might be a bit longer than that", said Rachel.

Pegg left them and collected Fred from the front of the Landrover. He left the site and went on the same route as he went last time. He decided to give Pat Worthington a call. He got her voicemail. He decided to send her a text; *"WHAT ARE YOU DOING THIS WEEKEND? HOW ABOUT SOME FELL WALKING? CALL ME THIS EVENING. ARCHIE PEGG."* He sent the message and continued walking after forty minutes he returned to the site, put Fred back in the Landrover again, and joined the others in the 'van.

The two women were still viewing the laptop, and Amiya had filled her notepad with several pages of shorthand.

"Archie, I don't know who gave you this information, and I don't want to know, but it blows the cases against the alleged "war criminals" wide open", Rachel said, before continuing. "Any case that goes before a judicial hearing would be so full of holes that the prosecutor would have to throw the towel in before any trial starts."

"So, where does my friend Tony stand regarding these allegations?" asked Pegg.

"Well not only do I think that the evidence against him does not stand up, but I also think that any case against him would be thrown out. I am determined not only to clear his name, I will be claiming his legal costs back, and also try and obtain some compensation for him", she replied. "I think that we have enough here to refute any claims made against Mr Spratt, so there is a very good chance that the case will not even get to court."

"So, what happens now?" asked Pegg.

"Well we'll go back to the office and review what we've got, and then I shall be in contact with the Services Prosecution Authority. The SPA is the body which would review what evidence the BWIT has obtained and act on it. In this these cases the SPA is responsible for bringing them to court."

"Would you like me to make you some lunch before you go back? I can do some sandwiches, or there is a pub down the road. They do some decent bar meals."

"Thanks all the same but we need to get back to Manchester. It has been a very fruitful morning, we appreciate all you've done so far, Archie," said Rachel, continuing continued, "we'll keep you informed as to how the case concerning Mr Spratt, and if you uncover anything else which you feel is relevant please let us know."

The women packed up their stuff, and after saying their farewells, left the site. Pegg went over to the Landrover and let Fred out. He went into the 'van again and prepared some lunch, which consisted of some sandwiches and some coffee. He ate and when he had finished, he cleared up. He had uploaded the contents of the 2 memory sticks onto his laptop, before giving them to Rachel. He decided to view some of Mr Ali's emails, especially those from rickhos666@gmail.com. It would appear that a third party was feeding information to this email address regarding details of British Service personnel who have served in the Balkans, including Kosovo. He needed to find out more and to do this he would need to access this email account.

He sent a text to Angie's mobile, which gave the address of the account; this was accompanied by a message *"CAN YOU WORK YOUR MAGIC, WILL CALL YOU ON HOUSEPHONE IN A COUPLE OF MINS"*. Five minutes later he phoned Angie on her land line number. The phone was picked up immediately.

"Hi Archie, just got it," said Angie.

"Are you alone?"

"Yes, Ross is doing some shopping he's taken Catherine Rose with him; I'm doing a bit of work for one of my clients."

"Okay I'm sorry to do this behind Ross's back but the less people know the better. If you feel you are unable to help me, no worries."

"No, I'm fine honestly. I'll have a look for you, and I'll let you know what I can find out."

The next ten minutes were taken up with talk about what she and Ross had been up to and what they were going to at the weekend. She said a bit of work had come in since the last time they had spoken, so she was tied to her desk for a bit. Ross was going back to work next week, but he'll be at Norwich Airport for the foreseeable future. Pegg told her he had not made up his mind whether to stay for another week or not. He said he should come to a decision by the weekend. He ended the call and went back to his laptop.

He accessed the Nottinghamshire Police's website; he was looking at any reports of break-ins in the Mansfield Road area of Nottingham. He scrolled down to the city beat areas. There were no details of any crimes reported. Pegg thought that this was normal as details of victims would be confidential, but no harm checking. He checked the local press. The Nottingham Post had details of crimes, but nothing in the Mansfield Road area. Pegg thought that maybe LPJ had not discovered that the premises in Mansfield Road had been entered and Mr Ali's computer had been used and data removed from it, or they knew but were keeping quiet. Pegg could see why LPJ would not want the police snooping round the offices and especially their IT equipment. Pegg logged out and turned his laptop off.

In the morning he would go over to Buxton and to GDF Supplies and see if he could get there before the van came to pick up New Start Car Wash's supplies. He was determined to get to the bottom of the attempt to interfere with his caravan's heating system. The only people who were not happy at his involvement with Spratt's case were LPJ and Richard Hoskins. Why take such drastic action, had he come across some major conspiracy to pervert the course of justice? It appeared to Pegg that certain people wanted to stop his snooping into their nefarious activities. He was still thinking about what he had uncovered when his mobile rang. It was Pat Warrington.

"Hi Pat, thanks for getting back to me, well do you fancy going out for the day?"

"Yes, Archie I really fancy that, it seems to be set fair for the weekend, if you believe the long-range weather forecast, where do you want to go?"

"Well I thought we could spend the day up at your end of the Peak National Park, maybe get a pub or café lunch halfway through the day. I'll meet you at yours and we can take the Landrover, plenty of room for the animals. Shall I drop by yours at about nine on Saturday morning?"

"I had not got anything planned for this weekend; that sounds perfect. Mum and Dad are away in Leeds staying at Mum's sisters."

"Oh, that's a shame I would have liked to have met them; maybe another time," Pegg said.

"Do you know how to get to me?"

"Just give me your address and post code, and Google will do the rest."

Pat gave him the details which he noted down. They spent the next five minutes with small talk before they ended the call.

Pegg prepared an evening meal, which he ate, before getting Fred his feed. After clearing up he went to the shower block and washed all the days used crockery, cutlery and pans. He returned to the 'van and stowed away the washed items. He looked at the time. It was getting on for seven. He took Fred out again, when he returned to the 'van he spent the rest of the evening reading and listening to music on the radio. At ten-thirty he went to bed.

CHAPTER 16

Pegg woke up at six, he felt refreshed and ready to start what might be a very active day. He started by going out for a walk with Fred, before returning and going for a long shower, followed by a shave. He returned to the 'van, dressed and made breakfast. He made up a flask of coffee and some sandwiches. He packed these items away in the ruck sack together with some food and water for Fred. He drove out of the site at eight continued to the industrial estate, where he found a parking space from which he had a good view of GDF Supplies. A couple of vehicles called at the premises. Both were small vans, one was from a company of domestic cleaners, and the other was from a firm of office cleaners. The drivers were both women.

After an hour a white Ford Transit pulled up onto the firm's forecourt and backed up to the main door. Pegg noticed that the vehicle's offside brake light was not working. The driver got out and went through the smaller door into the counter area. The man was slim built, about five feet seven tall and was wearing blue jeans and a fluorescent jacket. He had dark hair and a swarthy complexion. "I reckon you are from the Middle East or Eastern Mediterranean, chap. Pound to a penny you're from the car wash," thought Pegg.

Pegg waited. After about five minutes the man came out again and went to the back of the van and opened the back doors. The large door shutter opened up, and the man and a member of GDF's staff proceeded to load up the van with boxes and large twenty litre containers of liquid. Once the van was loaded, the large door was closed, the man shut the doors to the van, and got into the front. A couple of minutes later the van drove out of the estate. Pegg started up the Landrover and followed it. He saw that when the van stopped at the junction prior to exiting the estate, that the van's offside brake light continued to be inoperative. Pegg had noticed that there was a lay-by in a wooded area about a mile ahead on the road into Buxton. He continued to follow the van, and he started to sound the Landover's horn and flash its lights. After a short interval the van indicated to turn left into the lay-by, which was free of any other vehicles. The van stopped, and Pegg pulled up in front of it. He got out and went over to the driver's side of the van, the engine was still running. The driver stayed where he was, the widow was open.

"Sorry to stop you chap, but one of your brake lights isn't working, the police are red hot around here; you don't want to get stopped do you?"

"What you talk about brake light," the man said.

Pegg pointed to the back of the van, "Brake light not working, come and look, I'll press the brake pedal, you go to the back and see."

The man reluctantly got out, and went to the back of the van, Pegg reached inside and depressed the brake pedal a couple of times, "see what I mean?"

"Okay I get fixed, thank you." Pegg switched off the van's engine and took the van's ignition key out and put it in his pocket.

"Hey please give me keys", the driver said as Pegg went to join him at the back of the van.

"In a minute I want to speak to you first and then you can have your keys back". He produced the invoice he had found underneath the caravan on Monday morning. "Is this yours?" he asked.

The man said nothing

"I'll ask again is this yours, start speaking or we're going to be here all day. I've got plenty of time on my hands, but I expect the boss at New Start Car Wash will be waiting for the stuff you've just collected."

The man said nothing. Pegg leant against the side of the van and started whistling. The impasse continued for a couple of minutes.

"Finally, the man said, "Okay I just collect the stuff, and drive it back to Nottingham, and I take it out and put it in the store."

"Do keep the invoices?"

"No, I give this to boss man."

"He's the guy who deals with all the invoices yeah, what's his name?"

The man said nothing.

"Well looks like we wait here then. I bet your boss is really going to be pissed off with you."

The man thought a bit, and then said, "Look he is very sad man I frightened for him, there are men who will do bad things to the boss."

"Just give me his name I won't tell him you said it to me, nobody will know, and you can be on your way."

"Okay," said the man, he like me Albanian, he called Afrim Babic.

Pegg got out a notebook and wrote it down, he showed it to the man who took Pegg's pen and corrected the spelling.

"And who are you."

The man said nothing. Pegg started to whistle again.

"Okay, okay, I Endrit Bejko", he wrote it down it Pegg's notebook.

"I'll keep this invoice and I'll give it back to Mr Babic myself. I'll not be telling him about our talk, will you?"

"No, no I shut up."

"Good, don't forget to get that brake light fixed, "said Pegg as he reached into his pocket and gave Bejko back the keys to his van. Bejko got back into his van and, started up and drove off. Pegg watched him go. He thought to himself that the man was scared for Babic and would stay quiet about Pegg's conversation with him. Pegg went to the Landrover and put Fred on his lead. He let the dog out and walked him about the lay-by for about 10 minutes. Whilst Fred nasally investigated the edge of the lay-by, Pegg was forming a plan to confront Babic. It seemed that he was a good candidate for the tinkering of the caravan's heater. But he would not have just done it; somebody had put him up to it and may be have used some coercion. The only person in his view who wanted to do him harm was Hoskins. His suspicions were reinforced by what he'd heard on the answering machine on Mr Ali's desk. Hoskins must have some form of hold over Babic. It's time to pay Mr Babic a visit and confront him.

Pegg walked back to the Landrover, Fred jumped in and sat on the passenger seat. Pegg got in and retrieved the business cards that Hoskins and Walker had given out to both Pegg and Spratt. Pegg sensed that there was a rift between Hoskins and Walker. He decided that this could be exploited to his advantage. He saw that he had a good signal, so he phoned Raymond Walker. There was a voicemail message which informed callers to call a landline number. Pegg made a note of it and dialed the number. The call was answered by a female,

"Hello", the woman said.

"Hello, my name is Pegg may I speak to Mr Raymond Walker?"

"Just a minute," she said and then in a raised voice continued, "Ray, telephone for you."

Pegg heard the phone being placed down after a few seconds it was picked up again.

"Hello Mr Pegg, Ray Walker, how may I help you?"

"Well where do I begin, it's complicated. Since I've been helping my friend Mr Tony Spratt regarding these outrageous war crimes claims, I've had an attempt to kill me."

Pegg heard a gasp from the other end of the line. "Oh God, I am so shocked to hear that. Are you all right, what happened?"

Pegg briefly described what had happened, before continuing, "I have to speak to you regarding the way the investigations against British Military Personnel are carried out on behalf of BWIT."

"Before we go any further, I have resigned from Valhalla, and as a result I am no longer doing any work for BWIT."

"Oh, I'm sorry to have troubled you. In that case I'll say goodbye."

"No don't hang up, I'd like to speak to you a bit further, can we meet up somewhere, I don't want to speak over the phone."

"Sure, where are you? Can I come to you, or would you like to come to where I am, or maybe another venue?"

"Are you anywhere near Chesterfield?"

"Well I'm at a place just a mile or so outside Buxton."

"Ah your about 40 miles away. Maybe that's a bit far."

"No that's okay, it'll take about an hour to get to you, let me have your address."

Walker gave him the address.

"How about if I come and see you today?" said Pegg.

"That should be okay, I've nothing on and the misses is out all afternoon."

"Great said Pegg, I'll see you in about an hours' time."

He hung up and looked at his watch it was about eleven. He decided to eat a sandwich and poured a cup of coffee. After he finished, he gave Fred some of his dried food and a drink. At about midday day he left the lay-by and headed off to Buxton where he took the A6 and then the A619 to Chesterfield. Walker lived on the west side of the town. It was nearing one when he arrived at Walker's home address.

CHAPTER 17

Raymond Walker's house appeared to be a three-bedroom detached dwelling set back from the road. The house was solidly built, probably constructed in the 1930s. On the ground floor there were bay windows either side of a central semi glazed front door. On the first floor the windows above the bays were flush with the frontage of the house. A detached garage was situated to right side of the house. The drop kerb at the edge of the street led onto a ten metre driveway and a graveled apron in front of the house and garage. The area was devoid of any vehicles. Pegg decided to leave the Landrover parked on the street directly outside the house. He left Fred in the vehicle whilst he took his file and his laptop and walked up the driveway towards the front door. Walker must have seen him getting out of the Landrover, because the front door opened as Pegg approached it.

"That did not take you too long", he said as Pegg entered.

"No, I was quite lucky with the traffic, and the Lanny is not the fastest conveyance around.

"Right I thought we should go to the dining room; you can put your paperwork and laptop on the table in there", Walker said.

The front door led into an entrance hall, with a door immediately to the left, and a staircase which was also on the left but about four feet back from this door. The hallway floor was covered with a runner under which there were floorboards. The walls were painted light beige, and there were pictures of various animals on both sides of the hall. There was a door at the end of the hall, which was open and led to what appeared to be the kitchen. Walker ushered Pegg through an open door to the right and which was set back about ten feet back from the front door. The dining room had a table with four chairs round it and in addition there was a Welsh dresser on one side of the room and an ottoman under the bay window. The table had some papers and files on it. Walker tidied these up as they sat down. Pegg took out some fresh paper from his file.

"Do you mind if I make some notes?" he asked.

"No, you go ahead", said Walker, before continuing, "As I said to you on the phone I have resigned from Valhalla Investigations, so I'm in a position to continue with what I did before I started working for VI."

"What was that?" asked Pegg.

"I'm going back to doing jobs for the insurance industry; claims investigation and loss adjusting, that sort of thing. I'm not too worried, I work for some of the big boys, Cunningham Lindsey and Brownsword as well as others. Cunningham Lindsey has said that they have plenty of jobs for me. I only went over to Valhalla because they offered an opportunity for me to do other type of work, and also to take on stuff abroad."

"So, what made you quit?"

"At first VI gave some really interesting stuff that seemed really worthwhile. I was investigating stuff such as money laundering scams, insurance and VAT fraud. I loved it, and for about 6 months I got some good results. Then VI won a contract to carry out investigation work for the Services Prosecution Authority. As I am a fully qualified member of the Association of British Investigators, I was accepted to do this work. My background is with the insurance and financial sector. I have never been in the services or the police. On the whole the way I carried out my work was guided by the Civil Procedures Rules, but this new contract meant that we would work within the parameters of the Police and Criminal Evidence Act or PACE as it is known.

"At first I thought that we would be involved with genuine war criminals. I was naïve enough to think that I would be helping to bring justice to victims of ghastly mistreatment. So much for that; I was soon brought back to the real world when I found out that we would be investigating British service personnel. Mr Spratt was the fourth person I had interviewed; he and the other three were clearly not involved."

"So how did you get the jobs?" asked Pegg.

"VI has an office in Manchester, and it gets sent instructions from the SPA's office which is located at RAF Northolt in Ruislip just outside London. Depending on the whereabouts in the country an interviewee lives, a local agent will get the job to visit that intervicwee. Normally it is two of us who go. Initially we would get a letter sent out to the potential interviewee. This is to arrange a time to see the person in an informal environment; I think SPA's thinking is to reduce the stress to the interviewee, rather than arresting the person and formally interviewing them. If as a result of the informal interview it is ascertained that there is enough evidence to formally interview a, I don't like to use the word, "suspect". We then ask them to attend a local police station where the that person would be interviewed under caution."

"What if the alleged suspect refuses to attend a police station, surely you have no powers of arrest?"

"No, we don't, and this is where I get really uneasy. We get a regular police officer to arrest the "suspect" and he is then taken into police custody and is treated as a suspected offender within the parameters of PACE. The whole thing leaves a nasty taste in my mouth. It really came to a head when we came to interview Mr Spratt. In a way I'm glad you were there. I could see that Mr Spratt was clearly innocent of any wrongdoing, and that the accusations against him were clearly ludicrous."

"I could see that there was an altercation between you and Hoskins in the car park after you both had left Tony's office, what was all that about?" asked Pegg.

"Give me strength! That man is a real pain in the arse. His attitude is appalling as far as he's concerned every man is guilty until proved innocent. He says he used to be a policeman. I find that very difficult to believe."

Pegg said nothing; he decided not to tell Walker what Hoskins exploits were with the Norfolk Constabulary. He also decided not to mention the fact that he was a serving officer in the same force.

Walker continued, "He was all for us to get Mr Spratt arrested and taken into custody. I said that there was not a shred of evidence, and any custody officer would refuse charge. But Hoskins was having none of it; he said that we could make up a story and get the evidence at a later date. I'm not a policeman, but even a cursory glance at the PACE Codes of Conduct would tell me that this was completely out of order. I was going to drive off. It was my car after all, and I was going to leave Hoskins to find his own way back to Manchester."

"Is that where he lives?"

"I believe so. I picked him up from Chesterfield railway station, and then we went on to Mr Spratt's place of work in Buxton."

"I don't suppose you know his address."

"No but VI's Manchester office may have it."

"Have you worked with Hoskins on any other jobs?"

"Yes, we have been to three other people; one of them was a serving soldier actually. We went to his base, which was near Warwick, Kyneton I think. He was a major, something to do with bomb disposal, ammunition tech or something like that. It was a complete disaster, Hoskins was his obnoxious self, and even the RMP SIB guy who accompanied us was appalled. The major's commanding officer had us escorted off the base; we were told not to come back until we had some solid evidence. I mean the guy had not even been in contact with any civilians, he had been at an abandoned Serb ammunition dump south of Pristina doing some inventory work and making some of the ordnance safe. I'm no expert but it seemed obvious that his account of events was true. Hoskins was having none of it, he slandered the poor major, who apparently had been decorated for gallantry. The other two cases involved were former junior ranking soldiers, I think a private and a corporal; they had been involved relief work in the south of Kosovo, supporting the refugee feeding stations. The day we came to see Mr Spratt really was the last straw for me. I decided to get out of the whole BWIT thing as I had a gut feeling that with people like Hoskins involved there would not be any good ending to any case we worked."

"Did you say anything to VI about it?"

"What about me resigning?"

"No about how the whole BWIT thing appears flawed?"

Not yet, you see I am not directly employed by VI. I work on the same principal as I do for Cunningham Lindsey and Brownsword; that is to say that I'm known as a contractor I get the jobs and when I have completed them I invoice VI and my fees are paid direct to me. I am really what you would call a self-employed investigator. Unlike my other work, the job working for VI on behalf of BWIT does take up so much of my time, I had to temporarily give up taking on jobs from my other clients."

"Has Hoskins had anything to say about you resigning?"

"The day after we had spoken to Mr Spratt; he phoned me and said he was sorry about some of the things he said about me and mentioned that he was submitting a report back to VI, recommending that Mr Spratt should be formally arrested, and interviewed. I disagreed and this led to a torrent of abuse from him. I lost it completely, I told him what I thought of him, and hung up on him. The next day I contacted VI that I was not available to carry on working for them. They want me to go over to their Manchester office next week. I think it's something to do with signing some non-disclosure documentation. I've already signed the OSA, so really I'm in breach of that speaking to you."

"Don't worry, I'll not be telling anyone. But I'm going to look into the way BWIT is operating. I am concerned about the way that BWIT is getting the names of suspects and how the complainants are identified. The majority of the complainants are allegedly Kosovars, but they are in fact Albanians from Albania proper. I know for a fact that one of the complainants is actually an Albanian national who was born in Tirana the country's capital."

"I never knew that," said Walker.

"I am in contact with a firm of solicitors who are representing the interests of service personnel accused of alleged war crimes. I'll give you their name and contact numbers, would you be interested in telling them what you have told me?"

"Leave the firm's details, and let me think about it," replied Walker.

"Well that's about it for now, Mr Walker. I really appreciate your time. I've got your contact details on the card you gave me."

"No don't use that; they are details VI gave me. Let me give you one of my business cards I use for my insurance and loss adjusting work."

He retrieved a card from amongst the papers on the table and gave it to Pegg. Pegg wrote down his contact details and also that of OJA and Rachel Gluckstein on a sheet of paper and gave it to Walker. Pegg packed up his papers and laptop. As they got to the front door, he said:

"I am not worried if you tell someone about my visit to you, but in view of what happened to me, you might want to keep what I have told you under your hat."

"Don't worry Mr Pegg I'll be careful what I say."

They said their farewells and Pegg returned to the Landrover.

CHAPTER 18

It was a bit after five when he got back to the site. He called in at
the site office.

"Ah Mr Pegg," the receptionist said, "I've got some mail for
you, and also there was a foreign sounding chap who came earlier
this afternoon. He asked about "the man with the Landrover". I did
not give him any details about your whereabouts. I asked him to
leave his details, but he refused and left."

She gave Pegg a buff coloured A5 sized envelope, which Pegg
could see had come from Angie.

"Thanks," he said before adding, "this visitor what did he look
like and did he come in a car."

"He was slim, not very tall, light brown curly hair, and very
distinct green eyes. He was wearing a leather jacket and light
coloured clothing. He parked his car right in front of the office on
the visitor's car park. It was a black Vauxhall Astra, I did not make
a note of the registration, he would have done that on the visitor's
book, as he refused details, I was not able to complete an entry in
the book. He seemed quite agitated."

"Well thanks for that. If he should call again, if I'm on site I'll
see him, if I'm not, give him my mobile number, you've got that I
believe."

The receptionist confirmed she had that. Pegg got back into
the Landrover and drove down to his pitch. He took Fred up to the
dog walk, and let him wander around for a few minutes, before
returning to the pitch and going into the 'van. He fed Fred and

sat down at the table taking Angie's letter and reading through it, there was also a memory stick included. He sent a text to Angie acknowledging receipt of her letter and its contents.

The letter mentioned that she had been able to access the account rickhos555@gmail.com. She had put the contents on the memory stick. The rest of the letter was about what she had been up to, and other small talk. Pegg had not mentioned his near-death experience and had no intention of doing so at the moment. He put the memory stick into the laptop and started to view the contents. It appeared to be a treasure trove of items which were linked to account holder's nefarious activities. There was one item in the inbox which took Pegg's attention. It mentioned the names and ranks of the same ten soldiers that the account holder had emailed to Mehmet Ali at LPJ. Pegg looked at the address of the sender; it appeared to be a private email address pdm225@tinyworld.co.uk. He scrolled further down the inbox and there were more emails from the same sender. Some contained names of service personnel others were requests for payments. Pegg noted down the email address and the names of the soldiers. His next question was how I get the details of the account holder, and where were these emails being sent from. He set the laptop's browser to search "account holder emails". A number of headings came up. He clicked onto "reverse email look-up". There were a couple of options available, one of which was Facebook. If the email address is entered in the search box, the name of the account holder may come up. Pegg hoped that the account holder had not got any privacy settings in place.

He entered pdm22 HYPERLINK pdm225@tinyworld.co.uk into the search box. He gasped when a name came up. Gregor Henderson, Pegg clicked onto his profile. It gave Mr Henderson's hobbies job family. He looked under Mr Gregor's career. Civil Servant, educated Glasgow University, obtained BA in English and Literature. Works at The Army Personnel Centre.

Pegg knew that the old RE Records Office used to be located in Glasgow. He checked the address of the Army Personnel Centre, and it was located at Kentigern House, Brown Street Glasgow; it was the same address as the old Records Office. Pegg tried to search

Facebook for the account holder of rickhos@gmail.com. There was no match. He tried another way by searching using a Google tool. This time he was more successful; and sure enough the account holder was Richard Hoskins.

He now had the picture as to how the whole rotten system worked. Henderson would identify which theatres military personnel had served. He would then send the selected names and their units to Hoskins. Hoskins would then send these details to LPJ. LPJ would then find "victims" to fit the alleged crimes. It really was a pretty amateurish set up. Pegg could not understand how the Services Prosecution Authority could be so easily duped by this bunch of crooks. It was time for the whole business to be exposed.

He selected the Word programme on his laptop and spent the next hour typing up a report detailing what he had uncovered. He printed the report off and wrote a covering note which he stapled to the four-page report. He placed them both in an A5 envelope, which he addressed to LPJ. He fixed a stamp and sealed up the envelope. He would contact Rachel in the morning and let her know what he had uncovered.

It was after seven o'clock by the time he had finished. He decided to go to the same pub he had visited the previous Thursday for an evening meal. He stowed away his paperwork and after putting on his coat, took Fred's leash. He decided to set the 'vans alarm as he left. On his way out he posted the letter to LPJ. He continued on to the pub, arriving there twenty minutes later. There were about a dozen people in the lounge bar and about half the tables in the dining area were occupied. Pegg ordered a pint of bitter and steak and ale pie. He ordered chips and peas to go with it. He asked if he could eat at one of the tables in the lounge bar, as he had the dog with him; the barmaid said that would be fine. Pegg took his pint and sat down at the table near to the fire. Fred settled down on the carpet near to the fire and dosed off.

Pegg thought about what had been achieved so far in helping Tony Spratt to counter the allegations which had been made against him. The alleged victims appear to be Albanians and not Kosovars. Tony and his unit were working in an area of Pristina which in which the majority of the population was Serb. He and his men were clearing mines and unexploded ordnance; they had nothing to do with handling the local population. Pegg had uncovered a serious conspiracy to pervert the course of justice. The integrity and impartiality of the SPA's investigators was seriously in doubt. LPJ were not actively seeking victims of war crimes, instead they were being fed names of service personnel, and then finding "victims" to fit the alleged crime. He knew that the evidence he had gathered was obtained illegally, most as the result entering LPJ's premises without permission. None of this information could be used in court in its present form due to the method it was obtained. Neither could the information Angie had obtained be used in a court owing to the method she used, illegal hacking of email accounts. He had put everything he had found out in the report he had sent to Rachel Gluckstein. Her firm OJA would have enough information to challenge the SPA's case against Tony and the other soldiers. It would put pressure on the Ministry of Defence to have all the BWIT cases reviewed and the possibility of the whole flawed organisation shut down.

The food Pegg had ordered was brought to his table by a young waiter, together with cutlery and napkins. The young man went away and returned with a basket of cruets and sauces. Pegg thanked him and prepared to eat his meal. Fred sat up and looked longingly at Pegg's plate, his nostrils twitched, and he licked his muzzle.

"Forget it boy," muttered Pegg, "don't beg."

The dog let out a big sigh and lay down again. Pegg finished his meal and ordered another pint of beer, which the barmaid put on his tab. He returned to the table and sat down. His mobile rang; it was Pat Warrington.

"Hi Pat, I'm fixed to come up and see you Saturday morning."

"Archie, there's a change of plan."

"Oh, I'm sorry to hear that", said Pegg the disappointment very apparent in the tone of his voice.

"No, I am still going to meet up, but as I have got Friday off, I'd like to come and meet up Friday afternoon, I'll book in somewhere in the Buxton area, and we could make a weekend of it"

"That sounds a great idea. Look before you start booking anything, there are some static caravans on site. Do you fancy doing that?"

"Yes, are they okay with pets though? I' m bringing Zena with me."

"Of course, I can't see it being a problem at all. The site advertises the fact that "*well behaved animals are always welcome*". I'll sort something out first thing and I'll call you."

"Well I've got a few things to do tomorrow morning; I may be out and about."

"Not a problem I'll send you a text."

They then went on to discuss what they would do and places they could visit. Pat said she had a long weekend and she would not have to be back at work until Tuesday morning. After a further five minutes Pegg ended the call. He felt quite lightheaded and was looking forward to being away from the events of the past few days.

Pegg picked up Fred's leash and attached it to the dog's collar. He went to the bar and paid off his tab. The walk back to the site was uneventful. He arrived back at his pitch at about a quarter to ten. In view of what had happened previously, he decided to do an external check of the Landrover and the 'van and awning. It was dark, but the lamp he had carried with him all evening, gave ample illumination for the task in hand. After this and after finding nothing untoward, he entered the awning and unlocked the 'van. He disarmed the alarm and took off his coat. He decided to go to the shower block, where he showered and shaved. He returned to the 'van and gave Fred some food. He listened to some music on the radio for a bit, before going to bed.

CHAPTER 19

Pegg slept well and was ready for another day; hopefully this would not be as hectic as yesterday. He listened to the Today programme for about ten minutes, before tuning into Classic FM, the second movement Mozart's beautiful clarinet concerto filled his ears; it was going to be a good weekend having Pat for company. He thought of Cath and felt a twinge of guilt. He did not know if he was going anywhere with Pat regarding a relationship. He was just meeting up her and going to enjoy her company over the weekend, that was as far as he thought it would go.

Pegg got up, had a wash, and dressed. He took Fred up to the dog walk and let him sniff around and perform his necessary bodily functions. He retrieved a poop bag from his pocket and picked up the results of the dog's efforts, after placing the bag in the waste bin, Pegg returned to the 'van, where he made some coffee, and ate a breakfast of cereals, boiled egg and toast. He cleared away the breakfast things and made the bed. He put on his jacket and with Fred following, made a tour of the site, heading to where the statics were. There were a number of them, of various sizes. It would appear some were already occupied. These had small gardens around them, together with neat picket fences. One of the occupants of a larger static was pottering about with the garden. He was an elderly man and judging from his accent was from the county. Pegg exchanged pleasantries and asked if any of the statics were for short term rent. The man pointed to a row of 4 statics at the end of the line. Pegg thanked him and wandered over to them, they were all empty except the one at the end of the row. Pegg made his way to the reception and went into the office. He asked the receptionist if any of the statics were available for the weekend. She looked at her computer screen and said:

"We are all fully booked for the following weekend, but there are three available for the next three or four days."

Pegg's heart leapt, he said, almost too eagerly, "I have a friend and her dog coming over for a long weekend, so could I book one for her?"

"That will be fine, we charge a rate of ten pounds a day for the dog, to cover any damage or cleaning, should there be no issues with that, we will refund half that amount when the guest leaves. Is that okay?"

"Yes, that's fine."

He booked Pat and her dog in from today until Monday morning. He paid for the stay. The receptionist took a key from the board behind her desk and accompanied Pegg to where the static was. It was the first one in the row. She unlocked the static and showed Pegg around. There were two bedrooms, a bathroom, toilet and a living room, which also incorporated a kitchen area, and a small dining table. There were also a fridge and storage cupboards. She showed how the heating worked. Pegg took a few pictures of the interior and the exterior of the static. They walked back to the reception office. Pegg decided to pay for the static; after which he left the key with reception.

He returned to his pitch and went into the 'van. He sent a text to Pat together with the pictures he had taken of the static. He finished the text by saying that keys are in the reception office. Next he phoned PJA and asked to speak to Rachel; when she came onto the line, he gave her a brief summary of what he had discovered, before mentioning the report he had posted to PJA, which described his findings in more detail. He mentioned that he would not be doing any more work over the weekend. Rachel said she looked forward to reading the report, and she would contact him later in the day on Monday. Pegg then phoned Angie and was given a run down what her plans for the weekend were. Pegg mentioned his plans, without going into too much detail, and with that the call ended. He put the

phone down, and was going to make a cup of tea, when it bleeped.
Pegg picked it up again, and saw that he had a text from Pat.

*"GREAT! IT WILL SUIT ME & ZENA! WE SHOULD BE
THERE BY 2-00PM. PAT."*

Pegg texted back, *"SEE YOU THEN. REGARDS ARCHIE."*

He put the phone down again and went back to putting the kettle
on. He had just made a cup of tea when the phone rang again. Pegg
picked it up again. The caller was the receptionist.

"Mr Pegg, the same foreign gentleman who came yesterday is
here, shall I send him down to you, or do you want to come up to
the office?"

"I'll come up and meet him," he said and ended the call.

Pegg put Fred in the front of the Landrover and walked up to
the reception. He could see a black Vauxhall Astra parked up in
the visitors parking area. A man was standing outside the office
smoking. As Pegg approached the office the man walked towards
him, he nipped the end of his cigarette and dropped the butt in the
bin outside the office.

"Are you Pegg?"

"Who wants to know?"

"What?"

"What's your name and why do you want to see me?"

The man said nothing, he appeared extremely nervous, he was
not too tall, Pegg was a good head higher than him. He hesitated
before saying:

"My name is Afrim Babic," his English was quite fluent, and
when he spoke it was with a slight accent, "I need to speak with
you, Mr Pegg."

Pegg froze at the mention of the man's name. Was this the man
who tried to kill me? What does he want? There's only one way to
find out.

"So, what have you got to say to me?" asked Pegg.

Babic looked at Pegg, the nervousness in his demeanour had
changed, his face had taken on a look of sadness and his eyes were
watery.

"Oh, Mr Pegg I've done a terrible thing, I am so sorry."

"Come on Mr Babic let's go somewhere a bit more private."

Pegg escorted Babic back to the pitch. As they passed the Landrover, Fred stared intently at them from his place in the driver's seat. They entered the awning, Pegg indicated to one of the chairs, Babic sat down whilst Pegg took the other chair.

"You have a story to tell me, so let me hear it," said Pegg.

Babic sat there and after a long pause said:

"My friend Bejko said that you had spoken with him yesterday on his way back from Buxton. He said that you were coming to see me. He mentioned the invoice you had found. I tried to see you yesterday, but the lady at the office said that you were out."

"What was it you wanted to see me about that was so important that you drove all the way from Nottingham?"

Babic said nothing; he looked down at the floor, unable to make eye contact with Pegg.

"Was it you who came to my caravan, and tampered with the gas flue?"

"Yes, I'm so sorry Mr Pegg, what can I do to make things better?" he murmured.

"What the fuck did you think you were doing? Me and my dog were poisoned with carbon monoxide, we could have died; that's attempted murder in my book Babic. Give me one good reason why I should not go to the police; you've admitted to me what you've done."

Babic said nothing, he started to sob. Pegg had no intention of getting the police involved; instead he wanted to know why Babic did what he did.

"Come on Mr Babic why did you do it? What have I done to you to deserve what you did to me?"

Babic looked up, tears were streaming down his cheeks; he said:

"Mr Pegg it is a long story."

"I'm listening."

"I came to this country as a twelve-year old orphan. I am from the old Yugoslavia, from a part of Serbia called Kosovo. My parents and brothers and sister were killed, and I managed to escape to the south. I was in a refugee camp. The British Army set it up and was running it. They saved me, as had no family I had a chance to go to the UK. This country fed and clothed, she educated me. I worked in a few jobs after I finished school. One day I got a chance to set up a business. I was working in Nottingham when I met an Albanian, who was looking for someone to manage a car wash. As I was an Albanian speaker, and my English is fluent I was "just the person he was looking for". I thought this was the opportunity I needed to get on the management ladder."

Babic paused.

Pegg said, "Go on I'm listening."

Babic continued:

"It seemed a good idea at the time and if I had known what was going to happen I'd have walked away. But I was so keen to be my own boss, I did not think things through. First of all, I had to "buy" the franchise. I did not have any ready cash, and I could not get a bank loan. The guy said this is not a problem, he could advance me the money, and I could pay him back through the takings from the car wash. In the end I agreed, and we set up the business at the back of a filling station on Arnold Road in Nottingham.

"Most of the stuff I needed was supplied through the Albanian guy. It was quite basic really, a few hose pipes and an old pressure washer. I had a couple of guys working for me to begin with. We got going and there were plenty of customers and although it was hard work the money started to come in. I ploughed some of the money into upgrading the old kit and obtained newer and better stuff. As a consequence, we got busier and busier. I needed more staff. The Albanian got me more people, even a couple of Brits, but the others were from places like Albania, Romania and even Afghanistan. The earnings went up and I thought I could pay off what I owed. But the Albanian said that the price had gone up. This is when things started to go bad."

"What happened," asked Pegg.

"Well because the payments I had to make to clear my loan had increased so much, I was not breaking even. I said to the Albanian that I would have to close down as it was no longer viable. I was told that I would still owe them money. He came around to my house with two other Albanian guys; he said that things could be very difficult if I did not make the payments. I realised that I was being threatened. If I went to the police, they would inform them that some of my workers were in the country illegally. You know I had been foolish and maybe I had not asked enough questions when I took my workers on. I wanted to be a success, and this clouded my better judgment."

"You mention "The Albanian" who is this person and what does he do."

"Oh yes he is some sort of lawyer, his name is Mehmet Ali."

Pegg said nothing; he waited, before he said:

"Look, let me make us something to drink, tea or coffee"

Babic was taken aback he eventually said, "Coffee please Mr Pegg, black with two sugars."

"Right come up into the 'van, take a seat," said Pegg.

They both entered the 'van, Babic sat down on the bench, whilst Pegg busied himself with making the coffee. Five minutes later, he poured them two cups, sugaring one and giving it to Babic. He looked at his watch it was a quarter past ten. He had at least 3 hours before he would be meeting Pat. He decided to continue with his conversation.

"How long have you got before you have to get back to Nottingham?"

"Oh, I'm fine for this morning; I've got to settle my account with GDF Supplies. I'll do that on my way back to Nottingham."

"So, tell me more about Mehmet Ali, or "The Albanian" as you call him."

"As I told you I met an Albanian guy, not Mehmet Ali, who was looking for someone to manage a car wash. I said that I was interested. The next thing I went to meet Mr Ali at leisure complex just outside Nottingham. I thought he was a businessman. He spoke English with no accent, certainly not like a foreigner would. I speak good English as you can see but even I have a slight accent. Anyway, after a bit the conversation switched over to Albanian. He noted that my accent was Kosovan. After giving him my early history, he said that I was just the person he was looking for. Well, one thing led to another and I ended up running the New Start Car Wash on Arnold Road.

"The car wash had just the basic stuff, and I wanted to improve it by getting things like pressure washers. I did not have the money for the improvements. I tried to get a bank loan but was not able to get one. Mr Ali must have heard about it, and he offered to loan the money. In fact, he gave me five thousand pounds. I wanted to set up a repayment schedule, but he said just pay him back when I could. I used the money and updated the equipment, and with my guys we really did well, and the car wash was thriving. We were making some three hundred pounds a day, going up to five hundred pounds a day at weekends. I banked the profits and I was able to pay my guys a decent wage. I realised I would need to get an accountant. I asked Mr Ali who he would recommend for this. He said not to worry he would take care of it. As you can see I put a lot of faith into Mr Ali. Anyway, I managed to put aside the five thousand pounds I borrowed from Mr Ali. I wanted to pay him back and be free of debt; when I went to him with the money, he told me that because of interest and other charges the amount owed was now six thousand pounds. I was very angry and said that this was unreasonable. I would be paying him some interest of one hundred and fifty percent on the loan, it was not fair.

"I was told that if I didn't like it, I could walk away but I still had to pay. He said that he would inform the tax people that I owed VAT. I did charge VAT on the car washes, and I put these sums in the bank. Ali said he would look after the accounting side of the business when I first started up. I kept a record of my receipts and invoices, in this book I worked out the VAT and kept it separately. Ali was supposed to be arranging for the accounts to be audited for tax purposes, and as part of this arrangement Ali became a joint account holder"

"So, you say Ali was using this debt to coerce you in to doing stuff you didn't want?" asked Pegg.

"Yes, and in the end I had to take on people I had no idea of who they were or where they had come from. My suspicions were that they were illegals. I put my concerns to Ali, but he just said that it was no longer my problem. I noticed that lots of money was being paid in and paid out of the car wash's bank account, again when I asked about this, I was told it was none of my business. So, you see all my work that I did setting up my business was all in vain; for all intents and purposes it has been stolen from me, and I am forced to do stuff I don't want to do."

"So how did you end up coming to my caravan and blocking off the gas flue?" said Pegg, who continued, "I want you to know I have no intention of going to the police, providing you are straight and honest with me. I'd like you to explain to me how you came to nearly kill me and my dog. What on earth have I done to you?"

Babic sat there and said nothing.

"Well I'm waiting."

Babic paused and took a deep breath, before saying, "I am so sorry about that, but Ali had me by the balls. He could at any time pull the rug from under my feet and I could end up in prison or worse. I am really ashamed that I did not put my foot down at the beginning. It started with what I suspected of money laundering, all that money going through New Start's account, and then the illegals who were working for the company. Then I was asked about me putting in a complaint about being mistreated by British soldiers when I was a refugee in Kosovo. That is something I would not do; the British saved my life and they gave me a new start, how could I turn on people who were good to me? This for me was a line I would not cross, and I was prepared for Ali to do his worse. But strangely enough Ali did not press me on this issue."

"Does Ali know that you are here seeing me?" asked Pegg.

"No, as I have said I am collecting stuff from GDF Supplies and settling our account, as you know the amount I owe, you have the invoice."

"No problem my man, I'll let you have it before you go. Now are you prepared to help me to nail Ali? I will make sure that your name will not be mentioned in any of this."

"Mr Pegg, you are a good and honourable man. The UK is my country now, and as I have said before it has given me so much. I must give it something back. I will help you in any way I can. I am not frightened of Ali anymore, so if my name comes out, well so be it and to hell with the consequences."

"Right then I'll get this whole murky situation into the domain of people who I know will assist in bringing Mehmet Ali down, and you will be a key person who'll help us to get this thing done," said Pegg.

"Is there a way I can contact you in confidence, without anyone else knowing about it?"

Babic wrote down a telephone number and an email address. Pegg gave Babic a mobile number, and informed Babic that he may be getting calls and emails from Rachel and her firm of solicitors. After speaking for a further five minutes he escorted Babic back to his car. He waited until the man drove off, before making a phone call to Rachel. Her secretary answered.

"Archie Pegg! You have really started something! We have been very busy following up your findings which you describe in your report."

"Thanks, I got a bit more information for you. I'll write it up and send it as an email attachment. Then that's it for the weekend. I'll be in touch at the beginning of the week, Monday or Tuesday. Will Rachel be in?"

"Well at the moment she is contacting the Law Society about LPJ. I can't say too much about this at the moment. Thanks to your efforts we have a lot to do; I expect Rachel will be in on Monday morning, but she is in court all of Monday afternoon."

Pegg ended the call and made his way back to his pitch. He let Fred out of the Landrover, and the dog followed Pegg into the awning. After clearing up the cups and plates, he got the laptop out and wrote a report detailing what Babic had told him. He wrote a covering email to Rachel and before sending it, attached the report, that job completed, the laptop was packed away.

He sat down and reviewed what he had achieved over the past eleven days. It would appear that the case against Tony Spratt has fallen apart. As this was the main reason for him being involved in the whole business, he was satisfied with the way things had turned out. There was one more thing to sort out. He needed to make sure that Richard Hoskins gets his just desserts. As he was pondering what he was going to do to achieve this, his phone rang.

CHAPTER 20

"Mr Pegg, Miss Warrington is at Reception."

"I'll be right up, see you in a minute."

Pegg put Fred on his leash and walked up to the Reception Office. There he saw Pat's Nissan X-Trail parked outside the building. He walked to the office and met Pat, she patted Fred, who licked her hand.

"Is Zena with you?"

"Yup, she's in the back of the car."

The receptionist gave her the keys to the static. She asked about how much she owed and was informed that the stay had been paid for. She looked quizzically at Pegg but said nothing; she waited until they were outside.

"Archie, I should be paying for this."

"Well they wanted a deposit, and rather than paying for part of the cost, I thought that I would pay for the lot. We can settle up later if you want."

"Archie Pegg, I'll hold you to that!"

"Come on, hop into your transport and follow us, I'll show you where your lodgings are."

He walked down to where the statics were parked, Pat followed When they got to Pat's static Pegg showed her where to park. She parked the Nissan up, and got out. There was whimpering coming from the back of the vehicle.

"Alright Zena, just let me get in and I'll come and sort you out," she said.

They climbed the steps that led up to the static's door. Pat unlocked the door and went in, followed by Pegg.

"This'll suit us for the next few days. It's bigger than I thought," said Pat. She walked through examining the two bedrooms, and the shower and WC. "I've brought Zena's bedding, so no excuse for her jumping up on the beds."

"I thought that this would be better than a B & B, much more of your own space, and you can come and go as you please."

"It's perfect; I'd have never thought of it. You're full of good ideas Mr Pegg!"

"Thanks. I'll let you settle in then I thought we could take ourselves off for walk with the dogs. By the way have you eaten?"

"Yes, I had something before I left."

"Right I'll give you a hand to unload your stuff if you want."

"No that's fine. I'll give you a call when we're ready to go."

Pegg walked back to his pitch. He made himself a sandwich and gave Fred something to eat. He took his map out and planned a route for the afternoon. The weather was warm and there was no sign of any rain. He'd been lucky with the weather for the past week, and it looked to be set fair for the weekend. He made himself a mug of tea and pondered his plans for the weekend. He had enough food and drink in, but he'd thought that he would take Pat for dinner at the pub he had been using for the past week; that's a point I need to give them a ring and order a table for this evening he thought. He dug out a menu he picked up on his first visit, looked up the number and gave the pub a call. He ordered a table for seven o'clock.

Pegg's phone rang. It was Pat who informed him they will be ready in five minutes. Pegg said he will meet her up at the Reception Office. He put away the lunch things and got himself ready. He took his small rucksack which contained the essentials plus compass and 1/25000 OS map, and after securing the 'van made his way up to the Reception Office. He got there and saw Pat and her dog walking towards them. The dogs greeted each other in the way canines do. Fred seemed delighted at seeing the German shepherd again. Zena for her part was a bit stand offish. Oh well thought Pegg, it's a dog thing.

"Right Pat I've planned a route which will take us a couple of hours or so, are you up for it?"

"Lead on Archie, I need to stretch my legs, having been cooped up in the car, and Zena really needs a good run as well."

"Great, let's do it then!"

They left the site and very shortly afterwards they were on the footpath. They let the dogs off their leashes and the animals immediately began a game of chase, scampering around as if they were a couple of pups. The weather was clear and dry; a slight chill in the air gave a hint that it might be a cold night.

"Well what have you been up to Archie, since we last met?"

Pegg thought before he replied, at this stage he did not want to go into detail what he had been doing. He certainly wasn't going to mention the attempt on his life.

"I've been enjoying the area, as well as a meeting up with an old friend from my army days. I spent a nice Sunday with him and his family. The poor old boy is in a bit of a muddle actually."

"Oh dear, I hope it's not something too serious."

"Well there is some bad stuff in his life at the moment, and it's all to do with his time in the Army. I expect that you have heard of the trouble in the Balkans about 10 years ago, Bosnia and all that."

"Oh yes, NATO were involved weren't they, and there were British troops out there?"

"Yes, that's right. Well my friend was out in Pristina, which is the capital in what was then Serbian province of Kosovo. Kosovo's majority population is Albanian speaking Kosovars, and the Serbs are the minority. In Pristina the population is divided roughly north and south, the Serbs being in the north of the city and the Kosovars in the city's south. There was always bad blood between the two people. The late president of Yugoslavia, Marshal Tito, managed to keep the diverse union of countries which made up the Republic together. The Republic was made up of several countries; Serbia, Slovenia, Croatia, Bosnia-Herzegovina, Macedonia and Montenegro.'

"My friend was part of a small group of Royal Engineers, which was attached to an infantry company, based in the northern part of the city of Pristina. Their job was to work with some of the infantry company's assault pioneers in the job of making safe and destroying ordnance and munitions left behind by the Serbian forces. He was not involved in any of the policing operations that were taking place in the city. Unfortunately, there have been allegations against the British troops, spurious in my view, that Kosovars were mistreated. There are a number of questions regarding these alleged incidents, the main one being that British troops were not in the areas where the Kosovar population of the city are located. The main body of British troops were in the south of the province, where they were constructing and running refugee camps for the Kosovars who had fled their homes and communities.'

"My friend has received notification that he is being investigated by an organisation called the Balkan War Investigation Team or BWIT for short. These people have a remit from the Services Prosecution Authority to investigate veterans of the Balkan conflict with a view to prosecuting them."

"That's so awful", said Pat, "these brave people out there serving their country and helping to protect defenceless Kosovans, only to be stabbed in the back for doing their job, it really makes me ill."

"Yes, it does leave a nasty taste in your mouth, especially when you know the allegations are false. Anyway, I managed to get my friend the help he needs. It looks like he'll be able to walk away from it all."

"I'm glad to hear it."

They'd been walking for an hour, and Pegg decided to take a slightly different route back to the site and not just turning around and retracing their steps. The walk back was uneventful, and they did not meet any other walkers. They arrived back on the site.

"I've booked a table for seven, what about the dogs? The pub is quite dog friendly."

"I think it would be best if Zena did not come in as she tends to wander and wants to be everyone's friend. I think I'll take my car and leave her in it."

"Fair enough then Fred can keep her company, is that okay with you?"

"Of course, I'll meet you in a bit."

"We'll come over and meet you at about quarte two."

Pat agreed to that and went back to her static. Pegg returned to the pitch, and had a wash, and changed. He decided to wear slacks a shirt and a sports jacket. He gave Spratt a call. The call was answered almost immediately. He gave Tony a summary of what had happened and informed him that in all probability the investigation involving the allegations against him would be stopped, and that Rachel will be informing him that no further action will be taken. He would not even be interviewed any more. Spratt appeared to be choking with emotion,

"Archie, I don't know how to thank you enough, I'd be up shit creek without a paddle if it hadn't been for you."

"We go back a long way Tony, I could never have left you to fight this outrage alone. Now just enjoy the weekend, and chill."

"Thanks again Archie, we'll speak soon."

Pegg ended the call and phoned Angie. The phone went to voice mail; Pegg left a message to say he'll call again on Sunday evening. He realised that by the time he went back to work, he would have to give the Norfolk Constabulary a decision as to whether he will continue in service or retire. If Cath had been alive, the decision would have been easy; now she had gone it was a question of having a focus on his life. He was fit, and there was no reason why he could not continue with the police for quite a few more years. He even considered applying for a sergeant's post. He already had passed the sergeants written exam but had never bothered to follow it up. His "difficult" attitude that many of the supervisory ranks in the Force perceived he had, made him reluctant to pursue the matter. One thing that was making him have a rethink about this was what Bill Grimes had said to him. Here was a young and rising star in the Force who appreciated Pegg's qualities; maybe it might be worthwhile having a crack at getting his stripes. His thoughts were interrupted by the ringtone of his phone.

"Come on Archie, have you forgotten?" said Pat.

Pegg glanced at his watch it was ten to seven.

"Oh gosh Pat, be with you in thirty seconds."

He grabbed his jacket and locked up the 'van. He put his laptop and the paperwork he had accumulated into the Landrover, placing the items under the passenger seat, and with Fred on his lead, sprinted to the Reception. There he saw Pat's X-Trail parked outside. Pat got out and Pegg stared at her. She had changed into a light blue skirt and dark blue blouse over which she was wearing a beige lambs-wool jacket. Her auburn hair was loose to her shoulders and she had applied minimal make-up. She was beautiful.

"What's up Archie? Don't just stand there put Fred in the back with Zena."

Pegg came to again and walked to the back of the car, where Pat was holding the tail gate open. Fred jumped up into the back and Pat closed the gate.

"Gosh Pat you look beautiful."

"Thank you kind sir," she beamed, "you don't look so bad yourself Archie! Now tell me which way we go."

Pegg explained and less than five minutes later they pulled into the pub's car park. Pegg was glad he had booked a table earlier; the pub appeared quite busy judging by the number of vehicles in the car park. Pat found a slot and deftly maneuvered the X-Trail into it. She checked the dogs and followed Pegg into the pub. After ordering their drinks, a waitress showed them to their table; it was a fairly reasonably sized affair, laid out for two diners. About half the tables in the restaurant area were occupied, but the majority of the clientele were in the bar area.

The waitress gave them each a menu and left to collect their drinks. They scrutinised their respective menus. Pegg decided on the steak and ale pie again, and Pat thought that she would go for the Cajun chicken. The waitress returned with their drinks, a pint of the guest bitter for Pegg and a white wine for Pat. The waitress took their order and left them.

"Well this is nice Archie, have you been here before?"

"I came here a couple of times this week; it is nice and convenient for the caravan site. The food is good, and the staff are attentive and friendly."

They continued to make small talk until their food arrived. The waitress returned with a small tureen of vegetables and left them. They ate their food; Pegg put down his knife and fork and asked:

"Well Pat I know that you live just outside Sheffield and that you work at the city's university, are you doing anything special there, or is what you do confidential?"

"Our department, mechanical and electrical engineering, is involved in a lot of stuff. As well as running the students courses, and there are a number of postgraduates doing their PhD's, there are some really interesting research projects."

"How are you financed regarding the research work," said Pegg as he spooned some more vegetables onto his plate.

Pat had put some food into her mouth and chewed thoughtfully before swallowing she continued:

"The money comes from a variety of sources. There is of course money from the government, and also we get some finance from industrial enterprises, plus individual benefactors contribute as well."

Pegg took a mouthful of beer before saying:

"So, what are you currently involved in, or is that a need to know thing."

"Not really, we are actually developing a type of wind turbine. It is slightly different from the conventional type. Instead of having rotors which resemble propellers, the turbine we are working on is cylindrical. The concept is not new, they are being used on a small scale, but we want to get some really serious machines developed so that they can be manufactured commercially. There is a lot going for this type of wind generated power; for a start these turbines themselves do not take up so much space as the normal turbine, so you can put them closer together if needs be. They could be installed on or next to buildings, and they are far less damaging to birds."

"That sounds like really worthwhile stuff to be doing, how far is it to becoming commercially viable?"

"We are nearly ready to go. We've had a bit of issue with metal fatigue on the blades and that is what I've been involved with, but we've now cracked it, if you'll excuse the pun. So, watch this space!"

They finished their food. The waitress returned and they ordered dessert. They both ordered the cheesecake; the waitress cleared their plates and left them. They continued to talk. Pat had mentioned the last time they met that she had been engaged. She started to expand on this. Apparently her fiancé had been seeing other women behind her back. She found out when she had inadvertently saw a text message on his phone. The person sending the text had left a lewd message, and an attachment. The attachment was a "selfie" of a woman exposing her breasts. Her fiancé was out of the room at the time. She confronted him, and he rapidly conceded that he had been seeing the woman. She said that she let it go after he had reassured her that this was a "one off". Things carried on but Pat started to have doubts as to his commitment to the relationship between them. Her doubts were confirmed when she phoned him one evening when she was in Denmark with members of the university's mechanical and electrical engineering facility's research team. His phoned was answered by a female. That was the final straw, and on her return to Sheffield she broke off with him. This happened about 18 months ago, and since then she had buried herself in her work. Their dessert arrived and they ate in silence for a bit, before Pegg said:

"You know Pat, in a way we're both in a similar situation. I've lost my soul mate, and you have also, through no fault of your own, been deprived of a potential life partner. I know that this sounds a bit strange, but I'd like us to be friends. How do you feel?"

"I like you Archie, but I do not think I want anything more than friendship at this time."

"Oh Lord Pat, I didn't mean to give the impression I am after replacing my Cath. I hope I have not in any way offended you."

She reached across the table and touched his hand:

"No dear man you haven't. I would like to be a good friend."

"Me too, so have you got an idea where we should go tomorrow?"

"I thought that we could head off to the High Peak. We can park up at the Upper Derwent Visitor Centre, and then we can do some serious walking taking in the Derwent Reservoir and Hope Forest. You'll love it."

"That sounds like a great plan. Shall we take a packed lunch?"

"We can do that, or we can find somewhere to eat. I am very familiar with the area and I know of a couple eateries."

"Well we can eat out. I'll still bring a flask."

They finished their dessert. Pegg asked if Pat wanted a coffee, she declined. She went to get her purse out of her bag. Pegg said that he was paying.

"Archie, this is my shout, put your money back. You can pay for lunch tomorrow if you want; that's an end to it!"

She got up and went to the bar and settled up. She came back to the table and picked up her coat.

"Just off to the girl's room, see you in a couple of minutes"

Pegg went to the gents, after which he waited at the entrance door. Pat joined him shortly afterwards, and they walked across the car park to Pat's X-Trail. Pat drove back to the caravan Park and stopped at Reception.

"Do you want to come to mine for a drink?" asked Pat.

"That sounds a plan, but first I'll take the dogs for a quick walk, is it all right if I bring Fred back to your static, if not I'll put him in my 'van."

"No bring him in; I'll fix up some drinks and nibbles."

Pegg collected the animals from the back of the car and led them off to the dog walk. Pat drove off to her static. He reached the park's dog walk and opened up the gate and let the animals in, closing the gate again before letting them off their leads. Although it was dark, there was enough illumination from a light at the entrance to the enclosed area for Pegg to see what the dogs were doing. Neither animal defecated which was a relief as he did not have any poop bags with him. He let them both sniff around for five minutes before going back to the entrance. He called Fred, who trotted back to him, followed closely by Zena. He put the leashes back on them and walked back to Pat's static.

CHAPTER 21

Pegg knocked on the door and said, "We're back."

"Come in, come in," said Pat from inside, "there's a towel just inside the door on the mat for wiping the mutt's feet. Give Fred's paws a rub, and I'll do Zena's."

"No worries I'll dry them both."

After wiping the feet of both dogs, Pegg entered the static. The door led into the lounge/kitchen area of the static. The room had a dining table with three chairs around it, there was a window seat which ran the whole width of the room, as well as a couple of armchairs. Pat set out some bottles of drink on the dining table. On an occasional table between the window seat and the two armchairs, she had set out a couple of bowls with mixed nuts and raisins in one and kettle chips in the other. Pat had lit the gas fire. The dogs wandered in and looked longingly at the bowls of snacks.

"No", said Pat, "settle down."

The animals sighed and made their way to the fire and lay down in front of it. Pegg removed his shoes and walked over to the window seat.

"What would like to drink, Archie?"

"A whisky please, with a drop of water"

Pat poured him a scotch and added water from the mixers, before pouring a vodka and tonic for herself. They sat side by side on the window seat. She offered Pegg a bowl of nuts, before taking some for herself. They sat in silence sipping their drinks and munching on the nuts. Pegg said:

"It has been so good to see you again Pat, I've really enjoyed our evening together."

"Me too Archie, you're really good company."

Pegg blushed he felt like an awkward teenager on his first date. Although he had not known this woman for long, he was starting to feel a strong bond towards her. He had no intention of displaying any overt signs of affection towards her, especially in view of what she had said in the pub, regarding forming anything more than friendship.

"Well what time should we start out tomorrow?" he said.

"If we're ready to go by seven thirty, we should be at the Derwent Visitor Centre an hour later. That'll be a good time to get some serious walking in before we stop for some lunch."

They talked for a long time, consuming chips and nuts as well as a couple of more drinks. Pegg looked at his watch, it was already past midnight.

"I think that it is time for me to turn in. It's going to be an early start tomorrow," he said.

"Yes, you're right Archie," she said, stifling a yawn.

They cleared up, and Pegg got Fred's lead.

"Thanks for this evening, Pat, I think that we'll take my Lanny tomorrow, I'll be outside here tomorrow at half past seven."

"Thank you too, we'll be up and ready to go."

She went over to him and took his hand, before kissing him on both cheeks. Pegg left and made his way to his pitch. As he neared his awning Fred growled; in view of what had happened previously Pegg approached cautiously. He did not say anything to the dog, he noticed that the entrance to the awning was unzipped and on shining the light inside, he could see that the door of the caravan was open, the lock had been forced. He looked inside and found that the 'van had been ransacked.

He checked around the 'van and the outside of the awning, nothing appeared to have been damaged except the 'van's door. He went to the Landrover, the doors were still locked and no sign of any attempt to gain entry. He unlocked the vehicle and checked under the passenger seat; he was relieved to find that the laptop and papers were still there.

He went to have a closer look at the door to the caravan. The edge of the door around the handle and lock was bent outwards. The lock itself was damaged beyond repair. He shone his torch close to the area around the lock. There were what appeared to be glove marks on the surface of the door and on the side of the caravan around the door handle. He looked at his watch, it was getting on for one. He definitely did not want to call the police. It would not help him to have policemen nosing about at this stage.

He had a look around the inside of the 'van. All the lockers were open, and their contents were strewn over the floor, seats and bunks. His bedding had been pulled off his bunk and was lying on the floor along with his clothes. Fortunately, the food items were still in their packaging and containers, nothing had been spilt. He had a look around, seeing if there was anything which might have been left by the intruder. There were no marks, blood or any other items which may point to who the person was. He checked to see if anything was missing. He had his phone and wallet with him when he went out. Nothing appeared to have been taken. So, the perpetrator or perpetrators were not your common or garden thief. Pegg pondered what they were looking for. The information he had on Tony Spratt's case was on his laptop, and in the file he had built up. This was all the stuff he had gathered over the past few days that would be damaging to both Mehmet Ali and Richard Hoskins. Fortunately, he still had both the laptop and the file items. He had passed on most of the information to Rachel, but there were a few bits he had held back. Another reason that he was glad that nobody had taken his laptop was that the contents could be point to Angie's hacking activities. He would wait until the morning and see if any other outfit had been broken into, before coming to any definitive conclusions regarding who was responsible. In the meantime, he tidied up and stowed clothing and food away again.

He was not going to let this stop his day out with Pat. He remade the bed, and fifteen15 minutes later he got into it and tried to get some sleep.

CHAPTER 22

Pegg had a poor night, waking up several times. He gave up and got up at six. After a shower he took Fred up to the dog walk, on the way he looked surreptitiously at the various outfits as he passed them. He could not find any sign that either caravans or vehicles had been interfered with. He made his way back to his pitch and had a look around. There was nothing to suggest that any attempt had been made to break into the Landrover. He found no marks on the doors, window edges or the tail gate.

He would have to get some sort of repair done to the caravan door. But that could wait until Monday. He was going to enjoy his day out with Pat, and he was not going to let these bastards get to him. There had now been two occasions that he had been targeted, "I must be getting up some shithead's nose," he thought to himself. "So, I'm on the right track."

He went back to the 'van and made some breakfast. After finishing he made a flask of coffee, and a couple of rounds of sandwiches; he then filled up some bottles with water for the dogs. Having packed these items and some dried food and bowls in a rucksack, he got ready for his walk across the Peaks. He put Fred in the back of the vehicle and drove to Pat's static. As he approached her pitch, she was already coming out of the door. She had a rucksack with her and was dressed in a red Berghaus jacket and blue craghopper trousers, and on her feet was a pair of brown walking boots. Her dog, Zena was at her heels. Pegg pulled up beside Pat's

X-Trail; he got out and opened up the back of the Landrover. Zena, with no hesitation jumped in and took her place beside Fred.

"How are you Pat? Did you get a decent night's kip?"

"I was out like a light the moment my head hit the pillow!"

Pegg did not mention his misfortune; nothing was going to ruin the day. He did not want Pat to cancel today's sojourn because of some scrote's nefarious activity.

"I'm so pleased. Well I guess we need to get going," he said, taking Pat's kit and putting it in the back.

They got into the Landrover and Pegg drove out of the site. It was another glorious autumn morning, some cloud cover but in the main the sun was coming up, promising a beautiful day. There was a slight breeze which gave a pleasant feel to the air. It was ideal walking weather; and in spite of everything Pegg was looking forward to it.

There was very little traffic on the roads, and they arrived at the Upper Derwent Visitor Centre in a little over an hour. Pegg drove into the car park and parked up in a fairly open section of the facility. They got out and let the dogs out of the back, both animals wandered round the immediate area, before they were put on their leashes. Pegg and Pat put their rucksacks on.

"Right, Pat, you're our guide today, lead on!"

"Follow me, I'll show you a good time Archie Pegg!"

They walked out of the car park and were soon on a trail beside the reservoir. After two hours they reached the Hope Forest area of the Peaks. It was a steady uphill trek, and they found a spot to pause and look back on the route they had taken. The sun had burnt off the cloud, and the view was a picture. The sun shining on the foliage of the trees enhanced the autumn hues. The palette ranged from light yellow, gold, red and brown. An artist would be hard put to replicate them on a canvas. Pegg reached into his rucksack and brought out a bowl and a bottle of water. The dogs drank, emptying the bowl which Pegg refilled. He emptied some dried food into another bowl. Neither animal was really interested in eating. He poured a couple of cups of coffee, and gave one to Pat.

"Sandwich?" he asked.

"Thanks, it will be a couple of more hours before we have some lunch."

They ate and sipped their coffee. The dogs lay down nearby. Pegg asked Pat what her plans were for Monday:

"I've got to get the X-Trail in for its MoT test. It's booked in for eleven o'clock; and then I promised mum that I'd help with a couple of things in the afternoon."

"If you want, I'll give the car a quick look over tomorrow."

"That would be great. I think it's OK, but a fresh pair of eyes could be an advantage."

They finished their break. Pegg packed everything away in his rucksack, and they continued on their walk. They took a large circular walk before arriving back at the Upper Derwent Visitor Centre at two. They made their way back to the Landrover.

" Where can we get a late lunch?" asked Pegg.

"I know just the place, it's about 3 miles to the south in Bamford, it's called the Yorkshire Bridge Inn. I've been there quite a few times. You'll like it Archie".

"Great! Let's do it!"

Pegg opened up the back of the vehicle and the dogs jumped in. He drove out of the car park and headed south, after fifteen minutes they were pulling into the pub's car park. It was still a warm afternoon, so Pat decided to get a table in the outside seating area. It was not too crowded. Pat sat with the dogs whilst Pegg went inside to get a menu and some drinks. He returned about five minutes later; a glass of beer for himself and a white wine for Pat. They studied the menu. Pegg decided on cod in beer batter and chips; Pat wanted the chicken chili and rice. Pegg went back to the bar and gave their order. He returned to Pat. She had spotted a bowl of water to the right of the seating area and had taken the dogs to it. Both animals were lying at Pat's feet with water dripping from their muzzles.

"I think that tomorrow I'll give your X-Trail a good looking over. I'll do it fairly early, and if there are any bits I need, I can go and get some stuff from Halfords or some such store."

"Well not too early Archie, "said Pat, "It is a Sunday you know!"

"Well we'll see how it goes," he said.

They continued to talk about the way they had come. After a bit their food arrived; carried by a young man, and followed by a young woman, who was carrying cutlery, cruets and sauces. After placing their plates on the table, the young man left. Pegg asked the young woman if they could have some more drinks and some water in a jug. Pat asked for another white wine, Pegg another beer. They started on their food.

"Mmm this fish is delicious Pat, what's the chicken like?"

"It's very tasty thanks. As I 've said before I've been here a few times; I've never been disappointed."

They continued eating; the young woman returned with a tray, on which were, Pat's wine, Pegg's beer, a jug of water, and two fresh glasses. The waitress took their old glasses and left.

"After I've sorted your motor out tomorrow, what do you fancy doing?"

"I haven't really thought about it. Maybe a visit to that nice pub where we had supper, and a walk around the local area. How about you?"

"Yeah, that sounds like a plan. We'll see how the day pans out."

The waitress returned and cleared up their plates and cruets. She asked if they wanted a dessert, reciting the dessert menu. Pegg ordered apple crumble and custard, as did Pat. Pegg had finished his beer and poured himself a glass of water.

"So how far do you live from here, Pat? You seem to have an encyclopedic knowledge of the local area."

"Gosh not so far, High Bradfield is about fifteen miles north of here. I'm out on the Peaks most weekends. I just love it. Sometimes I have to give it a miss in the winter, as the snow closes off access."

"Well maybe I can persuade you to come to our neck of the woods. There is the coastal path now, which runs from Lynn through to Great Yarmouth, not many hills but lovely views of the sea and marshes."

"Now there's an idea Archie Pegg, something to look forward to!"

The waitress returned with their desserts. They waited until she left them.

"I've something to tell you Pat, I did not want to mention it before as I did not want it to spoil our day out together," said Pegg.

Pat stopped eating and looked anxiously at Pegg:

"What is it you want to tell me?" she asked.

Pegg went on to explain about the break in and ransacking of his 'van, whilst they were out having a meal at the pub. He explained about the laptop, and the file.

"So as far as you know, nothing has been taken?"

"No, there was not too much of value for an opportunist thief. I mean there was a small money box with some silver and pound coins, as well as a radio, my camera and binoculars. These were not missing when I checked, so my gut feeling is that the intruder was after something else. I am well aware that there is a lot of stuff on the laptop that certain people would want erased."

"Oh my, Archie! You really have got involved in something quite serious."

"Nothing I can't handle, but I do not want you worrying about it. It has nothing to do with you. I just thought that I need to let you know, as you will be aware that something has happened when you see the door to my caravan."

Pegg went on to explain how he had done a check of other outfits on the site and found no sign of any break-ins to either vehicles or caravans. His outfit was the only one which had been interfered with.

"So, on Monday I'll be doing one or two follow-up enquiries, and then I'll think about going back home. But I want to spend the rest of the weekend with you, if that is alright with you Pat."

"I wouldn't want it any other way," Pat said.

They finished off their desserts.

"Do you want anything else," he asked Pat.

She looked at her watch before saying:

"No, I'm fine; how about stretching our legs for a bit. We can leave the car here and go for a wander across the moor again. I think that the dogs would like that."

"Yes, let's do that," replied Pegg.

They donned their jackets again, and with their respective animal on a leash, walked out of the car park, across the road, and onto the moor. They followed a trail, uphill and away from the pub. After five minutes the dogs were let off their leases. Pat took hold of Pegg's hand. They continued walking hand in hand, whilst the dogs trotted on ahead of them. The weather continued to be set fair. There were a few clouds but there was a slight chill in the air. There could be a slight frost later in the night, Pegg thought. They continued to walk for another thirty minutes before Pat said:

"It will be getting dark in a couple of hours; I think we should think about getting back to the car."

Pegg nodded in agreement, and they returned to the car park. They loaded the dogs into the back of the Landrover, and then climbed into the front of the vehicle. Pegg started the engine and drove out of the car park, and back to the site. The journey back was uneventful, and an hour later they were pulling into the caravan park. Pegg pulled into his pitch and parked up. It was starting to get dark, and the clear sky confirmed Pegg's belief that a frost was in the air. They looked at the damage to the caravan's door. It would not take too much to put it right Pegg thought. The door itself was not buckled or bent; it was the catch mechanism which was damaged. He'd look around at some of the dealers and see if he could get a replacement, in the meantime he'd make a temporary repair.

"There are some evil people about, Archie. How are you going to sort it out?"

Pegg told her what he intended to do; after this he went to the back of the Landrover and let the dogs out.

"Do you fancy coming over for some supper, say about eight?" asked Pat.

"Yes, I'd like that. Is there anything you need from here? I don't know what you want, I've got some salad stuff, or tinned soups."

"No thanks I've got a few things I can rustle up."

"Okay then I'll see you then. I'll bring a couple of beers, and I've got a bottle of wine as well."

Pat stood in front of Pegg, she put her arms on his shoulder, and kissed him fully on the lips. Pegg was somewhat startled, but instead of pushing her away, put his arms around her waist and held her.

"Thank you for a lovely day", she whispered in his ear.

"You too Pat, I've enjoyed it as well."

"See you in a bit Archie," she said, before continuing, "come Zena let's sort ourselves out before our guests come to supper."

She left and walked away to her static with Zena following behind her. She'd left Pegg in a somewhat flustered state. He went into the 'van and sat down, Fred jumped up onto Pegg's lap.

"Dear me boy, what do you make of it? Here I am, heart fluttering like a little bird's wings, short of breath." The dog looked at Pegg and whined softly. Pegg tickled the animal's ear. "Well I suppose we'd better get ourselves ready then."

He changed into a sweatshirt and jogging bottoms, grabbed his toilet bag and a towel, and made his way to the door of the 'van.

"Fred you look after the 'van for 10 minutes whilst I go to the washroom," he said to the poodle, before shutting the door, and walking over to the shower block. Pegg shaved and then had a shower. He dried himself, before donning his sweatshirt and jogging bottoms again, and returning back to the 'van again. Fred was where he had left him, lying on the blanket, which was draped over the seat.

He changed into a pair of clean jeans and a long-sleeved shirt. He took a shopping bag and placed a couple of bottles of beer and a bottle of wine, which he had taken out of the fridge, into it. Next he went to the Landrover and took the laptop and file from the compartment under the passenger seat. He brought these two items back into the 'van and placed them in the shopping bag as well. He had decided to play safe and keep these things with him; not that he thought his 'van would be targeted again. He looked at the clock; it was quarter past seven. He picked up his phone and called Afrim Babic. The phone rang for quite a time before it was answered.

"Yes" a male voice answered softly.

"Mr Babic, it's Archie Pegg. You alright?"

"Ah Mr Pegg, I'm not too good; I'm sorry I meant to call you, but I am a bit hurt."

"What happened?"

Babic hesitated before answering, "You promise not to tell the police or anyone?"

"I'll not tell the police, come on my man, out with it"

"Yesterday morning I received a visit from Mehmet Ali and two of the Albanians he works with. I haven't seen them before. They asked me if I knew you. I denied it. They knew I had been to the site, as Richard Hoskins had told them. I was given a beating. They told me to go to your caravan and search it. They were after any sort of computers, paperwork, you know, stuff like that. They wanted me to steal these things. I refused to do it. The two thugs then beat me some more, Ali just stood there and watched. I do not remember anything else, I must have passed out. I came to on the floor of my house. I have a few cuts and bruises, but I do not think anything is broken. They made a mess of my house"

"You need to get yourself checked out. So, you have been at home all this time."

"Yes, I've tried to clean myself up a bit, but I think I'll stay in for the rest of tomorrow."

"You do that; I'll try and get out to you on Monday. My caravan was broken into last night, whilst I was out. Have you any idea who might have done it?"

"I'm so sorry to hear that Mr Pegg; the only person who knows for sure where you are apart from me is Hoskins. But he could have told Mehmet, and either he or one of his men may have done it."

Pegg thought for a moment before he said:

"I think it was some of his muscle; I can't see either Mehmet or Hoskins getting involved. Look I've got to go now. I'll speak again on Monday and fix a time to see you. Remember keep indoors, and if you feel yourself in any danger, dial 999 and ask for the police. Hopefully it won't come to that."

Pegg ended the call. Monday is going to be a busy day he thought to himself.

"Right Fred, time for us to go and see Pat and Zena," he said, putting on a fleece and gathering up the bag and Fred's leash. He shut and secured the 'van's door as best as he could, before zipping up the entrance to the awning, and making his way over to Pat's static. When he got there and climbed the steps to the door, he heard Zena bark. Pat came to the door and let them in.

"Come in boys and make yourselves comfortable," she said.

She was dressed in a pair of jeans and a light blue sweatshirt. She had laid the table and there was something in the oven. She had prepared a salad, which was in a bowl on the table together with some bowls of potato salad and coleslaw. Pegg produced the bottle of wine and the bottles of beer. He filled two glasses, and gave one to Pat.

"Well thanks for today and here's to us, "he said, clinking Pat's glass.

"Cheers Archie, I really enjoyed it. The dogs seem to be worn out", she replied indicating towards the two animals who were lying down in front of the low burning gas fire.

Pat took a sip of her wine before putting it down and taking a quiche out of the oven and putting it down on a mat beside the salad bowl.

"Right take a seat, I'll cut this up, help yourself to salad and stuff."

Pat quartered the quiche and put a piece on Pegg's plate and one on hers. Pegg helped himself to some of the salad, before passing the bowl onto Pat. He spooned some of the potato salad and coleslaw onto his plate as well.

"Not very exciting fare, but we had quite a good lunch."

"Absolutely Pat this is fine for me."

They ate and drank some more of the wine.

"Right tomorrow Pat, I'm going to give your X-Trail the once over, so it'll be ready for its MoT Test. If there's anything that it needs I'll try and get it sorted."

"That's very kind of you Archie, I don't want to impose on you too much."

"No, I said I'll do it, and that's an end to it."

They went on to discuss what they were going to do in the following week. Pat explained that she was going to Denmark again on Thursday. The research team were hoping to convince the Danes at Aarhus University to adopt some of the turbine designs she and her team had been working on. Pegg said that there were a few loose ends he wanted to tie up before returning to Norfolk. They cleared up the table and washed up the dinner things, after which they sat down. Pat refilled their glasses with the last of the wine. They continued talking for another hour, when Pat stifled a yawn.

"It's been a long day, Pat and there is a lot to do tomorrow. I think we both need our beauty sleep."

"You're right Archie, time for some shut eye."

"I really have enjoyed it, and I hope that we will be able to do it again, maybe next time you'd like to come and do some walking in Norfolk. It's a bit flatter than the Peaks, but just as beautiful, especially the coastal paths."

"You can count me in on that!"

"Right Fred let's be getting back. Do you want me to take Zena to the dog walk?"

"I'll tell you what we can go up together I could do with a bit of fresh air before I turn in."

Pegg put his fleece and Pat donned a Berghaus jacket. She put Zena's leash on, and they and the dogs walked up to the dog walk, where the dogs were let of their leashes. After five minutes, the dogs were on their leashes again and Pat and Pegg walked back to the main site. Outside Pat's static they talked for a bit before they bade farewell to each other. They kissed and Pegg returned to his pitch. After undressing and finishing off in the washroom, he went to bed, and shortly after went to sleep.

CHAPTER 23

It was another crisp autumn morning when Pegg woke up. There had been a slight frost overnight, but it had become heavy dew. The rising sun shining through the foliage on the trees was throwing dappled patterns on the damp grass; this combined with the gossamer threads of countless spiders' webs gave the cut grass the appearance of a shimmering lake.

Pegg made his way to the dog walk with Fred, after finishing there he returned to the pitch, left Fred in the Landrover, collected his washing gear, and made his way to the washroom. Half an hour later he was finishing his breakfast. He phoned Pat and arranged to be at her static for half past nine. He spent the time sorting out his tools and placing them in the back of the Landrover. He donned a set of coveralls and placed the laptop and file in the space under the passenger seat. By the time he had completed these tasks it was nearly half past nine. He put Fred in the front of the Landrover, and after securing the 'van as best he could, drove over to Pat's static.

He parked up beside her X-Trail. By the time he had got out of the vehicle, Pat was already at the open door of the static. She was dressed in a pair of Levi's and a red sweatshirt. She had her hair in a ponytail, secured with a red band. She looked gorgeous thought Pegg to himself. Zena was beside her, and on seeing the Landrover, went over to it. She jumped up at the passenger side door, resting her front paws on the window ledge. Fred looked at her and started to whine softly. The two animals continued to stare at each other.

"Good morning Archie, did you sleep well?"

"Gosh, I dropped off the moment my head hit the pillow, and you?"

"Likewise, I was out until eight o'clock. I've just cleared up after breakfast. Did you want a tea or coffee?"

"Not just now thank you, I think that we need to get going, I don't know how much has got to be done to your motor. I'll leave Fred where he is for now, he'll only start ragging with her, and we don't need them playing chase around the site!"

"Okay, I'll tether her to the steps, and we'll begin, what do you want me to do?"

"Gosh where do I start, well I would like you to be at my side for most of the time. We'll go through a general check of your car first, this will identify some faults, but I do not think that we will have too many major problems."

"How does the vehicle feel when you drive it?"

"Generally okay; but at times there is a bit of a squealing noise when I apply the brakes."

"Is it when you apply the handbrake or foot brake?"

"It's when I use the foot brake mainly."

"Right let's get going then, you ready, Pat?"

"As ready as I'll ever be!"

Pegg went to the back of the Landrover and took his toolbox out and carried it to the side of the X-Trail. Next he laid a ground sheet next to the vehicle, and taking a headlamp, put it is elasticated band around his head. He lay down and switching the lamp on, examined the brake pads on the front nearside wheel. He got up again.

"It appears that the front nearside brake pads are worn, that being the case, it'll be the same with the other 3 sets of pads."

"Oh dear, is that a problem?"

"Well it could be a failure on the MoT. It's easy enough to rectify, we'll pop out and get some. There's bound to be a Halfords or something. In point of fact if you can look online and find the nearest branch."

He went to the front of his vehicle, and reaching under the passenger seat, took out his laptop, and powered it up. He gave it to Pat who took it and sat on one of the top step to the door of the static. Zena sat beside her, staring at the screens laptop.

After about five minutes Pat said:

"Here, Archie, there's a Halfords in Ashbourne, it's about twenty miles away, they are open from ten to five on a Sunday."

"That's great, give them a call later after ten and see if they stock brake pads. Right come here and sit in the driver's seat, and we'll have a check over."

"Okay, I'll just make a note of the stores telephone number."

After doing this she joined Pegg. She got into the driver's side and put the key in the ignition.

"Okay start her up said Pegg."

The engine started and was slightly revved up and left idling. Pegg went to the driver's side.

"Switch on the lights."

She did so, and Pegg walked around the vehicle. He went to the back of the vehicle.

"Press the brake pedal on and off."

She did that, and Pegg went to the driver's side again.

"Looks like the near offside brake light is out, otherwise all the lights are working, we'll just check the headlights again. Switch to main beam and dip again when I get to the front."

He walked to the front of the vehicle and stood about 20 feet from it. He nodded to Pat who switched the lights from main beam to dipped beam several times. Pegg held his arm up and walked back to the driver's side.

"That looks fine, so it's just the rear brake light which needs fixing. Right we'll look at the windscreen washers and wipers. Switch the wipers and washers on."

The wipers started up; there was a very weak jet of water coming from one washer and nothing from the other.

"Oh, dearie me Pat! When was the last time you checked the windscreen washer bottle?"

"Umm well......"

"Never mind we've all been there! Right slip the bonnet release catch."

Pegg then lifted the bonnet and secured it. He checked the screen washer bottle, it appeared to be devoid of any liquid content.

"Can you get a jug of water or failing that a kettle with cold water."

Pat switched off the engine and went inside the static. Pegg meanwhile went to the back of the Landrover and retrieved a bottle of washer fluid. He also fetched some a tin of needles from his toolbox. He proceeded to clean the nozzles on the front washers and did the same with the rear windows washer nozzle. Pat came back out and was holding the electric kettle.

Pegg unscrewed the top of the washer fluid bottle and poured some of its contents into the screen washer reservoir.

"Okay Pat start to pour some water in, I'll want you to stop halfway and I'll add some more of this to the mix."

She did so, pausing halfway through the operation to let Pegg add more washer fluid, before finishing as the level of the liquid reached the top of the bottle. She put the kettle down at the foot of the steps. Zena gave it a cursory sniff, before settling down again.

"Okay back in the driving seat and switch the ignition on."

She operated the washers again. A powerful stream of liquid squirted out of the nozzles and onto the front windscreen. Pegg got her the switch on the front and rear wipers the jet from the rear washer nozzle was as powerful as those on the windscreen.

"Okay switch off, Pat. If you could top up the washer bottle again, and I'll have a look at the wiper blades."

"Do you think I'll need new ones?"

"Not necessarily I'll give the blades a clean."

"Have you got any vinegar?"

"Yeah I think there is some in the cupboard."

"Great! If you can mix some warm water; and some vinegar in a bucket for me, only about a litre or so and pour in about three tablespoons full of vinegar.

Pat returned to the static, picking up the kettle on the way. Pegg meanwhile got a cloth and a roll of Kim wipes from the back of the Landrover. Shortly afterwards Pat returned with a bucket containing the water and vinegar mix. Pegg proceeded to clean the front and rear wiper blades. When he was satisfied that they were all clean, he asked Pat to turn them on again, at the same time operating the washer. The result was a 100% improvement in the devices performance.

"Perfect!" exclaimed Pegg. "Right all we've got to do is to ring Halfords at Ashbourne and see if they have disc pads and brake light bulbs in stock. Make the call Pat!"

"Yes sir!"

She returned to the static and five minutes later, she went back to the X-Trail, where Pegg had secured the bonnet.

"According to the call taker the said items are on the shelf," she said.

"Right we'll go in my car, I'll leave my bits in the back of the X-Trail if I may; there 'll be more room for the dogs in the back."

"That's fine, whilst you're doing that I'll take the dogs up to the dog walk."

Pegg gathered up his toolbox and the rest of his stuff and put it in the back of the X-Trail. He got out of his coveralls and placed them on top of the toolbox. He returned to the Landrover and cleaned off his hands with some wet wipes, then he retrieved his laptop and put it under the driver's seat. By the time he had finished Pat had returned with the dogs. She put them in the back of the Landrover. She walked to the static, collected her handbag, and locked up. Pegg was already seated in the driver's seat of the Landrover when Pat got in the passenger side.

"Right let's head off to Ashbourne. Halfords is located on the Waterside Retail Park area of the town. You've been to Ashbourne before, haven't you Pat?"

"Yes, I was there last year. You need to go into Buxton and then follow the A515 southbound; that will take us direct to Ashbourne."

It was about forty-five minutes later, that they entered Ashbourne, and fifteen minutes later that they had parked up in front of Halfords on the retail park. Twenty minutes later they were walking out of the store with four sets of brake pads and a rear lamp bulb for the X-Trail.

They decided to return to the site without stopping for a lunch break. Pegg said he had to fit all the brake pads before the end of the day. The drive back was uneventful and by one o'clock they were parked up at Pat's static. They had a light lunch of sandwiches and coffee, in Pat's static. After they had finished Pegg said:

"I'll get started; it should not take too long to get those pads fitted."

"I'll take the dogs out for a walk whilst you do that. I'll be about an hour."

"Great! I'll not be finished by the time you get back, but I'll try!"

"Don't bust a gut Archie."

Pegg proceeded to take off the near-side front wheel. He removed the brake pads, cleaned out the calipers and washed off the brake dust. He fitted a pair of new brake pads and replaced the wheel before repeating the process with the off-side front wheel. He was removing the rear offside wheel when Pat returned with the dogs.

"How's it going Archie?" she asked.

"It's going a lot better than I hoped. The old pads are coming out quite easily. I should be done in an hour then we'll take the vehicle for a test run."

"That's brilliant; I'll make us a mug of tea."

She went into the static, the dogs followed her. Pegg continued removing the wheel. By the time Pat joined him again with two mugs of tea, the wheel was off and the old brake pads were out. Pegg continued working on the calipers and cleaning up the disc, whilst taking sips from his mug. After an hour all the new brake pads were in place. Pegg fitted the final wheel, and after tightening the wheel nuts, went around the vehicle and checking the nuts on the other wheels. He changed the defective bulb in the rear light cluster.

He packed his tools away and placed the detritus which had accumulated during the afternoon in a bag including the disposable gloves he had worn. He removed his coveralls and cleaned his hands with some wipes. These joined the gloves in the bag.

"Right Pat time for a quick road test," he said.

"Okay, do you want me to drive?"

"Absolutely, you need to be aware of the new brake pads. At first you need to pump the brake pedal a couple of times before we drive off. The calipers which grip the brake pads need to be closed up a bit. I had opened them out to fit the new pads."

Pat put the dogs in the back and got into the driver's seat, whilst Pegg put his tools in the back of the Landrover. He carried the bag to the back of the X-Trail and placed it near the tailgate. Zena sniffed the bag, and as there was no sign of edible material, lost interest and lay down again. Pegg climbed in beside Pat.

She started up and pumped the brake pedal until it became firm. She drove towards the site entrance, stopping to allow Pegg to deposit the bag in the skip located next to the site office. They drove for about fifteen minutes during which time Pat applied the brakes several times. The squealing that Pat had previously mentioned had gone. She drove back to the site and parked up again outside the static.

"You should not have any problem with the MoT tomorrow, as far as I can see. I think the emissions level from the exhaust will be within the parameters, it's not smoking or anything like that. Tyres are fine and all the lights work," said Pegg.

"I'll treat us to dinner, Archie it's the least I can do."

They decided to go to the pub down the road. They'd walk there with the dogs. Pegg said that he would meet her at her static at seven. He had to get cleaned up and needed to give Angie a call. He drove the Landrover back to his pitch and parked it up. He entered the 'van. Fred followed him and settled down on his blanket. Pegg grabbed his washing gear and made his way to the shower block, where he showered and shaved before returning to the 'van. He changed into a clean pair of slacks, shirt and pullover. He then phoned Angie. She picked up the phone after the second ring.

"Archie, how is it going up in sunny Derbyshire?"

"That's a very apt description! The weather has been absolutely wonderful!"

"Did Pat turn up?"

"She certainly did. She's going back home tomorrow."

Pegg went on to describe their weekend. How Pat had hired a static on the site. Their trip out to the Derwent Reservoir, and how he had spent Sunday sorting Pat's car out prior to its MoT on Monday.

He was well aware about how Angie might feel regarding Pegg having another person in his life. It was a bit over six months since he had lost Cath.

"Pat's going back home tomorrow; I've got a few loose ends to tie up this end before I come back to Norfolk."

Angie asked him about the way things were panning out regarding Tony Spratt. Pegg told her he was waiting to hear from

Rachel. It was looking good, and there was a real possibility that the allegations against Tony would be dropped. She went on to describe how they had spent their weekend. They had taken Catherine Rose to see Ross' parents and spent the day with them. Ross had to go to work on Tuesday, but at least it was at Norwich Airport, so he would be coming home each evening.

They continued talking for another ten minutes, before Pegg ended the call. He said that he would call again on Tuesday. Angie told him he could phone any time, as she was working from home. Pegg looked at his watch; it was about five minutes before he was due to meet Pat. He put his fleece on, put Fred on his lease, secured the 'van, and made his way to Pat's static. He tapped on the door, Zena barked and a short while later Pat opened the door and let them in.

"We're just about ready; bear with me," she said and went back into the bathroom. A few moments later she joined him.

She was dressed in a pair of red corduroy trousers and a navy sweater. He hair was down, no pony tail this time. She donned a Berghaus jacket and put Zena's lease on. They made their way out of the site, and onto the road. Twenty minutes later they were seated in the pub at a table near the window. Pegg had a pint of bitter and Pat was sipping a glass of wine. They had ordered their choices at the bar at the same time they got their drinks. Pegg was having a chicken and bacon pie, whilst Pat ordered the lasagne. Pegg said:

"I hope that we can continue to see each other. You know I've enjoyed your company and the time we've spent together these past two days. We have our own lives to lead."

"Well I am glad I decided to spend the weekend here. I know in a way it's my own back yard, but it gets me away from my home and work. But having said that, I love my work, and I am very close to mum and dad. But I need a break from them sometimes!"

"Yes, I know I know what you mean. Perhaps you should come down to Norfolk. As I've said before, it's a lot flatter than the landscape you are used to, but there are some really good coastal walks and we could take a boat and sail on the Broads."

"We'll do that," she said.

"When I get back, I've got to decide whether to retire from the police or continue. I really do not know what to do. I am shortly going to be fifty-five, and nowadays that really is no age."

"I can't really advise you Archie; but if you are happy in what you are, why not continue?"

"I think you're right. Since Cath died, I've been in a bit of a rut. I must admit my job and my stepdaughter's family have kept me going."

Pat was silent.

"No please don't take this the wrong way," said Pegg. He continued, "I want you to be a friend, I am not looking after a person to replace my Cath."

Pat reached across the table and squeezed his hand. Before Pegg could say anything more, their food arrived. They waited until the waiter had left them before Pat said:

"Look Archie, as I have told you before; at this time, I am quite content for us to be friends, and if it goes further, well time will tell."

"I'm completely with you on that. So, we'll stay in touch, and I'll keep you up to speed regarding my future work arrangements. I've got a couple of months before I have to give the police my final decision as to whether I continue, or I leave."

They ate their food. Pegg asked Pat about her ongoing trip to Denmark. She said that the Danes were quite interested in the new wind turbine design Sheffield was working on. She will be going to Aarhus University with the team, and also they will be meeting with the management of DONG, the major manufacturer of wind turbines. Pegg, being an electrician by training, had an interest in electricity generation. His knowledge of renewable electricity generation was quite substantial, and so he was able to have a deep and meaningful conversation with Pat. It was quite a relief to Pegg that the subject of their conversation was steered from their relationship to another topic. They finished their meal and ordered some more drinks. The pub had filled up a bit since they first arrived. They continued to talk for a further two hours, during which time they consumed another two rounds of drinks. Pat said:

"I think it's time for me to think about turning in. The car's got its MoT tomorrow. I don't have to drive it to the garage, as I've arranged for it to be collected from home; but I expect that they'll be quite early to pick it up. They said it will be between eight-thirty and nine. I'll have to be home by eight. So, Pat my girl, it's a really early start."

"If you want I'll get the static handed over for you tomorrow," said Pegg.

"That'll be great if you could, I'll drop the keys off with you before I go."

"No worries, we'll probably be up."

"Right then I'll settle up, and we'll make tracks," said Pat.

She went to the bar and paid off their tab; whilst she was doing that Pegg put the leashes on the dogs and led them out onto the car park. A few moments later Pat joined them. They walked back to the site and down to Pat's static.

"Thank you for the dinner and a really good couple of days, I hope that it'll not be too long before we see each other again. Give me a call tomorrow to see if the X-Trail has passed its MoT."

"I'll do that, and hey, thank you for a great couple of days; and yes, I'll look forward to coming to Norfolk. Let me know what you decide regarding retiring or not," she said.

She put her arms round him and kissed him.

"Good night Archie, see you in the morning."

They parted company and Pegg headed back to his pitch. He let himself into the 'van, and Fred followed. He undressed and got into bed. He lay awake for a while and thought about the weekend he'd spent with Pat. He put these thoughts away and concentrated on what he was going to do during the coming week. He needed to see Babic and try and find a way to get Mehmet Ali and his thugs off the poor man's back. He also needed to get an update from Rachel Gluckstein, but that would have to be mid-week. He eventually fell into a dreamless sleep.

CHAPTER 24

Pegg was woken up by Fred barking. He heard a tap on the door of the 'van. He got up and slipped on a pair of track suit bottoms and a sweatshirt. He opened the door:

"Good morning, Archie, I hoped that you slept well," she said, before handing him the keys to her static.

"I had a really good nights kip. What time were you up this morning?"

"About five-thirty, I need to get going if I'm to be home before half past eight."

Pegg glanced at his watch it was coming up for seven, he stepped out of the 'van.

"Well, have a safe journey, and thanks again for your company this weekend," he said.

He gave her a kiss on her cheek; she put her arms around him and kissed him full on the lips. She slowly pulled away before whispering in his ear:

"Take care of yourself dear Archie Pegg, we'll speak soon."

She left him and made her way back to the X-Trail and drove out of the site. Pegg watched her drive away; he remained standing for a long time before he went back into the 'van again. He realised that Pat had made a huge impression on him, and that their relationship was on an upward course.

He took Fred up to the dog walk and waited until the dog had finished, before returning to the 'van and collecting his washing kit. After washing and shaving in the shower block, he had breakfast.

After he had finished, he dressed and got his file and laptop out. He needed to get an update from Babic. He gave him a call; the phone was answered almost immediately:

"Afrim, it's Archie Pegg, how are you today?"

"I am okay, a bit sore, but better than I was when I last spoke to you."

"How's your head are you getting headaches or having dizzy spells? You haven't been to get medical help, have you?"

"No, Mr Pegg, my head is sore, but I am not getting any headaches or dizziness."

"Okay I'll be out to see you, in the next hour or so. Is there anything you need.? I've got some medical stuff and I'll bring that with me. What about food and stuff, if you've been in all weekend, you'll need to be re-stocking."

"Thank you so much Mr Pegg."

"Archie, Afrim, Archie!"

"Sorry Archie. I have not been out at all. I stayed in as I do not know if Ali or his men are still about. I will be very grateful if you could get something in for me; I'll pay you for everything."

"You stay where you are I'll be with you as quick as I can."

Pegg went back to the laptop and turned it on. He waited until the Wi-Fi engaged and clicked on to his email inbox. There were three new emails, two were from Rachel Gluckstein's office, and the third one was from Splash Waters.

He opened the emails from Rachel. The first one informed Pegg that the entire operation of the BWIT has been suspended, and the SPA has contacted the MoD Police to assist them with a criminal investigation. This was as a result of information sent to the SPA by Rachel's firm OJA. The second email notified Pegg that Mehmet Ali's firm, Lawyers for Personal Justice was being looked at by the Law Society. The third email from Waters informed Pegg that that the two suspects arrested at Whissonsett, had been charged and that they were appearing at Norwich Crown Court at a date to be fixed. They were both remanded to HMP Norwich, as they were a flight risk. Pegg was pleased with the way things had played out. After he had got involved, Spratt was no longer going to be investigated, and there was a good chance that future investigations of other Kosovo veterans would not take place. Ali's firm of solicitors has been shown for the corrupt and dishonest enterprise it was. Now it would be likely the Law Society will close the whole rotten edifice down. The MoD Police are going to investigate the Services Record Office in Glasgow regarding the leaking of the names of personnel who had served in Kosovo to Ali's firm via Hoskins.

Pegg got his things together and secured the 'van as best he could. He put a spare coat and his bag containing the laptop and his paperwork inside, as well as his First Aid kit which he had packed into his rucksack into the back of the Landrover. He opened the passenger door and Fred jumped in. He drove out of the site and headed into Buxton where he stopped briefly at a Co-op and picked up a few groceries. He then took the A6 to Belper and from there to Eastwood. He found Afrim Babic's house on a small estate off Dovecote Road. It was a semi-detached bungalow, which was set back from the road. A path ran to the centre of the building from the pavement. The front doors were side by side. There was a small front garden in front of each dwelling.

Pegg phoned Babic, the phone was answered almost immediately:

"Afrim, it's Archie Pegg, I'm outside on the road."

"I see you Archie. Come up the path, and go to the right, I'll meet you at the side door."

"That's fine, I'm bringing some medical stuff; I'll leave the dog in the car."

"No bring him in, I want to see him."

Pegg hung up and gathered his things together. He had all the medical kit packed in his rucksack. He left his laptop in its place under the passenger seat. He took a notebook and pen with him, placing them in one of the rucksack's side pockets. He put Fred on his leash, before making his way to the side of the bungalow. By the time he reached the side door, he found the door open and Babic standing in the doorway.

Pegg was shocked at what he saw. Afrim Babic had received a severe beating. His face was swollen, and he had two black eyes. He was wearing a gray T-shirt which was heavily soiled, many of the dark stains were probably blood, in addition to the soiled top he was also wearing blue jogging bottoms. There were bruises on his arms.

"Come in Archie, I'm sorry for my appearance and the mess, "he said, he sobbed, before continuing, "I do not normally live like this."

The back door led into a small kitchen. The place was in a complete mess. The cupboards were open, and their contents had been strewn over the floor. Babic led Pegg into the living room; he was limping and clearly in a great deal of pain. The furniture in the living room had been tipped over, but the chaos was not as bad as that in the kitchen. Pegg picked up an armchair and set it back in place, he up-righted the sofa.

"Sit down Afrim and tell me what happened."

Babic made his way to the up-righted armchair, and sat down, uttering a grown. Fred went and sat beside him and licked his hand.

"Fred leave him be."

"No, no he's alright," Babic said, stroking Fred's head; he continued, "as I mentioned on the phone, on Thursday morning. Mehmet Ali paid me a visit. There were two guys with him, both Albanians, one of them works with Ali at his Nottingham office. I was not too worried at first, as I thought it was something to do with the car wash."

"I let them in, and they came into the living room. Then without any warning one of them hit me across my face and my nose, my nose started to bleed. Ali then told me that I have not done what I was told. He said that Hoskins had told me to sort you out. I said I did not know what he was talking about. Then the same man hit me again."

"After that I think I must have passed out. The next thing was I felt water on my face. I was picked up again, and they kept asking where were the papers and stuff that I had taken from you. I kept saying I had nothing. They went through the house going through all my things.

"After this Ali said that there is nothing here. Before they left, Ali told me that if I went to the police his boys would make sure that I would never talk to anyone again."

Pegg was silent for a few minutes. Fred decided to climb onto Babic's lap.

"Fred get down, Afrim is hurting, off boy, now!"

"Please Archie, leave him be. It is so nice to have him so close." Babic started to weep before continuing, "and to think I might have killed him."

"That's enough of that, Afrim! It's over; I'd forgotten about it, and it looks as if that daft dog has as well! Now let's get you sorted out. Nothing personal Afrim, but you need to get cleaned up. We'll start with a shower or bath, and then I can see to your cuts and bruises."

Pegg left Babic and Fred where they were and went into the bathroom. It appeared that Ali and his thugs had not left much of a mess in there. It was apparent that Babic was a person who looked after his house, and prior to Ali's visit the house must have been in a high state of order and cleanliness. There was a shower curtain across the bath, and a hand shower attachment was fitted to the taps. Pegg turned the hot water tap on, which resulted in a stream of hot water issuing from the tap.

"At least these vindictive bastards did not muck up the boy's plumbing," Pegg muttered to himself. He went out and checked the bedroom. Here things were in a more chaotic state. Looking at the state of the bedding and especially the sheets, Babic had taken to his bed after the beating he had taken and had stayed there. The sheets were blood stained as were the pillowcases. Pegg went to the hall and opened a small door which revealed an airing cupboard. Here again the uninvited guests had been rummaging through the stacked spare bedding and airing laundry. Pegg picked up the items which had been thrown on the floor. He stacked the spare sheets and pillowcases on their respective shelves again and did the same for the clean laundry. He closed the airing cupboard door again and went back into the living room.

"Right Afrim, before I see to your injuries we need to get you cleaned up. I'm going to run you a bath. A soak in hot water will help to ease your aches and pains.

"Okay Archie, maybe it will do me good. I just do not seem to have the will to do anything."

"No worries, I'm here and between the two of us we'll get you sorted out. Do you have any family or friends nearby?"

"The couple next door are very kind, but they are away on holiday in Spain. I'm supposed to keep a look on the house. They did not give me the key or anything, but just to take parcels and stuff like that, as well as keeping a check on strangers coming to the house. They are very good to me, but as I say they are not here. The guys at the car wash I guess are too scared to come and see me. I have phoned some of them, but they said Ali told them they'd be sorry if they contacted me again. As you know I am an orphan, I have no family in the UK."

Pegg left him and went into the bathroom and started to fill the bathtub. Whilst the tub was filling up, he got a clean towel, and replaced the used one which had been draped over the towel rail. By the time Pegg had done this, the depth of the water in the tub was sufficient for a bath. Pegg tested the water; it was quite hot, he left it to Babic to adjust the its temperature.

"Right Afrim let's get into the bathroom, I've left a clean towel for you."

Pegg helped Babic up, Fred had jumped off Babic's lap by this time, Babic made his way to the bathroom.

"I'll leave you to it, if you need any help, give me a shout."

"Thanks Archie, but I think I will be okay."

Pegg shut the bathroom door and went into the bedroom. He stripped the bed and put on fresh sheets, pillowcases and duvet cover. After placing the soiled bed linen in the now full laundry basket, he tidied up the bedroom. He passed the bathroom and asked through the closed door:

"You okay in there?"

"I'm fine Archie, this feels so good."

"Have a good long soak, I'll find some fresh clothing and put it through the door."

Pegg went back into the bedroom, and in the chest of drawers he found underwear and socks. A further search and he got a T-shirt and a pair of jogging bottoms. He returned to the bathroom, knocked on the door and said:

"Afrim there's some stuff for you to wear, I'll leave it outside the door. I'm just going to do a bit of tidying up, yell if you want any help."

He was answered by a low mumble, "I'll be okay Archie."

Pegg then went and did a bit more tidying up in the living room, before going into the kitchen, where he proceeded to deal with the mess that Ali and his thugs had left behind them. Half an hour later he was finishing the last task, the floor, which he mopped clean. He proceeded to the bedroom, where he found Babic already putting on the jogging bottoms.

"Right Afrim, let's have a look at you."

Pegg examined his torso, they was some bruising to the left side of his chest, he pressed Babic's rib cage.

"Does it hurt when I press here and here."

Babic winced slightly when Pegg pressed the bruised area.

"A little but not as bad as it was."

"Take a deep breath, and let it out slowly"

Babic did so.

"And again."

Babic repeated the action a few more times.

"Did it hurt when you did that?"

"No."

"That's good, I do not think you have any broken ribs. Have you got any blood showing in your pee, or in your poo? Sorry to ask you these personal questions, but it is necessary in case there is any damage to your insides.

"No, I think I am okay, there seems to be no sign of blood."

"Okay I'll leave you to get dressed then. After that we'll get some food into you."

Pegg went and prepared a light meal of scrambled eggs and toast. He laid out a place at the small table in the kitchen, and when he had finished cooking he served up the meal. He called Babic, who a short while later shuffled into the kitchen. He was dressed in the clothes Pegg had left out for him. He sat down and started to eat, at first picking at the food, but then devouring the plate of eggs as if there was no tomorrow.

"Good grief my man you were hungry!"

"Thank you so much Archie," said Babic buttering a piece of toast, "I don't seem to have eaten for such a long time."

"Well if you want some more I'll get something else going, but I think that is enough for now. Here's a mug of tea, you finish off. I need to pop out to the car and retrieve my phone."

Pegg left him and went outside to the Landrover. He got his phone and saw that there were a load of voicemails and text messages, several were from Pat.

Pegg cursed himself, he'd meant to monitor his phone, but with all that was going on with Babic he'd forgotten to do it. He checked the texts. The first was from Pat that she had got home in good time, and that the garage had picked up the X-Trail. The other text was from Rachel, asking him to phone her as soon as he can. There was also one from Bill Grimes his inspector. He read it and was surprised to learn that Bill was looking for a sergeant for the Dereham Section. The crafty sod thought Pegg, he's so keen to keep me in the job, it's embarrassing!

Next he phoned Rachel.

"Archie I've been trying to get hold of you for ages, don't you ever answer your phone?"

"I'm sorry about that, I've been a bit tucked up."

He briefly explained what had happened to Babic, and how he was assisting him. Rachel was appalled to hear the way Ali's thugs had treated Afrim Babic. Pegg then asked the reason for the urgency in her tone.

"Things are moving a lot faster than I thought they would. Briefly it looks like the SPA is dropping its contract with Valhalla Investigations. A couple of MP's on the Defence Select Committee have arranged for the head of the SPA to appear before them after my firm had sent a report regarding the way VI's investigators have been working. A civil servant, working at the Service Records Office in Glasgow is being investigated by the MoD Police. It seems this guy has been leaking the names of military personnel who had served in Kosovo.

"I have sent a letter to the Law Society regarding the activities of LPJ. The Law Society is not the fastest of agencies when it comes to investigating the nefarious activities of its members."

"I'm pleased to hear that, so what about your clients and the pending cases against them?" asked Pegg.

"Well I have contacted the SPA and informed them that I will be applying to get all cases dropped. I will be saying that the investigations are completely flawed and any continuance of proceedings against my clients will be a gross miscarriage of injustice."

"And Tony Spratt?"

"Thanks to you any charges against him are shown to be completely fictitious. I think that his will be the first of these cases to be dropped.

"Well I've a few loose ends to tie up here, and then I shall be heading back home in a couple of days. You have my phone number and email address if you want to contact me. The next time I'll not be so tardy in responding to your calls!"

"I'll keep you to that Archie! Take care and thanks again.

As he was reflecting on what Rachel had told him his phone rang; it was Pat:

"Hi Pat, what do you say?"

"Archie I've just got my car back, all serviced and with a new MoT Certificate! Thank you so much for doing all the work. No advisory notes on the Test report."

"I'm glad to hear that. What are your plans for the rest of the day?"

"I've been in touch with work, they are emailing me a draft interim report on the project I've been involved with. I'm going to read through it and make amendments where necessary. We've got a meeting tomorrow where we'll be discussing it before presenting it to our Danish colleagues. So apart from taking Zena for a walk, that's my day taken care of. What about you?"

"I've got one or two loose ends to tie up before I go back to Norfolk on Wednesday."

He went on to explain what had happened to Babic, and what he had done so far to assist him. She suggested that it might be a good idea to get Afrim checked out at an A & E department. Pegg explained how reluctant Babic was to get the authorities health professionals or otherwise, involved. Pegg said that he would have another go at persuading him.

He added that he would phone once he got back to Norfolk.

Pegg returned to the bungalow. Babic had cleared up the breakfast things and was in the process of washing the few items up.

"I could have done that for you Afrim, you need to take it easy."

"Thanks Archie, but I need to do things. I hate living in shit, after the pasting Ali and his bastards gave me, I had almost given up. Your presence here and with you helping me out, it has given me the push that I needed to sort myself out."

"That's good to hear, but I really think that we need to get you checked out. I don't think you have broken anything. But there may be something I missed. If you don't want to, then fair enough, but promise me, if you start to feel bad you'll get medical help."

"I'll do that Archie."

"Right, if you feel up to it, we'll make a shopping list and then go and get some food and stuff in for the next few days."

"Yes, I think that we need to do that."

"Right go and get yourself ready and I'll just take Fred round the block."

Pegg located the poodle who had ensconced himself on Babic's bed. He jumped off at Pegg's cursing. He put the dog on his lead and went out. After about fifteen minutes he returned to the bungalow. Babic had dressed in a pair of jeans, sweatshirt and a fleece.

As they were walking out to the Landrover Pegg asked Babic:

"Have you got any transport?"

"No, I had a car which as you know was a black Astra, but I did not own it, it was leased. I originally had the lease, but when Ali took my car wash business from me, his firm took over the lease. So, you see I've not only lost my car but also my business."

"Are you short of money now?"

"I have some money saved up, which should tie me over for a bit, until I can get further employment."

"Mmm, well let me have a think about that."

They drove to a local supermarket, a venue that Babic used on a regular basis. There they purchased groceries which would last Babic for a few days. After which Pegg visited the supermarket's petrol station, where he topped the Landrover up with diesel. He declined Babic's offer to pay for the fuel. They returned to the bungalow, as Pegg pulled up two men got out of a car which had been parked outside the bungalow. Babic went pale.

"Those are the bastards who worked me over and messed up my house."

"You wait here," said Pegg who stepped out of the vehicle.

"Can I help you guys? Is there a problem?" He asked the larger of the two men, who he did not recognise from the previous visit he made to the offices of LPJ. But he was about five feet nine tall and of a slightly obese build, his companion was a bit leaner and shorter. He spoke good English albeit with a heavy accent.

"There will be if you don't let us talk with that person you've got in your car."

"Listen to me and I will say this once only. Your boss Mr Mehmet Ali is in a great deal of trouble. He is up shit creek without a paddle. Your best bet is to abandon whatever Ali has told you to do and go and find another job."

"Who the fuck are you to tell me what to do?"

"Well let me see. You have committed the offences of aggravated burglary, criminal damage, and grievous bodily harm, to name but a few. In this country the courts take these offences seriously. The person whose home you have violated and whose person you have seriously injured, has not made an official complaint but I'm sure when he does, the police will arrest you both. He has not made any complaint yet, so I suggest you disappear sharpish."

The man looked at his companion and said something in a language which Pegg assumed was Albanian. This was later confirmed by Babic who had the passenger window open and was listening to what was being said.

Then the ringtone of a mobile phone sounded, and first man reached into his jacket pocket, retrieving a smart phone. He spoke into the mouthpiece, after a short conversation he spoke to his companion in Albanian, after which both men rushed to their car and drove off to the sound of screeching tyres. Pegg was left standing there looking perplexed. Was it something I said or what, he thought?

He heard the sound of the Landrover door closing behind him, he turned around to see Babic next to him with Fred at his side.

"What was all that about Afrim, what did they say to each other?"

"Well after the fat man finished speaking on his phone he said something about not going back to the boss's offices as the police have arrived and they are searching the place."

"Well it seems that the chickens are coming home to roost! Right Afrim let's get your shopping into the house."

They unloaded the groceries and carried them into Babic's house, Fred trotting behind them. After they had unpacked, Babic made them each a mug of tea. They took their drinks into the front room, Babic sat in the armchair and Pegg seated himself on the sofa. Fred jumped onto Babic's lap, ignoring the frown Pegg made. Babic supped his tea and caressed the dog's ear.

"Afrim where do you stand as far as the car wash is concerned?"

"After Ali's visit on Friday I have not been down there, I assume that it is still going. I am the owner and manager, but after Ali stole it the business from me, in name only."

"Well we'll have to get it back for you."

"How can you do this?"

"The less you ask the better, Afrim. Leave it to me. Right I need to get going, I'll be back later. Any sign of those goons turning up, dial 999 and get the police. I don't think they will as it seems Ali has all sorts of problems now. Right let me have your bank details."

"Why do you need these, Archie?"

"Afrim the less you know the better, bank details please."

Babic took his wallet out of his jeans and gave Pegg his bank card.

"I need to take this with me. I'll give it back to you later. This account has nothing to do with Ali, I mean he is not a joint holder or anything like that?"

"No this is my own account. Ali would not let me have card for the joint account."

"Good, can you look after Fred for me, I've got some food for him. Give him something to eat at about six if I'm not back by them."

"Of course," said Babic.

Pegg left them and went out to the Landrover.

CHAPTER 25

Pegg got out his laptop and opened it up. He turned it on and inserted one of the memory sticks, he opened up a file and retrieved James Smithson's email address and mobile telephone number.

Right he thought to himself let's hope that my plan will work. He dialed the mobile's number. He half expected that his call would go to voice mail, but was pleased when the called was answered:

"Hello James Smithson, how can I help?"

"Mr Smithson, I am calling on behalf of Mr Afrim Babic, I believe you may be able to help us. I need to speak to you personally sooner rather than later."

"What's this about, I am a bit tied up at the moment, can you give my secretary a call and make an appointment," he said. He sounded quite flustered."

"Are you in your office, I understand the police are there."

"How do you know. Who are you?"

"Never mind who I am, but it may be to your advantage if you hear me out. I have evidence that your partner's bully boys have broken into a domestic dwelling, and badly beaten up an acquaintance of mine."

There was a moan on the other end of the line before Smithson replied:

"Oh, I rue the day I ever met up with Mehmet Ali. You know it was going so well, but as we are an LLP, that is to say a Limited Liability Partnership. If only he had listened to me and stuck with

what we had set out to do together. I am not responsible for Mr
Ali's conduct in involving our firm. I really have nothing to do with
his side of the business. Look the police are swarming all over the
offices, it is difficult to speak at the moment. Can I call you back?"

"I really want to talk to you now. There's a pub around the
corner from you, do you know it?"

"Yes, I do, but not there. I'll meet at my home address in about
twenty minutes." Smithson gave Pegg the address. It was about
fifteen minutes away in Hucknall.

"I'll be there, make sure that you are alone, I don't want any of
Mr Ali's heavies there to meet me."

"Don't worry about that."

Pegg ended the call and drove to Hucknall. He arrived there in
good time to see blue Volvo C40 parked on the driveway outside
the house, which was a modest 3-bedroom detached dwelling, built
around the beginning of the Millennium. The property was situated
in a small cul-de-sac to the south of the town. The front of the house
gave way to a small lawn, around which was a flower bed, taken up
with a colourful display of roses. Pegg parked the Landrover outside
the house and walked up the driveway past the Volvo and along the
path to the front door. The door was opened before Pegg reached it.

The person who opened the door was a thin man aged between
forty and fifty years old. He was fair haired, clean shaven, and was
wearing rimless spectacles. He was dressed in a dark blue suit,
wearing a white shirt and blue tie. He looked drawn and haggard, he
looked up along the road that Pegg had come.

"James Smithson come in Mr Pegg. I hope that this is not going
to take long. I don't know whether the police will be visiting me
or not. They seem to be more interested in Mr Ali's side of the
business."

He ushered Pegg into a small study off the main living room,
and indicated a chair, which Pegg sat down on whilst Simpson took
a chair from behind the desk and sat opposite Pegg.

"So Mr Pegg what have you got to say to me," he said glancing
at his watch.

"I've been helping an old army friend of mine out. He has had
allegations made against him, regarding his service in the Balkans,

namely Kosovo and especially in Pristina. As a result of me getting involved, the evidence against him has been shown to be false and entirely fictitious. Your firm, Lawyers for Personal Justice, has been fed the names of military personnel from the Services Records Office by a rogue civil servant via an investigator."

Smithson lent forward in his chair, putting his elbows on his upper thighs, and his head in his hands.

"I never wanted the firm to get involved in war crimes claims. The debacle over Phil Shiner and his Public Interest Lawyers made me think that this is not a route we wanted to go down. I deal with and always been involved with personal injury claims. You know the sort of things like industrial accidents, "trip and slip", and car accidents and so on. When Mr Ali and myself set up the firm this is all we did, and even if I say so myself we were quite good at what we did. I always insisted on complete honesty from our clients. Any feeling I may have had about the veracity of a claim, I would not take it on. We got quite a good reputation, especially among the insurance companies. It paid off, because when we submitted a claim to the insurers, only on very few occasions was it disputed. It was good for the client and good for us."

"So, what has gone wrong do you think."

"Well although I was not directly involved with the alleged war crimes side of it, I did advise Ali on many occasions to do what I always did on my side of the business, make sure that the claim and claimant were genuine. He got quite angry telling me that I was questioning his competence. We had a lot of arguments. I was very much aware how some firms of solicitors were taking on claims from Iraq and being reckless as to whether they were dealing with fact or fiction. In the end he ignored my advice and carried on. He brought some of his own people into the firm, not as paralegals but as his personal gofers. I did not know what they were doing, because Ali was being quite secretive. May be this should have rung alarm bells. Anyway, I continued with my side of the business, and did not pay much attention to what Ali was doing with his side of things. Hindsight being twenty-twenty vision, I wish that I'd put my foot down earlier and got him to stop, or even parted company; but we are where we are. I don't know what I'm to do to get the company back on the rails again."

Pegg realised that the man was opening up, and so decided to probe a bit further.

"So, what is the situation at the moment regarding things?"

"Oh dear me Mr Pegg! Where do I start? This morning I got into work at normal time. Mondays tend to be quite busy. There is a lot of stuff to catch up on. New potential clients tend to respond to our advertisements we have on the media and our messaging services. So, a great deal of time is spent responding by both phone and email. I went about my normal routine, that is to say collating our replies and getting the staff to send out claims packs. I noticed that Mehmet was not in the office first thing, he did not come in until mid-morning. When eventually he arrived at the office he was in a bit of a state. He was shouting at everyone, myself included, things about how he is being undermined by his colleagues and there is no loyalty anymore.

"I followed him into his office and tried to calm him down, he was in an absolute rage. He was saying someone had reported him to the Law Society, and that somehow the MoD Police were involved. He went on further to claim that somebody in the office had made these allegations, and that in view of my disapproval of him taking on alleged war crime claims, it might even have been me. Well you can imagine how I felt. We'd spent years building up the business, and although I say it myself, we were good at what we did. I didn't help matters by telling that if he had not got himself involved with war crimes claims and some of the other sidelines he was engaged, and concentrated on what we were doing before, none of this sorry state of affairs would have occurred.

"At this point I left him and went into the main body of the office to try and calm things down a bit. The staff were clearly very upset, some of them were in tears. I spent some time going around the office and speaking to everyone individually. Eventually things settled down and we got on with the day to day routine. I left the office to visit the Nottingham County Court, whilst there I heard that the Police had raided the offices. They were more interested in Mehmet than my side of things but in any case the office was closed and those staff who weren't needed were sent home. I decided to stay away, if I my presence was required I would return."

"So, what is happening now?" asked Pegg

"Well where do I start? The member of staff who called me said that the police were detectives from the MoD Police, and they had a warrant to seize documents and computers. It appears that Mehmet Ali is their main person of interest. I've got to get some sort of agreement from the investigating officers to let the personal injury claims side of the business to continue."

"Well," said Pegg, "I have a problem which I hope you will be able to rectify. A friend of mine has had his business stolen from him by Ali. Ali loaned this person some money to set up the car wash. The person paid back the loan in installments, and it was going to be clear that the loan would be paid off quite soon. Ali decided that the price of the repayments were not high enough and raised them so much that the person could not afford them. One thing led to another and eventually Ali coerced him to hand the business over to Ali. Now I have evidence of Ali's criminality against this person, and rather than presenting my evidence to the police, I want Ali or your firm to do the right thing; that is to say give the business back to the rightful owner."

"I don't know how we can do this. I mean that I can access the general account, but I think that I would need to get Ali to counter sign any cheque."

"Never mind about cheques, why can't you use the BACS? You can transfer funds straight into this chap's account. I pay my creditors by using the same system."

Smithson thought about this and did not say anything for a couple of minutes, before he answered:

"Right I'm sick to my back teeth with all this. Ali through his own actions and nefarious behaviour, has wrecked the reputation of the firm which I spent years building up. I don't know how we are going to recover from this. But to hell with it, the process starts right now." He took a laptop which was sitting on the right side of the desk, opened the cover, and switched it on. He tapped the keys and waited before saying:

"Right Mr Pegg, have you got the person's bank details?" Pegg gave him Babic's bank card. "What was the amount that Ali lent him?"

"It was a loan of five thousand pounds, to be paid back over three years. The monthly repayments were to be one hundred and fifty pounds, so the cost of the loan was five thousand four hundred pounds. Ali kept putting up the repayments eventually when it got to be four hundred pounds a month, the borrower could not afford the repayments, so Ali took over the business but still wanted the loan repaying, eventually getting his thugs to beat the poor man up. He told me he had already paid Ali some three thousand pounds since he took the loan out six months ago."

"This is outrageous, we are a firm of solicitors not a bunch of crooks. Right I'm going to credit this poor chap's account with five thousand pounds. If I can I'll add to this later. What do you think, Mr Pegg?"

"I think that is a very fair start."

Simpson tapped away on his laptop.

"Who shall I put as the payee?"

"New Start Car Wash, that's the name of payee's company. He uses that account for his business."

"Right it will show that J Smithson Solicitors is the agency paying the money in."

He glanced at his watch:

"Right Mr Pegg I got to get going now, due in the County Court in half an hour."

After thanking Smithson Pegg left and made his way back to Babic's house. Babic opened the side door as Pegg approached it.

"Anything happened while I was away?" asked Pegg.

"I had a couple of phone calls, one was from a guy at the car wash. He was very upset; he said a couple of Ali's muscle came and told us all to go, as the car wash was finished. Ali had been taken away by the police and everyone is leaving him, before the police come and get them as well."

"Well that's good news for you isn't it?"

"How can that be Archie; Ali's no longer around to finance the car wash."

"He doesn't need to be, you can do it yourself. Check your bank account."

"I do not have money for this."

"Do it"

Babic got out his phone and logged into his banking app.

"Archie!" he shouted, "What's happened five thousand has been put into the account!" He put his phone down. Pegg said:

"Good, and now you can get on the phone to your guys and tell them to keep working. The business is yours again."

Babic picked his phone up again. He spoke for about five minutes, in Albanian first and then to what appeared to Pegg, another call taker, this time in English. After he had finished he said to Pegg:

"Archie, to use an English expression it seems that the shit has hit the fan; Ali has apparently been arrested along with some of his henchmen. There is nobody in charge and the guys were just hanging about. I've told them to carry on, and that I will be able to pay them their wages. That'll keep them there. Come on Archie let's go!"

Five minutes later there walked out to the Landrover and with Fred sitting on Babic's lap, they drove off. After a time, they entered Arnold Road, and shortly after that they drove into the forecourt of the New Start Car Wash. There was not much activity. In front the small Portakabin which acted as the crew room, five people were sitting on chairs which had been placed at random around a table. Some were holding mugs sipping hot drinks and others were smoking. Pegg parked up in front of the crew room and got out. The people round the table remained where they were, a couple looking sullenly at Pegg. It was not until Babic, appeared from the far side of the vehicle that everything changed.

There were shouts of "Afrim", and one of the men, who Pegg recognised as the van driver, Edrit Bejco, rushed and embraced Babic. There was a garbled exchange between the two. The others crowded round him, some starting to pat him on the back and shoulders. Babic winced and said something, after which they settled down a bit. Pegg stood back. Babic started to explain what he was going to do. The first thing he wanted them to get back to work. He said something to one of the men. The man went into a shipping container at the back of the crew room and retrieved a trestle sandwich sign on which had been written "CAR WASH OPEN". He placed this at the entrance to the facility and came back. Pegg was surprised to see a couple of cars already waiting. Pegg eventually went over to Babic. He said:

"Afrim are you okay now? Do you want me to do anything more, like get you home or run you to the bank?"

"Archie you've done enough for me. I'm okay Edrit still has the van, and he can drive me home when we finish. I've a lot to catch up on, not least to sort out these guys wages. Those bastards have not paid them for the past week. I need to sort out who is owed what. On paper I'm still the owner of this business, so with Ali out of the way, hopefully I can carry on as such."

"Well I'll be on my way. If you need anything give me a call."

"Archie I'll not forget what you have done for me, in spite of the way I have behaved towards you and dear Fred. You are a good man, Archie."

He followed Pegg to the Landrover, he shook Pegg's hand and went around to the passenger side and opened the door. Fred, who was sitting on the seat, gave a soft whine and licked Babic's hand. Babic hugged the dog, and with tears in his eyes closed the door. Pegg drove out of the forecourt and onto Arnold Road. He noticed that the car washing had already started. Babic was standing alone looking at the departing Landrover.

Pegg looked at the time it was now coming up for half past four. He was going to do a drive past of LPJ's offices on the way back to Buxton and the camp site, but he thought the better of it and headed back to the site.

CHAPTER 26

He arrived back on the site at half past eight, drove onto his pitch, and parked up. He quickly checked the outside of the 'van and awning, before entering and unlocking the 'van. Everything appeared to be in order. He placed his file and laptop on the bench beside the blanket onto which Fred had already ensconced himself. Pegg took a bottle of beer from the fridge, removed its top, and poured its contents into a glass; taking a couple of gulps of the cool liquid, he sat down next to the dog, took his laptop, opened it up and logged on. He saw he had some new emails. The first was from Rachel Gluckstein. She gave an update as to what was happening. The whole sorry saga of the alleged war crimes in Kosovo had hit the news, and the media was in full cry. Word had got out that names of soldiers who had served in the Balkans were being leaked by rogue civil servants to solicitors involved in making claims for alleged war crimes.

Pegg decided to reply to this latest email from Rachel. He wrote to say that in his view James Smithson's of LPJ was not being run dishonestly, and that Smithson had nothing to do with Ali's side of the business. No doubt the Law Society would come to the same conclusions. He saw that the next email was from Pat. She said that after her trip to Denmark she would be going to the University of East Anglia at Norwich to assist their Department of Environmental Studies with a presentation about the new wind turbine design. It would be sometime in the middle of next month. Maybe we could meet up. Pegg replied to this, asking her to give details of her itinerary when she got them, and we'll come up with a plan. The next one was from Bill Grimes. Informing Pegg that there was a Sergeants Board coming up in the near future. Could Pegg contact asap in order that he could put Pegg's name forward. He never gives up does he, thought Pegg. He typed a quick reply saying that he was seriously thinking of continuing in the Job. He will be back at work on Monday 25th October; but he'll see him on Thursday. The rest of his inbox consisted of what would be classified as junk which Pegg deleted. He logged out and switched the laptop off. He made himself a meal of tinned stew and potatoes. After clearing up he picked up the phone and called Angie:

"Archie how's it going?"

"Great I'll be packing up and coming home tomorrow. Can I come and see you after I get back?"

"Yes of course, do you fancy having supper with us? Nothing fancy, bangers and mash."

"Sounds perfect," said Pegg. He went on to explain what he had been doing and what had happened. The conversation continued for the next ten minutes before Angie said she needed to get the baby off to bed, Ross was working late. Pegg agreed that he would see them all at around six tomorrow evening. He was promised that Catherine Rose would still be up. After finishing he decided to give Tony Spratt a ring on his house phone. The call was answered by Marge, Tony's wife.

"Hello Archie, how are you?"

"I'm fine more's the point how are you two?"

"Oh Archie, you don't know how relieved we are now that this awful business is coming to an end. Would you like to speak with Tony, he's just doing a bit of paperwork, I'll put him on?" After a short pause Tony came on.

"Archie! What can I do for you?"

"Well I'm going back to Norfolk tomorrow, I just wanted to know how things stand with you?"

Spratt went on to explain that Rachel's firm had informed him that the BWIT was ceasing its investigation against him. She would be sending him written paperwork regarding this. Pegg asked him to let him know what the outcome will be. He spoke for a further five minutes before ending the call. Pegg took Fred out for a final time before retiring for the night. He took him up to the dog walk and let him have a good sniff around for the next ten minutes. When he got back to the 'van, he made the bed up, undressed and had a quick wash. He got into bed and within five minutes was fast asleep.

CHAPTER 27

Pegg woke up at seven having slept solidly for eight hours. After a quick visit to the bathroom, he put on a pair of jogging bottoms and a fleece and took Fred out for a twenty-minute walk. It was a bright morning, the sun was coming up and the sky was clear, only a few clouds. The forecast said it would be a dry day, just the ticket for the drive home thought Pegg. I really have been lucky with the weather this past week, he thought. When he got back to the 'van he made breakfast, afterwards he made his way to the shower block where he washed and shaved. On return to the 'van he proceeded to pack up. He waited until the dew had nearly gone from the awning before he took it down and packed it away. By mid-morning he had the caravan hitched up to the Landrover, and with everything stowed away in both the caravan and the towing vehicle, he left the site.

The journey back to Norfolk was uneventful He stopped once at garage on the A17 at a Farm Shop, where he bought some flowers, and had a cup of coffee. On arriving back in Litcham Road, Gressenhall, he unhitched the van and maneuvered into its slot beside the garage. It was three o'clock. That done he secured it and fitted the wheel and hitch locks. Next he parked up the Landrover and closed the gates to the driveway. He let Fred out, and the dog proceeded to carry out an inspection of the entire outside area, both at the front and rear of the house. Pegg meanwhile had unlocked the back door, disarmed the alarm and went through the house. There was a fair quantity of mail, mostly circulars and junk. He gathered these up and put them on the hall table, before going out again and starting the long process of unloading the 'van.

He spent the next hour fetching food, clothing and toiletries from the 'van and bringing them into the house. By the time he'd finished it was getting on for five o'clock. He fed the dog, and decided to have a quick shower, after which he put on a clean shirt and a pair of corduroy trousers, as well as pullover. Thirty minutes later he was on the road again, he drove into Dereham, and then onto the westbound A47 towards Swaffham. The traffic was quite heavy heading west, and it was five past six by the time he had parked up outside Angie's. He gathered up some gifts he'd bought up in Derbyshire as well the flowers and made his way to the front door; Fred followed, and was already waiting at the door by the time Pegg had rang the doorbell. The door was opened by Ross who was carrying Catherine Rose, already in her pajamas. The baby squealed with delight on seeing Pegg and the dog.

"Great to see you again Archie," he said closing the door behind them.

"And you, how's my little girl," he said, giving her a kiss on her forehead. "I've got some stuff for you, I'll take her if you can take these things off me."

Ross handed the baby over, and took the flowers and the carrier bag, which contained the presents. The child had wrapped her little arms around Pegg's neck and gurgled contentedly. Pegg followed Ross into the kitchen where Angie was mashing up a saucepan full of newly boiled potatoes. She stopped what she was doing and came and gave Pegg a kiss on the cheek.

"It's good to have you back Archie. I expect that you have lots to tell us," she gave Pegg a wink.

"Gosh Catherine Rose has grown even in the short time I've been away, she seems to be a tad heavier. You're getting to be a big girl now!" The baby just smiled and buried her little head in Pegg's chest.

"Yes, she is, she's eating well, and putting on weight, nothing out of the ordinary, and she has some more teeth."

Pegg glanced at the smiling child and sure enough there were two upper and two lower ones.

"Thank you for the flowers, Archie."

"I'm glad you like them, there are a few little things for you all in the carrier bag. Mementos of my visit to the Peak District."

"We'll eat first then we can see what you've brought for us. Ross can you put the flowers in some water. Archie maybe you could put young madam to bed. Supper will be ready in about twenty minutes."

Pegg went to take the baby upstairs. Fred started to follow them: "Stay!" Pegg said.

"Oh, he's alright let him be," said Angie.

Pegg continued up the stairs. He entered the child's bedroom and went over to her cot. He pulled back the duvet and laid her onto the mattress, pulled the duvet over her, and pulled up the side of the cot. She turned her head towards the side of the cot and reached through to stroke Fred's muzzle. The dog had sat down and was enjoying the attention. Pegg picked up a book from the top of the chest of drawers. He looked at the cover and said:

"Right let's find out what Barney Bear did on his picnic." He took the chair from beside the chest of drawers and placed it beside the cot. Catherine Rose sat up.

Pegg commenced reading and after five minutes she was lying down, eyes closed and sucking her thumb. Pegg continued to read for a couple of more minutes, by which time the child was asleep. He gently kissed her on the forehead, and with Fred following, he tip-toed out of the room, turning down the dimmer switch of the bedroom light on the way out.

Pegg entered the kitchen where he found the table had been laid, and Ross was already sat at the end. Angie was taking a tray of sausages out of the oven. A bowl of mash and a bowl of peas were already on the table, and these were joined by the sausages.

"The young lady is fast asleep, I read her a bit of Barney Bear's Picnic. The dimmer switch on a low setting, is that okay?"

"She'll be fine with that we'll turn it off later," answered Angie, before continuing, "now Archie, we are having some wine, would you like some, or a glass of beer?"

"Wine would be great, make it a small one though."

"Okay," said Ross who went and fetched another wine glass before going to the fridge, where he retrieved a bottle of New Zealand Chardonnay. He poured the wine into the glass:

"Enough, thanks Ross," said Pegg when the liquid had half-filled the glass. Ross topped up the other two glasses.

"Right," said Angie, "let's eat. Archie you sit here," she said indicating a chair at the centre of the table.

They sat down and Ross raised his glass, "Here's to your safe return to us Archie."

All three said "Cheers," and took a sip out of their respective glasses. After serving up their food, Angie asked how the trip had gone.

"Well," said Pegg, "it's been interesting to say the least." He went on to explain how he had helped to Tony Spratt. He left out the bits where Angie had assisted with her hacking skills, he didn't think Ross would have been too impressed, and the incident with the CO poisoning, as well as his burglary of LPJ's premises in Nottingham. There was a slight look of relief on Angie's face, not that Ross noticed anything. He explained that it looks as if the MoD was dropping its investigation into alleged war crimes in the Balkans.

Pegg asked Ross about work. Ross went on to say that it looked as if he may be staying at Norwich for the rest of the year and into a good deal of the next. They were expanding the maintenance facilities at Norwich Airport, and he had been appointed senior engineer. He would be making trips to the company's sites, which are located in Bristol, Derby and Sunderland, but it would mean that for the next few months, he would be living at home with his small family. Pegg then said:

"There is something that I'd like to discuss with you both. As you know I'm coming up for retirement age with the police. I am going into Dereham tomorrow to let them know what my final decision is. As I have not thought of anything else, I am leaning towards remaining in the job. I have been toying with setting up as an electrician, but I've been off my tools for such a long time, I'd have to think about some form of re-training, the thought of which fills me with dread. As you are my family, I'd like your thoughts, with Cath not here to share my concerns, can you give me a bit of guidance?"

Angie reached and put her hand on Pegg's. She looked at him and with her eyes on the verge of filling with tears she said:

"I am sure we can do that for you. If you are happy in continuing with what you do, Ross and I are behind you."

"Absolutely, Archie," said Ross.

"Well that's it then," replied Pegg, before continuing, "There is another matter that I'd like to discuss, and that is the question of whether I should put myself forward as a candidate for the next Constable to Sergeant Promotion Board. I have sat the exam and therefore I'm qualified to be a candidate."

"Go for it, Archie, said Ross.

"I agree, you have so much to offer. How long can you continue working in the Constabulary?" Angie said.

"Well in theory, as long as I am fit and there are no health problems, I can work until the age of 65."

"There you go then," said Angie.

"Well thank you for your support. I shall let Bill Grimes, my inspector, know my decision when I see him in the morning."

They continued with their meal, the conversation turned towards Angie's work. She was quite busy with a number of new clients. Designing websites for them and advising on online security. Fortunately, she was able to do most of her work from home. Occasionally she visited some clients' premises. Childcare was not a problem as she took the baby with her. The firms she visited were on the whole small family affairs, and a lot of the bosses were young women, so there was a great deal of empathy regarding Angie and her baby daughter.

"You know that when I am on rest days or late turns, I can always step in to assist you if needed," said Pegg.

"I'll hold you to that Archie!" Angie replied.

After the meal was finished, Ross said that he wanted to do a bit of paperwork regarding a meeting he had in the morning. Pegg assisted Angie in clearing up. She started to wash up, Pegg assisted with the drying.

"Well," she said, "I'm waiting to hear, you've been holding back, come on spill the beans!"

"What?"

"Come on Archie, you know what! Pat!"

"Oh yes, mmm, well I don't know how to start. I'm not wanting to replace Cath. Oh shit Angie I did not mean it like that..."

Angie took the towel and dried her hands, she put her arms round him and hugged him, she looked into his eyes and said:

"Archie I know you loved mum, and you were a good husband. You are a good father and grandfather, and I know mum would only want you to be happy, so if you have found someone, I am comfortable with that."

"Well Angie, as far as Pat is concerned, we are not an item, but in the short time I have known her, I feel that there is a strong bond of friendship developing. I cannot say where this is going, but I want you to know what is going on."

"Your happiness is important to me. If you are ready to start a relationship, go for it."

She disengaged herself from him, and the washing up continued without any further comment from either of them. After they were finished, Angie asked:

"Right do you want some coffee?"

"I think I'll give it a miss, thanks. I have a long day tomorrow. In fact, I'll need to get going soon. Thanks for the supper and for having me."

"Oh Archie, you are always welcome here! Please keep us in the loop"

"Of course, you'll be the first to know."

Pegg said his farewells to them both, and before he did, he had quietly ascended the stairs and checked on the baby. He put on his jacket and with Fred trotting behind him, left the house and made his way to the Landrover. He drove through Market Place and out of Swaffham town centre, onto Norwich Road towards the roundabout and there he joined the east bound A47. Twenty minutes later he was pulling onto the driveway of his house. After securing the vehicle and going inside, he checked the phone for any further messages. Nobody had phoned whilst he was out. The time was getting on for half past ten. He decided to go to bed, as there was a lot to do tomorrow. After letting Fred into the garden for a last time, he locked up and went to bed.

CHAPTER 28

After a good night's sleep, Pegg was up, dressed and breakfasted by nine. It was a reasonably mild day. There was a gentle breeze, and the sun was up. He started to empty the 'van of clothing and bedding. He needed to do some of the laundry which had accumulated during the period he had been away. After filling the washing machine to capacity, he started it, selecting the coloured cycle. Once that was going, he decided to phone Bill Grimes on his personal mobile. It took some time for the call to be answered, after initially going to voicemail, Grimes picked up:

"Guvnor, it's Archie Pegg, can I come in and see you this morning?"

"Archie, I've been waiting for you to get back to me. I am currently at Thetford, but I'll be back in Dereham after lunch. Shall we say my office at one?"

"Thanks guv, I'll be there. Civvies okay?"

"Of course, you're still on leave man, for heaven's sake!"

"I'll see you then."

Pegg went out into the garden and picked some dahlias. There was still a good display, but there has got to be some serious deadheading taking place in the near future. He put the flowers in a carrier bag and collected some secateurs from the garden shed. He whistled:

"Come on Fred, let's go up and see Cath."

The dog came bounding out of the house and yapped excitedly. Pegg gathered up the dog's leash and an old Barbour jacket from the garage, and put it on. After locking up the house, and shutting the driveway gate behind, he set off. He walked along Bridge Street, past the green. The horse chestnut trees were bearing golden brown foliage which shimmered in the autumn sunlight. The bulrushes in the village pond all had the black tops which resembled cricket bat handles. A pair of ducks were floating idly on the surface whilst a third was grazing the ponds bottom, its rear pointing vertically upwards. Pegg and the dog continued up Church Lane, and ten minutes later they were entering Saint Mary's churchyard. There were a couple of cars unattended in the car park.

They made their way up the path towards the church. The main door was open; he went through and peeped inside, a couple of ladies were cleaning the nave. Pegg went back outside and made his way to Cath's grave. The flowers he had left were gone, they had been replaced by Angie. Angie's flowers also needed replacing. Pegg removed them and replaced them with the dahlias he'd brought. He refilled the vase with water and wiped the headstone with a damp cloth. He tidied up around the grave, picking up grass cuttings and putting them in the bag with the old flowers.

He knelt down, Fred sat beside him, Pegg put his arm around the dog:

"Cath, it's been a busy time away. I can't say that it has been much of a holiday, but we've got a lot done, and put a lot of things to right. Angie had us for supper last night. She and Ross are well; the baby is thriving and is as pretty as a picture. I've decided to carry on in the police, and I am also going to put in for my sergeant..... I'm seeing the inspector first thing this afternoon."

Pegg remained where he was for a few more minutes, before getting up and gathering up the items he had brought with him. He kissed the top of the headstone, before walking over to the wheelie bins at the side of the church. He deposited the bag with the old flowers and grass cuttings. He started to make his way out of the churchyard. As he passed the door of the church, the ladies who he had seen earlier were coming out. He exchanged pleasantries before making his way back home.

It was getting on for midday by the time he got home. He went inside and emptied the washing machine. He took the full laundry basket and a tin of pegs out into the back garden, where he pegged its contents onto the rotary drier. That done, he went back inside and made himself some sandwiches and a small cafetiere of coffee. Once he'd eaten, and finished off the mug of coffee, he went upstairs and changed. He decided to wear a pair of dark blue moleskin trousers, a checked shirt and a sports jacket. When he was dressed he got ready to leave. After securing the house he left in the Landrover, with Fred sitting on the front passenger seat. Ten minutes later he was entering Commercial Road. After punching in the code on the entrance barrier at the side of station, he drove in and parked up. He went around to the front entrance where the front office staff buzzed him in.

"Hi Archie," said Jenny, the public inquiry office clerk. "How's your leave going?"

"Oh, busy Jen, I'll be glad to get back to work for a rest! How's it been for you; busy whilst I've been away?"

"Oh, you know, ticking over."

"Is the guvnor in?"

"Yes, he got back about ten minutes ago."

"Thanks," said Pegg. He walked down the corridor to Grimes' office; the door was open. Grimes was reading some reports, he looked up and on seeing Pegg, stood up and said:

"Archie, come in." He came over and shook Pegg's hand and pointed to a chair. Pegg sat down. He went over and shut the door. He asked how his visit to the Peak District had gone. Pegg gave a brief resume of what he had been up to, leaving out details regarding the collapse of Ali's nefarious enterprises.

"Well I've taken the opportunity of getting a bit of paperwork together. It will save time later as you will see. Now first I'd like to know where you stand as regarding your future with the Norfolk Constabulary. You are nearing your fifty-fifth birthday, which gives you the opportunity to retire with full pension rights, so what are you going to do?"

"Well I've given it a lot of thought, and I have discussed it with my family. As a result, I have decided to continue with the job, subject of course to confirmation by the Human Resources Department."

"Good man! I'm delighted to hear that, Archie. I'm sure HR's decision is just a formality. I've got a couple of bits of paper here, which I have completed. I'd like you to read through them and if you agree with what I've written, to sign in the spaces indicated."

He gave the forms to Pegg who spent the next five minutes reading and re-reading through them; after which he signed them and handed the completed sheets of paper back to Grimes.

"Right now, to the second item I want to speak to you about. As you know I've been banging on about you receiving your sergeant's stripes. You've taken the exam, and as far as that is concerned you are qualified. You just need to appear before a promotion board.

"Now to give you a bit of background to the problem I have. Mark Styles one of the Relief Supervisors on my section, is going on long term sick leave; the poor old chap has been diagnosed with a serious illness, and will be requiring a great deal of treatment, the nature of which make it impossible to carry out his duties supervising Three Relief. I need someone to take over from him very soon; to that end I am offering you the job. To begin with you'll be an Acting Sergeant, which, unlike the Temporary rank, you'll be paid. What have you got to say?"

Pegg sat and said nothing, finally saying:

"Phew, it's a lot to take in. I really owe it to the family and myself to give it a try." He paused before continuing: "Right, I'll take on the post. What do you want me to do now?

" Well Archie, I've already prepared the way a little. There is the matter of seeing the Super in Thetford, but quite frankly it is really a formality. To tell the truth, and keep this to yourself, he has given me a free rein as regarding appointments within the Dereham Section. I've made no secret of the fact that I want you as a shift supervisor. You have all the qualities for the job. I am not going over the bullshit of interviewing you, it's not needed in my view. And in any case you'll get all that squit when you go before your Sergeants Board. Right I've been a bit naughty here Archie, I've arranged for you to see the Super on Friday morning at ten o'clock."

"Blimey gov, you don't hang about! I know you are on fast track, but this is really quick!"

Grimes laughed at Pegg's jibe. Grimes was on the accelerated promotion career path, which meant after six years' service he was already an inspector. Unusually for such a young fast track candidate, he was a first-class copper. As a probationer he had a record as a thief taker that was the envy of officers with four times the length of his service.

"Very droll, Archie. But there is method in my madness. I need you to start in your new post on Monday, when you are due back off leave. That won't be a problem, will it?"

"I'm always up for a challenge, so bring it on."

With that Pegg got up to leave, he asked if he needed to be in uniform when he was going to see the superintendent. Grimes informed him as he was still on leave, he could go in civilian clothes; he mentioned for Pegg to go to the Force clothing store and collect some sergeant shoulder slides; for this Grimes signed a clothing acquisition form, and gave it to Pegg, with that they shook hands and Pegg left. He walked out of the station, got into his Landrover.

He sat there with his arm around Fred, deep in thought. He really could not face retirement, being stuck at home, without Cath, maybe continuing with a job he was comfortable and familiar with is not such a bad thing. He knew he had the support of Angie and Ross regarding his future career path, but would he be up to holding a skipper's post? It seemed that senior officers were sure he was the person for the job, otherwise he would not have spent the past forty minutes in Grimes' office. He had often said himself that he could do a better job than some of the incumbents he had come across. Now he thought, "Archie here is the golden opportunity to put your money where your mouth is."

"Come on Fred, let's go to Wymondham and get some of the kit I need to be wearing when I start work on Monday."

He made his way out of the station, headed south out of Dereham and onto the B1135. It was coming on for three thirty when he arrived at the rear gate of the Norfolk Constabulary's headquarters complex. He keyed in the pass code at the barrier, and on the barrier opening, drove in.

"Looks like we're in luck boy, there's a spare slot just outside the clothing store."

Pegg drove into the parking bay and went into the store. He went to the counter and waited. He did not have to ring the buzzer as a member of staff came through from the back a few moments later.

"How can I help you?" she asked.

"I need some sergeants slides as I have just found out today that I am to start work as an acting sergeant on Monday." Pegg gave her the form Grimes had given him.

"So, what about numbers?"

"I'll be using my PC's collar numbers."

"Okay we'll make up some slides, two sets with your own collar. Do you want to wait for them, or shall we put them in the system.? They should be in the internal mail by tonight, so they'll be at Dereham sometime tomorrow or Friday."

"Perfect, I shall wait for what the postman brings me."

Pegg left and drove his vehicle out of the complex and headed back home. It was getting on for five o'clock by the time he got home. It was still quite light, as it was not until a week on Sunday before the clocks went back, ending British Summer Time (BST). He gathered in the washing in from the rotary drier, and took it in. As it was completely dry, he placed it in the ironing basket, to be sorted out later.

He took his laptop out and placed it on the kitchen table; and after switching it on and logging in, he fetched a bottle of beer from the fridge, and poured it into a glass. He took a couple of sips and sat down. He checked his email inbox; there were a number of messages, the offers and junk which he deleted, before opening the first of the remaining two messages. It was from Rachel Gluckstein, she had written:

Re: Update Regarding Tony Spratt and other matters

Archie

We have had official confirmation that the SPA is taking no further action against Mr Spratt. They have sent him an NFA Letter. It looks as if a number of our other clients are no longer going to be investigated regarding their operational service in the Balkans, but we are yet to receive official confirmation.

The Law Society is in the process of looking into the activities of Mr Mehmet Ali's firm. A contact we have in the police has hinted that the Nottinghamshire police has

*started an investigation regarding Ali, this in addition to
the MoD police enquiries.*

*I thought that I'd let you know that James Smithson has
been interviewed by the police, but it appears that neither
the police nor the Law Society are taking any further
action against him.*

We'll update you further when we get more information.

The second email was from Tony Spratt, there was an
attachment, a video clip, Pegg read the email first:

Dear Archie

*Again, so many thanks for all you've done for me. It's like
a huge weight has been lifted from my shoulders. Marge
is a different person, she has such a positive outlook on
things now. The same goes for the rest of the family.*

*Just a small cloud on the horizon; you know that guy
Hoskins? Well the twat came around to the yard the other
day. There was nobody in except me. All the lads were
out on jobs. He was asking where you lived. I naturally
told him to sling his hook. He started to put on his parts.
In the end I forcibly ejected him from the premises. He
was making threats against me and my family. I took
the number of the car he was driving. Luckily my CCTV
system has sound, and when I played the footage of
Hoskins' visit back, the verbals were clear for all to hear.
I attached some video clips of the footage. I have also
been in contact with Derbyshire police. They are now in
possession of the CCTV footage. I'll leave it with them.
I have also passed the details of Hoskins and his car
to our local security company, the one that patrols the
industrial estate, where my yard is located.*

*Please take care of yourself, Archie, you never know
what this bastard is capable of.*

*Thanks again old friend
Yours Aye Tony.*

Pegg decided to give Oak Tree Farm Camping Park a call:

"Hello Oak Tree Farm Camping Park, how can we help?"

"Hello, it's Archie Pegg here, I just spent some days with you recently."

"Oh Mr Pegg, you obviously got home okay; is there something you left behind? We checked your pitch after you vacated it, it was all clear nothing left lying about."

"No, it's nothing like that, but has anyone been asking for me since I've left; I am just wondering as I have been visiting a lot of people whilst I've been staying at the site. Someone may have still thought I was still there. I think I told everyone the day I was traveling back home."

"As far as I know there hasn't been anyone, I'll just check with my partner, hold on a minute."

The call taker put Pegg on hold. He waited for about a minute:

"Mr Pegg, I've spoken to my partner, there was a gentleman who asked after you. He told the man you had gone. The man wanted to know your address, my partner declined to give it to him as this would contravene our confidentiality policy. He was quite rude to my partner and left."

"Well thank you so much for that. The people who need to contact me have my address, so this guy is not someone I want to speak to. I look forward to coming again soon, thanks again."

"You're always welcome."

That was more than likely Hoskins. Pegg decided to give Afrim Babic a call.

"Archie my friend how are you?"

"I'm good Afrim, and you?"

"Oh, Archie we are so busy here, I've taken on a couple of more guys. A Polish and an English. Funny eh, you'd not think an English would want to work in a car wash! But she is a good worker."

"She?"

"Yes, why not, the Pole is a young lady as well. Very good workers and the customers love them. Here at New Start we are an equal opportunity employer. I pay good money and there are lots who want to work for me."

"Well good for you, I'm pleased it's working out for you. Have you had any visits from Ali's men or others"?

"Not Ali's men, but there was someone who came around, that guy Hoskins, the one who forced me to interfere with your caravan. He wanted to know where you were, and contact telephone and stuff. Archie I'm not frightened of the bastard anymore. He started to shout and threaten me. I told him to fuck off my forecourt. By this time the other guys came and rallied round me. Hoskins was virtually frog marched to his car. He'll not be back again."

"Well done you, thanks for keeping him off my back."

"No problems Archie, you've shown me that I must stick up for myself."

"Can you give me an update on Ali?"

"Well it seems that he is in deep shit now. I heard through the grapevine that he has been nicked by the police. It seems that he is also involved in the drugs trade, in addition to his war crime claims stuff. So, he is being investigated on all fronts. I don't think he'll be bothering with me any time soon."

"Great to hear that. I'll let you go now, look after yourself."

"Thanks Archie, give my friend Fred a hug, tell him Afrim misses him!"

"I'll do that, 'bye now."

Pegg logged off and switched the laptop off. He looked at his watch, it was getting on for seven o'clock. He couldn't be bothered to cook an evening meal, so he decided to go around the corner to the Swan. In view of what he had found out about Hoskins looking for him, he decided to arm the burglar alarm before he went out. He took Fred with him, shutting the gate as he left the premises.

CHAPTER 29

Pegg entered the pub, there were about half a dozen people sat at the bar, and a further seven were seated in the dining area. He greeted a couple of neighbours

"Evening Archie, what will you have?"

"Hi Joe, I'll have a pint of Adnams Broadside, and can I have the menu?"

"Coming up," said the barman, placing a menu on the bar before taking a glass and drawing off the beer.

He placed the glass on the bar in front of Pegg.

"Shall I open a tab, or do you want to pay now."

"Put it on the tab, I'll settle up when I go, I'll have the steak and ale pie, please.

"Chips or new potatoes."

"New potatoes and whatever veg you've got."

Pegg exchanged niceties with the two men and talked a bit about his visit to the Peaks, before taking his beer and sitting down at a table next to the bar. Fred settled down and laid at Pegg's feet. His meal arrived, and after taking a further drink of his beer, started to eat. He ate his food, and after finishing his meal, he drank up his beer. He went across to the bar and ordered another pint. He stood at the bar and talked with the two neighbours. They had been joined by a further three drinkers, one of whom was the owner of the small caravan site, located off the village green. It was what the Caravan and Motorhome Club designated a Certified Location (CL) He showed a great deal of interest in the site that Pegg had just stayed at in Buxton. From a professional point of view, he was keen to find out what the site offered compared to his own. Pegg explained the facilities offered, and the owner of the CL seemed pleased that his site compared well with the one which Pegg had recently visited, albeit on a smaller scale. Pegg stayed talking for another hour, before finishing his drink. He settled up with the barman, bade farewell to the other drinkers, and left. He took a detour in order to give Fred a walk, he went down Bridge Street, and turned onto the green by the Old Horseshoes public house. He continued walking until he got to the Reading Room and the village store. There he sat down on a bench and took stock of his situation.

As far as his friend Tony Spratt was concerned, it would appear that his problems are at an end. In order to achieve this Pegg was acutely aware that he had committed theft and burglary, and if he had been found out, and he could forget continuing in his present job. Fortunately, he had covered his tracks; his involvement in obtaining the information which brought an end to BWIT's current investigations in Kosovo was not known, to either the authorities or to Mehmet Ali and his acolytes. It was worrying that Richard Hoskins could not let it go. He seemed to be making great efforts in trying to trace Pegg. So, in Pegg's view it would appear that Hoskins' nefarious activities have been severely restricted or even curtailed completely. It is obvious that Hoskins is seeking some form of revenge, and in his view Pegg is a primary reason for all of Hoskins' woes. Well bring it on thought Pegg. I'm ready for anything he tries to do to me. This time I'll nail the bastard. Pegg got up and made his way back to his house. The gate was still shut as he approached the house he entered and unlocked the side door, disarming the alarm on his way in. He decided to have an early night. He had a lot to do in the morning.

CHAPTER 30

P egg was up and dressed by seven. He had had a good night's sleep and felt ready for whatever the day would. After breakfast he took Fred for a short walk around the Green, before calling in at the village store, where he bought a copy of the Eastern Daily Press. After returning to the house he read the paper for an hour. When he'd finished, he decided to clean the caravan and the Landrover.

After getting cleaning materials together, he started with the Landrover. He filled up a bucket with hot water, and adding some wax shampoo. He then fetched the hosepipe reel from the back of the shed, unrolled it, and connected it to the outside tap. After hosing the Landrover down, he used a sponge to apply the shampoo solution to the vehicles external bodywork. He rinsed it off with the hose and finished with a chamois leather.

Next he moved onto the caravan. He began by closing all its windows, before using the hose pipe. For the next thirty0 minutes he had hosed down, shampooed, and rinsed it off. After packing up the cleaning kit, and rolling up the hose reel, he stored all them away. He went back to the house and got out his laptop and switched it on. After waiting for the device to warm up, he logged on. He checked his email, apart from the ubiquitous adverts, there were 2 messages which caught his attention. The first was from Rachel Gluckstein:

Re: Further Update

Hello again Archie!

Just to keep you in the loop, our contact in the Nottinghamshire Police has informed me that Mr Mehmet Ali has been linked to a large cannabis production network. One of his co-defendants has spilled the beans, and it looks as if the police have evidence that Ali is up to his neck in it. I don't think he'll be practising law for a long time, if ever.

The other matter is that the MoD Police have only discovered the one rogue Civil Servant at the Army Personnel Centre in Glasgow, Gregor Henderson. He is still in custody being interviewed.

We have written to the Defence Secretary and have requested that the government close down all current and future investigations against service personnel who have served in the Balkans. There is at least one MP who is in contact with me, and there are a number of others who are in agreement with her. So hopefully there will be pressure in Parliament to bring about the above outcome.

The second one was from Pat:

Re: Attendance at UEA Norwich

Hi Archie

I do not know what you are up to or where you'll be, so I've sent you this email instead. As I have mentioned before a team from our Engineering Facility have been invited to attend the UEA as part of a symposium on renewable energy.

Well there is a great deal of interest in our new wind turbine designs. As a result of this we'll be bringing down a small working model.

Yours truly will be there to assist in setting up and running the small prototype.

We'll be down for a week. I am due to be in Norwich on Friday 31 October, when I'll be helping to get things ready for a start on the following Monday, the 3rd November.

I hope we'll be able to meet up.

Yours Pat.

Peg wrote a reply:

Dear Pat,

Great to hear you are coming to my part of the world. I am rostered to workday shifts that week, but I'll be around late afternoon and in the evening.

If you like I can put you up at my house. I've got masses of room. I'll give you a key and you can come and go as you please, I am only about 15 miles from the uni's campus. I'll not charge you for accommodation!

I'll give you a call tonight.

Regards Archie.

By the time he'd packed away his laptop it was getting on for lunchtime. He put the kettle on and made himself a mug of tea and a round of sandwiches. He switched on the radio and listened to the lunchtime news bulletin from Radio Norfolk. Same old stuff more roadworks on the city ring road, traffic accident on the A47 at the A11 junction. That'll keep the traffic policing lot busy he thought to himself. After hearing a local correspondent giving her report regarding a new development in the city, he switched the radio off. He had just finished eating when the house phone rang.

"Archie I've just got your email."

"Gosh Pat I didn't expect a response that quick, are you at home?"

"I'm at work, currently on my lunch break. I was checking my emails on my phone. As to your suggestion I use your place as a base when I come to Norwich next week that would be great. But I've a favour to ask you before that."

"Okay Pat, what can I do for you."

"Is it alright if me and Zena come down this weekend. I'm at a bit of a loose end, and I'm finishing early on tomorrow."

Pegg could scarcely hold back his excitement. What are thinking you're behaving like an excited adolescent he said to himself.

"Yes, that would be great. I should be home from early afternoon onward. You've got my address and postcode. Just feed it into your Satnav and you'll get to us."

He went on to explain his new situation, and his interview with the Super in the morning. They spoke for a further twenty minutes, until Pat had to go.

"I'll see you tomorrow then, Pat. If you get in a muddle getting here give us a buzz, and I'll come and guide you in."

"See you then Archie, 'bye."

Pegg spent the rest of the day cleaning the house and in doing so made up the bed in the one of the spare bedrooms. In view of Pat's impending visit, he decided to do some shopping, and to that end he prepared to go out this afternoon, instead of tomorrow morning, after he had seen the superintendent in Thetford. If it was going to be mild and sunny, he decided on a barbecue on the Saturday afternoon. At least that is what the weather forecast for the weekend said. Pegg phoned Angie and told her about Pat's weekend visit. He asked her if she would come over with Ross and the baby, and join them for a barbecue lunch, any time after midday. Angie eagerly accepted the invite on behalf of them all. Pegg then took Fred and drove into Dereham where he bought enough groceries to see him and his guests through the weekend. By the time he got back home again it was getting on for six. After putting away the shopping, he made himself something to eat. Having cleared away and washed up, he sat down and watched some TV. He then took Fred out for a walk around the Green. On returning to the house he decided to turn in. It was going to be a long day tomorrow. For a change Pegg was actually looking forward to the weekend.

CHAPTER 31

As an anticyclone was in control over the centre of the United Kingdom, the weather forecast had predicted a fine autumn weekend The prediction was not, when Pegg up the sunshine was streaming through the bedroom window., and in spite of a misty start it looked as if it was going to be a clear day. Pegg checked the barometer in the hall; 1028 millibars and set fair. Pegg was up, dressed and breakfasted by half past eight. He walked Fred round the Green; on his way back to the house, he called in at the shop and bought an Eastern Daily Press. Once he got back in, he changed into grey flannels, blazer with the Corps badge on the pocket, white shirt and Corps tie. At nine he drove out of the driveway, with Fred in his usual place on the front seat and headed towards Thetford.

He arrived at the police station at a quarter to nine, he drove to the barrier, enter the code on the keypad, and once the barrier opened he drove into the parking area at the back of the building. He found slot in a shaded area and left the windows open.

"Right boy, I don't know how long I'll be." he said to the poodle. He stroked the dog's ear and was rewarded with a lick to the back of his right hand. He secured the vehicle and made his way to the main building, and up the stairs. He knocked at the door of the Superintendent's Secretary's office

"PC Pegg," he said. "I've been asked to see the Super at ten o'clock"

"Come in Mr Pegg, sit down. There's someone in with him at the moment. He shan't be too long."

Pegg went in and sat down on a chair next to the secretary's desk. They exchanged small talk for the next couple of minutes. Eventually the door to the superintendent's office opened, and one of the detective sergeants (DS) walked out, he glanced into the secretary's office, and said to Pegg:

"Archie what brings you here? Nothing serious I hope?"

"I'll call in and see you before I go back to Dereham." With that the DS nodded to the secretary and went off.

The secretary got up from behind her desk, and knocked on the superintendent's office, and went in. After a minute she came out and said to Pegg:

"You can go in now, Mr Pegg."

Pegg got up and went into the office.

"Good morning, Archie how are you getting on? It must be very hard for you coping with the loss of Cath."

"Thank you sir. I'm getting there."

The superintendent looked at the open file on his desk.

"Well I'll not beat about the bush, Inspector Grimes has put in a strong recommendation that you be made up to Acting Sergeant. I have no hesitation in endorsing his recommendation. As of now you are an Acting Sergeant. So, to that end I have put your name forward for the next Sergeants Board, which will be taking place in about 3 weeks' time."

"Thank you sir. I take it that my application to continue my employment with the Constabulary has been accepted?."

"Of course, this has been fast tracked by Force Headquarters, we don't want to lose you Archie. Is there anything you want to ask me?"

"I understand I'll be taking over Mark Styles Relief at Dereham. Should I be successful on the Sergeants Board, I'd like it known that Mark Styles' post is my preferred option."

"I'll make a note of that."

For the next twenty minutes the conversation broached further into Pegg's home situation, before covering his future within the Force. Pegg thought to himself, if only folk knew how close to the wind he had sailed during his break in Notts and Derby, he would not have been having this conversation with the superintendent. The superintendents mobile rang.

"Sorry Archie I'll need to take this", he said, "hello can you wait a minute." He put the device on hold and got up walking over to Pegg's side of the desk. Pegg got up as well.

"Archie, I'm so glad that you are staying with us. Enjoy the rest of your leave, I appreciate you coming to see me. I'll see you at Dereham on my next visit."

Pegg shook hands with him and left the office, on his way out he said farewells to the secretary. He went downstairs and called in at the CID office. He spent the next half hour chatting with the DS he had met earlier. Apparently as a result of the arrests Pegg made in Whissonsett on Monday 4th October, a further five cannabis farms were identified and shut down. A number of arrests were made. The DS was sure that the illegal cultivation of cannabis had been severely curtailed within the county. Pegg said that it would not be too long before it all started up again somewhere else. The DS agreed with him. As long as people wanted to use dope, there are always those who'll supply it. After putting the world to rights, Pegg left.

He drove back to Dereham, and into the police station car park. He let Fred out of the vehicle and walked to the back door. He punched in the code on the keypad beside the door and went in. He walked towards the front office, passing the inspector's office. Grimes was not there. He walked to the report room, where he checked his pigeonhole. There were one or two bits of paper, and a jiffy bag. He checked the contents and found two sets of sergeants shoulder slides. He read through the items of paperwork. There was nothing that could not wait until Monday. He went to the sergeant's office, but it was empty as well. He called in at the front office.

Jenny was by herself, Fred was on Jenny's lap, eyes closed, and head nuzzled on her ample bosom.

"Fred you're nothing but a little tart!" The dog opened one eye and just sighed, making no attempt to vacate his comfortable situation.

"Oh Archie, can't you leave him here."

Pegg grinned, "You've got enough to do without that animal distracting you! I've got to get home now, I wonder if you could leave a message for the skipper, that I am going to take over B Relief on Monday as Acting Sergeant. It looks as if poor old Mark Styles will not be returning to work for the foreseeable future."

"Certainly, and congratulations are in order."

"Yes, but the circumstances are a bit sad. I really hope Mark gets through this."

"And so say all of us."

Pegg bade Jenny farewell, Fred reluctantly jumped down from her lap and followed Pegg out of the station. A short while later they arrived back home. He parked up and let Fred carry out a patrol of the garden. He went inside and put his things away, after which he made himself a sandwich and a mug of tea. He went into the living room and switched on the television. He tuned into the News Channel. His attention was drawn to the red news feed at the bottom of the screen.

Breaking News: Ministry of Defence to shut down Balkans War Investigation Team....amid claims of corruption and criminal activity.

Pegg was astounded, he punched the air, "Yes!" he shouted. The sound caused Fred to come running back into the house, barking furiously.

"It's okay boy, settle down," he said to the agitated animal. The dog jumped onto Pegg's lap and lay down.

There were no further details on the news feed, it just kept repeating the message. Pegg remained watching the programme, hoping that eventually a more detailed report regarding this item. Eventually his patience was rewarded; the anchorman said

"Now we have some breaking news, the Ministry of Defence has issued a press release regarding the Balkans War Investigation Team. I'll read the details:

"As a result of evidence uncovered by the Ministry of Defence and the Nottinghamshire Police Forces. A number of people have been arrested and charged with offences relating to misconduct in public office, false accounting, fraud, and theft."

There are no further details at this time. As soon as we do get more to this story we'll bring it to you. Now for some sports news......."

Pegg switched the TV off. He read the paper he had bought previously. Thirty minutes later the phone rang.

"Hi Archie, I'm about thirty minutes away from you, I've pulled over to get some fuel. It's a BP station, co-located with a Macdonald's Drive-Thru, near Swaffham."

"You're about ten miles from us. Keep going on the Norwich bound A47, and as you approach Dereham pick up the signs for the "Gressenhall Workhouse Museum." As you enter Beetley follow the sign to Gressenhall village. Give me a call when you get to the village shop, and I'll come and guide you in."

"I'll do that 'bye."

Pegg cleared up the detritus from his light meal. He went outside and opened the driveway gates. He then moved the Landrover, to a position directly in front of the 'van. He had left Fred inside the house. He wandered around the front of the house and picked up a few weeds from the flower bed. Twenty minutes later his phone rang. He wandered out of the gate and saw Pat's X-Trial parked at the side of the village store.

He waved, and the X-Trail moved off towards Pegg. Pat drove into Pegg's driveway and parked up beside the Landrover and caravan. Pegg closed the gates, and by the time he got to Pat's car she was already out. She flung her arms around Pegg's neck and hugged him.

"Oh Archie," she gasped, "I'm so glad you invited me to come." She stood on her toes and kissed him fully on the mouth. They held the embrace until the barking of Zena from the back of the X-Trail caused Pat to release him. She went to the back of the vehicle and opened the tail gate, whereupon the dog jumped out and greeted Pegg, after which she went into the back garden. Pat retrieved a wheeled suitcase, Pegg took it and went to the back door, on opening it, an excited Fred ran out and after a brief sniff at Pat ran out to the garden and joined Zena. After the usual canine method of introductions, the two animals started to engage in a game of chase.

Pegg said:

"We'll leave them to it, he shut the back door. Come on, I'll show you your room, and the facilities."

He carried the suitcase upstairs, and into the spare bedroom After placing the suitcase beside the bed. He showed her the wardrobe where he had cleared a space, and the bathroom.

"I'll let you unpack, do you want a cup of tea or something stronger?"

"It's a bit early for me, a cup of tea will be fine."

As Pegg was about to leave she said:

"Archie wait. There's something I want to tell you. Since I left you on Monday morning, I've had you on my mind all the time. I know that we have not been acquainted for very long, I have already got deep feelings for you."

Pegg said nothing. He just stood there looking down at the floor. Eventually he said:

"If I'm honest with myself, Pat, I feel the same. Right you unpack and freshen up while I go and make that cup of tea. I'll see you downstairs."

Pegg left her and descended the stairs. He went into the kitchen and heard scrabbling at the door. He went and let the two dogs in. He had kept the kitchen door closed.

"Right you chaps settle down whilst I make Pat and me some tea."

The dogs made themselves comfortable on Fred's bed. Pegg busied himself in preparing the tea. He glanced the clock on the cooker, it was three thwenty-five. He continued with the job in hand, and ten minutes later he had a pot of tea, two cups, milk, sugar bowl and a plate of biscuits laid out on the table in the kitchen's dining annex. He heard a tap on the other side of the kitchen door. Pat came in. Both dogs exited Fred's bed and went over to greet her. She patted each animal's head and walked over to the annex. Pegg indicated a seat and she sat down. He poured each of them a cup of tea. Pat helped herself to milk and sugar, Pegg just added sugar to his cup. He passed her the plate of biscuits and she took one.

"All unpacked and kit stowed away?" he asked.

"Yes thanks, all done." She sipped her tea and munched on a biscuit.

"Great. We'll dine in tonight, unless you'd rather go and eat out. I am not a bad cook. I've got the stuff in, but if you want to go out, we can have it some other time. I've got some lamb cutlets."

"Mmm sounds perfect. Now tell me what's happened since we last spoke on the phone."

Pegg explained what had been decided regarding continuing in the police. He described the circumstances which led to his new job as an acting sergeant at Dereham, before telling her about his going before a sergeants promotion board. He went on to say that he would like to have a permanent post in Dereham, as a shift sergeant.

"Have you thought of going to CID or any other department?"

"I have done a couple of stints as a temporary detective constable (DC). At the time there were some major enquiries going on, and the guvnors decided to throw some more detectives at them. I can't say I enjoyed it but, being the Good Soldier Pegg, I did my best.

'Don't get me wrong the CID guys do a great job, and we'd be in a right muddle if we did not have them. I am a hands-on copper, and I feel being a uniformed bobby I am closer on the ground to where the action is. Uniformed officers still nick criminals and solve cases. I've had my fair share of theft and assault cases where I've investigated and processed suspects, and got them to court, without a CID officer in sight. When you are a rural beat officer, you enjoy a degree of independence. Some of the more serious crimes which require specialist knowledge, then CID would be very much involved as they have the resources to carry out more detailed and deeper investigations.

"But if you are a sergeant won't that mean that you are stuck behind a desk and not out on the street?"

"That's a good point, Pat. Yes, I would be tied up to a certain extent, after all I would be supervising some eight or so constables. But I'm not one for letting my in-tray dominate my life! There will still be time for me to get out and about. And now we have these Police Investigation Centres, there is no chance of me being tied up in the role of custody sergeant.

"Police Investigation Centres?

"Yes, we've got three of them in Norfolk. Wymondham, King's Lynn and Great Yarmouth. They are basically a one stop shop. After a suspect is arrested, he or she is taken to one of these centres, where they are booked in, processed and interviewed. If there is evidence to charge them. They are charged and bailed to a magistrates court. In more in serious cases the suspect would remain in custody and put before a court. If there are decisions to be made regarding charging, or further inquiries need to be done, then the suspect would be bailed to return at a future date.'

"Previously all the main police stations in Norfolk would have had a custody suite, which meant that a custody officer at each of these stations. It was quite handy for local officers when making arrests, to bring their prisoners to their nearest police station. But the downside was that if the prisoner had health issues or was vulnerable, that is to say a juvenile or someone with learning difficulties, then there would be the problems of getting a clinician in, or an appropriate adult to attend the prisoner. With the Police Investigation Centres, it means that these facilities are on hand, and the whole system is much more streamlined."

"I never realised that arresting people was so involved," said Pat.

"Well we are guided by the Police and Criminal Evidence Act or PACE as it is known. Coppers will whinge about it being a pain in the neck, but really its procedures are just as much a protection for us as it is for the detainee. I've always stuck by it when I have made official arrests. When your case goes to court you know you have done everything by the book. And it's not so easy for a wily defence solicitor or barrister to get their clients acquitted on a technicality. I've still lost cases but they were not due any failure on my part in not sticking to the correct procedures.'

"Well I think that's enough of me going on about detention, custody procedures and court cases. I think we'll take the dogs for a walk, are you up for that Pat?"

"Absolutely, do I need to change at all?"

"No, we'll do a pavement walk, just put on a pair of working shoes."

Ten minutes later they and the dogs were walking up Bittering Street. Their route took them from Bittering Street and on to Common Drift, and into Beetley where they walked along Fakenham Road. With the exception of Common Drift, the animals remained on their respective leashes. They continued on Fakenham Road until they turned right into Litcham Road and back to Gressenhall. As they walked past the Gressenhall Museum and Workhouse. Pat asked about the building.

"Well it really was a workhouse, or house of industry as they liked to call it. Workhouses came about as a result of the Poor Laws. The Good Old Days were quite frankly pretty awful if you were destitute. Each parish was responsible for the poor of the parish. People who had no work or abode were committed to the workhouse, where in exchange for food and accommodation, they were required to work, they were not paid, the "full board" was the wages. If you've read Oliver Twist, there is a good account of what life within the workhouse was like."

"Yes, read it, seen the film and the musical. Not very nice for the inmates." said Pat

"Well this actual establishment ceased to be a workhouse at the end of the 19th century. It became a place where agricultural workers went after they became too old to continue working on the land. Many of them were in tied houses, that went with the job. The farmer would have needed the housing for replacement workers. What was so awful was those workers with wives had to live separately from their spouses. They were accommodated in dormitories."

"The establishment was closed in the 60s, and it was not until the end of that decade, some people, mainly locals, got the idea of opening the place up as a Rural Life Museum. This is what happened, and it took off. It developed into what it is today, although it is known as the Gressenhall Workhouse and Museum. Next time I'll take you round. There is a lot to see, and they have events throughout the year."

"I'd really like that." she said.

A bit later they were back at the house again. After taking off their jackets and shoes, and toweling down the dogs, they went into the living room. Pegg said:

"The plan tomorrow is that I'll be doing a barbecue here. Angie, Ross and the baby, Catherine Rose will be coming. The baby is very fond of Fred, and as a result she has no fear of dogs. Will she be alright with Zena?"

"She is fine, I have taken her to friends' houses, and she is very popular with the children. Even when toddlers pull her about, she does not mind them. If it gets too much she tends to retreat and find somewhere to get some peace."

"Catherine Rose is very gentle with Fred, so if Zena is the same, I can see there being no problems."

"Archie, can I say something?"

"Of course, what is it?"

"How will Angie react to me being part of your life? I don't want to be seen as usurping Cath's memory. I am a bit anxious to say the least."

"You want the honest truth?"

"Yes."

"First I've told her that we are good friends I have not said that we are an item. She is comfortable that I have met someone, and quite frankly she is looking forward to meeting you. So, wind your neck in my girl, it'll be just fine."

"Oh, you are such a sweetie," she said as she went over to him and put her arms round him.

They stayed like that until Pegg said:

"Right I've got to start prepping some food, otherwise we'll not be eating tonight."

"Is there anything I can do?"

"I think I am okay, why don't you go and sit down and chill, once I've got things going I'll come and join you."

Pegg spent the next twenty minutes or so preparing their meal, by which time the vegetables and potatoes, were in their respective saucepans and the lamb cutlets were seasoned and ready to go into the grill oven. He had a lamb gravy mix which he whisked up and place in a small saucepan as well. Having done that, he laid the table. He went to the garage and fetched a bottle of wine which he put in the fridge.

He put his head round the door to the living room and said:

"We'll eat at about seven I'll get it started now, and then I'll sit down. Do you fancy a drink, I've got some wine to go with the meal, it should be nice and chilled?"

Pat was sitting in the armchair reading the paper:

"I'll wait until we eat, thanks," she said.

Pegg went back into the kitchen and put the saucepans on the cooker and switched the hotplates on. He placed the lamb cutlets on a roasting dish and put it in the grill oven. After switching it on and setting the timer he went and joined Pat in the living room.

"As I've already told you the plan for tomorrow is that we chill in the morning. I've got everything in; no need to go out and do any shopping."

"What time are Angie and her family coming?"

"I've said anytime from midday onward. I expect that I'll start cooking at about one o' clock. There are one or two things I need to get done before they come, making some salad stuff up and so on."

They talked for a bit, the conversation was only interrupted when Pegg went into the kitchen to check the food. They were halfway through discussing Pat's impending symposium at the UEA, when the alarm sounded on the cooker.

"Right time to eat," Pegg said, getting up and going to the kitchen. Pat followed, saying

"What can I do?"

"Take the wine out of the fridge and sit yourself down."

Pat did that and took her place at the table. Pegg removed the meat from the oven and put it on a serving plate. After draining off the vegetables and potatoes, he dished them into serving bowls which he then put on the table.

Pat filled their glasses, raising hers she said:

"Here's to a great weekend."

"I'll drink to that!"

They ate. Pat complimented him on his culinary skills.

"It's nice to be able to cook for someone, one gets a bit bored just eating alone. It's a shame really I do enjoy cooking. When Cath was alive I did a fair bit of the cooking, and before we were together as single man, I had to do it anyway."

"Where did you learn to cook?"

"I picked it up in the army really. In spite of all the tales you hear, army cooks are not that bad. At the beginning of my career in the army, I did a spell in the cookhouse. The sergeant in charge of the cookhouse was a bit of a tyrant but he taught me a lot. My love of cooking stayed with me ever since. At one point I was thinking of transferring to the Army Catering Corps. But I never went through with it, so I continued as a sapper."

When they had eaten and cleared up, they returned to the sitting room. They talked and discussed their respective futures. Eventually Pat said:

"Archie, thanks for a great evening, I'm glad we stayed in. But now I think I'll turn in."

"I was thinking of doing the same."

"I think I'll take a shower, that OK?"

"Of course, there's everything you need in the bathroom. I hardly ever use it, as I've got an en suite. Whilst you're doing that I'll let the dogs out in the garden and shut up shop."

Pegg went and let the dogs out. He switched on the outside light. It was a clear night again, there was a bit of a chill in the air. The area of high pressure still dominated the weather and tomorrow promised to be a dry and sunny day. He wandered to the front of the house and checked the driveway gate. There were a myriad of stars. Like many of the villages in Norfolk, there was no street lighting in Gressenhall, which meant there was very little light pollution at night. The view of the endless constellations never ceased to amaze him. Pegg saw that the dogs were still wandering around the garden, he decided to leave them there and went back into the house again.

Pegg again took stock at what had been achieved since he had become involved in Tony Spratt's predicament. "It's all coming together," he thought. The one thing which still niggled him was the whereabouts of Hoskins. He had not yet been detained; he was clearly implicated in this whole business, and in being so, he had some serious questions to answer. And now it would seem he's on the lookout for Pegg. Pegg wondered if Hoskins had been listed as wanted by the police. He would have thought that if Mehmet Ali and Gavin Henderson are already under investigation surely Hoskins must be a person of interest. He would check the Police National

Computer (PNC) when he went back to work on Monday. He would also contact Raymond Walker again to see if the police have spoken to him. His thoughts were interrupted by the sound of Fred barking. Pegg made his way to the back door, and on opening it, found Fred and Zena standing outside.

"Right you guys let's get you settled down for the night." After letting the dogs in, he found an extra rug for Zena and placed it down on the floor next to Fred's bed. Fred climbed into his bed, and instead of lying down on the blanket, Zena joined Fred on his bed. Fortunately, the bed was big enough to accommodate both animals. Pegg shrugged his shoulders, and after turning off the outside light and locking the back door, he said, "Goodnight you two, see you in the morning."

There was no reaction from the poodle, he was already snoring. Zena looked at Pegg, and then sighed and rested her head on Fred's back. Pegg left a small worktop lamp on but switched the rest of the kitchen lights off. He went upstairs and into his bedroom. There was a knock on the door.

"Can I come in?"

"Of course."

Pat entered the bedroom, she was wearing a dressing gown, and had a towel draped round her head.

"Have you got a hair-drier I can burrow, I forgot to pack mine."

"Of course." He went and to the dressing table, and gave her the device. "The dogs are settled, and I was just getting ready for bed."

"That's fine I'll just dry my hair, and I'll give this back."

"No that's fine hold on to it for now."

"Well I'll wish you goodnight then," she kissed him fully on the mouth and left the room.

Pegg remained where he was for a minute and then undressed, he went to the en suite and had a quick shower. After finishing off, he got into bed, as was his habit he slept without pajamas. He turned off the bedside light and lay awake for a bit before he dosed off.

He was woken by the sound of the bedroom door opening.

"Is that you Pat, what's wrong."

"Nothing's wrong come on move over this girl's getting cold."

She slid into the bed beside him. He gasped as he realised she had nothing on. She snuggled up beside him. He smelt her hair and her skin, they had a faint aroma from the soap and shampoo.

"Oh, Archie you've got no jimjams on!"

"Makes two of us then you wicked girl!," he said.

She snuggled up to him and then ran her hands over his chest and down along his body. Pegg gasped as she took hold of him. She gently massaged him. Pegg moaned and kissed her. He stroked her flank and caressed her breasts. She kissed him and pulled him on top of her. They were passionate in their lovemaking, after which they laid in each other's arms utterly spent. They fell asleep, their bodies entwined as one, and slumbered on and on.

CHAPTER 32

Pat woke first, she was leaning on her elbow and looking down at Pegg's prone body, she caressed the side of his face with her index finger. Pegg opened his eyes, she kissed him on the mouth. He returned the kiss and they made love once again. Afterwards they lay back, Pegg looked at the bedside clock.

"Gosh it's nearly eight, I need to let the dogs out. Do you fancy a cup of tea?"

"No Archie, I need to get myself sorted out. I left my dressing gown in the spare bedroom."

"I'll get it for you."

"No need I'll go myself," with that she got up and made her way out of the bedroom. Pegg looked on appreciatively at her athletically honed body. She was beautiful, clever and intelligent and seemingly a good friend, what more could he want. He went downstairs and let the dogs out. He sat down at the kitchen dining table and thought. He had a slight pang of guilt. He was involved with another woman, and Cath had only been gone six months. But in view of what Angie had told him regarding finding someone else, he felt easier. The scrabbling at the door brought Pegg thoughts to the present. He let the dogs in. Fred went to the water bowl and Zena stared anxiously at the closed door to the living room. She whined.

"Don't worry girl, Pat's upstairs she'll be down soon."

Pegg laid the table for breakfast.

"Right guys I'm off upstairs to get shaved and dressed. I'll be down soon, behave yourselves."

Pegg left the dogs and went upstairs. He washed and shaved and got himself dressed. He decided to wear jeans and a sweatshirt. He knocked on the spare bedroom's door.

"Come in Archie, Pat said.

She was sitting at the dressing table, in her dressing gown.

"I'm doing breakfast, as we'll be having a "barby" lunchtime, I thought we'd just have cereals, toast and boiled eggs. Will that be okay?"

"Great."

"Tea or coffee, I am having coffee."

"Same for me please."

Pegg went downstairs again and started on the breakfast. He'd just finished boiling the eggs, and was putting them into egg cups, when Pat appeared. She was wearing a pair of red corduroy slacks and a lightweight jersey, her hair was done up in a ponytail. Zena came and greeted her whimpering and then barking. Pat settled her down and then came behind Pegg and put her arms around his waist. She whispered in his ear:

"I fancy a re-run of last night."

Pegg turned around and kissed her on the forehead.

"Come on you naughty girl, our bodies we need some fuel so let's at least have some breakfast first!"

They sat down and ate the breakfast that Pegg had prepared. Afterwards Pegg outlined the plans for the rest of the day. He had a bit of preparation to do beforehand.

"What would you like me to do."

"I've got some salad stuff in, can you prep it? I mean cutting up toms, cucumber, peppers that sort of thing?"

"Of course, I can do that."

"I've got to sort out the grill, I've got to take a gas bottle out of the 'van. There are some baking potatoes, which I'll do. I cheat on those, by precooking them in the microwave, and then browning them on the grill."

Pegg looked at his watch:

"It's a least a couple of hours before Angie and co arrive, so let's take the dogs for walk, and then that's their exercise sorted out for the day."

They got their things together and after putting the dogs on their leases, walked out onto Litcham Road and down Bridge Street. Pegg took them on a route of about three miles, which brought them back to the house. There was quite a bit of open country, with no livestock, so the dogs could run free. The morning was getting warm, and the sun was shining, there was some cloud but very little wind. Pegg and Pat walked arm in arm. He had not felt so happy and content in a long time. It looked as if it was the perfect day to be eating Al Fresco. After they got back they set about their allotted jobs. Just as they had finished, Ross' car pulled through the gates and parked up in front of Pat's X-Trail. Pegg and Pat came out to meet them.

First out of the car was Angie. She went over to them. Pegg introduced her to Pat. Pat held her hand out, but instead of taking it, Angie embraced her and kissed her. She released her and gave Pegg a kiss on the cheek, she whispered in his ear:

"Where did you find her, she's gorgeous." Pegg blushed and said nothing.

Angie took Pat by the hand and led her to the car where Ross was unbuckling Catherine Rose from her car seat. When Ross had extricated the child, Angie took her whilst Ross went to the back of the car and started to take stuff out. Pegg went and gave him a hand. After they had carried all the items into the house. He went to see what the women were up to. By this time Catherine Rose was in Pat's arms and being introduced to Zena. The baby squealed, as the shepherd licked her tiny hand. Pat remarked to Angie that the child had no fear of dogs. Angie explained that Fred had been around since the day she was born; both child and dog had developed a very close bond between them.

They all went inside. The women sat down in the sitting room, and Catherine Rose toddled about from piece of furniture to piece of furniture. Pegg and Ross sorted out tables and chairs for their Al Fresco meal, Pegg had also retrieved a child's highchair from the garage.

"Right Ross, can you sort the girls out with drinks, not forgetting yourself of course. There's beer and wine in the 'fridge."

"Right Archie, can I get you something?"

"Not now thanks, I'll have a beer later, I need to get the food going."

Ross went back inside, and Pegg started to get things going. He lit the gas barbecue grill. He wrapped up the precooked potatoes in foil and placed them on the corner of the grill. He followed this by laying out plates, cutlery, and the bowls of salad that Pat had prepared. He fetched the burgers, sausages, chicken pieces out of the 'fridge, and after donning an apron, proceeded to start cooking. The two dogs at this point had decided to join Pegg and both of them were sat and looking longingly at Pegg, as he started to cook.

Forty minutes later they were all sat down and eating. Pegg was sitting beside Catherine Rose, who was ensconced in the highchair. He was spooning mashed baked potato sausage and beans into her mouth. Ross was sitting on the other side of her. Pat and Angie were seated beside each other. They were chatting animatedly between mouthfuls of food. It was almost to the exclusion of the others.

After they had finished their meal, Pegg lifted the baby out of the highchair. He sniffed the child and said:

"Angie, madam needs changing. I'll pop upstairs and get it done."

He went upstairs, gathering up the kit to carry out the task in hand. The others cleared the table and put the uneaten food away. By the time Pegg had brought the baby back down again. Pat was washing the more heavily soiled pots, Ross was packing away the grill, having wiped it down, and Angie was stacking the crockery and cutlery into the dishwasher. They spent the rest of the afternoon sitting out in the garden. Pegg served up coffee and a plate of pastries. As the light was starting to go, they moved indoors. It was six o'clock when Angie and Ross got up and started to get their things together.

"Thank you Archie for a great afternoon. Pat I'm so pleased we met, and next time you come down I'm inviting you up to ours. We've got each other's telephone and emails, so let's stay in touch."

"I'll second that Angie."

The two women embraced and kissed. Ross said his farewell.

"When you are in Norwich maybe you can come and view our engineering facility at Norwich Airport, Pat"

"I'd really like that."

Angie took Pegg to one side:

"Archie whichever way your friendship with Pat develops, I am comfortable with it, from what I've seen of her, and having spoken to her, she is a good person, and I would value her friendship. I am happy for you." She kissed him and gave him a hug.

Ross strapped the now sleeping Catherine Rose into her baby seat, and after a final farewell Ross and Angie drove out of the driveway and back home to Swaffham. Pegg closed the driveway gates and joined Pat. She said:

"I'm so pleased that you introduced me to Angie and her small family. I must admit that I was nervous at meeting them, but Angie is such a sweet girl, I feel that I have known her all my life. We have a lot in common. Ross is a good man, and the little girl is a poppet."

"I was nervous too, in case we'd be walking on eggshells all afternoon! In the end it turned out not to be the case and things seemed to gel in a positive way. They are the only family I've got now, and they are very precious to me. And with you being with me, well that's the icing on the cake."

"Oh Archie, you say the nicest things!"

They went inside. Pegg suggested that they take the dogs for a wander around the Green. By the time they returned to the house, darkness had fallen. They went into the sitting room and Pegg poured Pat a glass of wine, whilst he poured himself a glass of beer. They sat on the sofa. Pat snuggled up to Pegg and he put his arm around her shoulder, she rested her head on his chest.

"Tomorrow I thought that we could have some lunch out. We could go to the King's Head in North Elmham, or I could do us something here. I don't know when you have to be back."

"I need to be home before too late as I've got to be at work for eight o'clock on Monday. So, can't we have some lunch here?"

"No that's fine, I've got to be in for the early shift at eight as well. I'll rustle up something, there's still salad stuff from today, and I think there's some chops in the freezer."

"Perfect!"

They spent the rest of the evening talking. It was half past ten when Pegg said:

"Well I'm ready to turn in, how about you my girl?"

"That sounds like a plan to me," she said giving Pegg a mischievous wink.

"You go on up and I'll sort the hounds out."

He went to the back door and let the dogs out. He shut the door behind him and went outside, wandering into the garden. It was a cold and clear night again, there could be bit of frost. It would at least be fine weather in the morning. He reflected on how the day had panned out, he was more than content with the ways things had gone. His concerns regarding how Angie would react to Pat proved to be entirely groundless. He went back in and waited in the kitchen for the dogs. He checked the water bowl; it was half empty. He rinsed it out and refilled it. Zena came in first, she went to her rug and settled down. A couple of minutes later Fred appeared, and without further ado entered his bed. Pegg shut and locked the back door. He turned to where the dogs were:

"Good night guys, sleep well."

He turned off the main lights leaving the worktop lamp on, as he had done the previous evening. He went his bedroom, where Pat was already in bed. The only illumination came from the one bedside lamp on her side of the bed. Pegg undressed and slipped on his dressing gown, before going into the en suite. After he had finished he slipped off the dressing gown and joined Pat. She turned off the light. They made love, rested and made love again, after which they fell into a deep sleep.

CHAPTER 33

As Pegg had predicted it was a bright frosty morning, the sun rising into a cloudless sky. After a long lie in, Pegg and Pat ate a full English breakfast. They then drove out Foxley Woods, where they went for a long walk, with the dogs. They got back to the house at one. Pegg made them lunch, after which Pat packed her things, by half past two she was ready to leave.

"Well I'll see you on Friday then, Pat. Here's a spare key so that you can let yourself in. I'm scheduled to work an eight til four shift, but the nature of the job means that I can't guarantee being home on time after work."

"That's fine our team will be leaving Sheffield mid-morning. After arriving at Norwich there are a few things to do, and we'll be setting the kit up over the weekend ready for a Monday start. So, looks like it'll only be the evenings that I'll be back."

"Well I'll be on day shift all week, having rest days on Monday and Tuesday. So, we'll still see a bit of each other."

"Thanks for a wonderful weekend, it was so nice to meet your family, especially Angie. I'll look forward to seeing them again."

They embraced and kissed after which Pegg loaded her bags into the X-Trail and let Zena into the back as well.

"Drive carefully and let me know when you're safely home."

"I'll do that."

She got into the vehicle and with a wave to Pegg she drove out of the driveway. Pegg did not close the gates, as he had decided to drive to the Police Station. It was his intention to familiarise himself with the current operational situation in Dereham and the surrounding patrol areas. In doing so he would be ready to lead his shift in the morning.

"Come on Fred let's go for a drive," he opened the passenger door of the Landrover, and the poodle jumped up onto the passenger seat. He went back into the house and fetched the vehicle's key, locked up and drove off, having closed the driveway gates on the way out. Fifteen minutes later he was in the police station. The station seemed deserted, he went to the sergeants office, nobody in. He wandered into the constables' report room. There was a young probationer sat down doing some paperwork. Pegg asked her where everybody was. She informed him that there had been a "polac", which is police parlance for any collision involving a police vehicle. It had transpired an agricultural vehicle had collided with one of the local patrol vehicles, fortunately nobody was hurt. This incident reminded Pegg that it is the job of an officer's immediate supervisor to investigate any collision involving his or her vehicle. Umm that was something to look forward to, he thought. At least this incident will be done and dusted before he starts in the morning.

He went and checked his pigeonhole, only to find it had been moved. Ah he thought, sergeants' office. He made his way there and sure enough there it was, only this time the "PC 443 PEGG" label had been replaced with "A/SGT PEGG". He checked through its contents, apart from a couple of crime files to be signed off by the shift sergeant, there was nothing important for him. After sitting down at one of the desks, he logged into the Force's Intranet system. He checked his emails; there was nothing much to note and he deleted most of them, except some notifications regarding his Sergeants Promotion Board. He next went into the PNC System. He entered Hoskins details and did a search.

"Gotcha," he said to himself. Hoskins was listed as wanted and as a person of interest by Ministry of Defence Police. He was to be arrested on sight for offences of Misconduct in Public Office and under the Official Secrets Act. Hoskins whereabouts are unknown, he has contacts in Manchester, and throughout the North of England and Scotland. Pegg noted the details on a sheet of paper and put it in his pigeonhole.

Pegg recalled that Hoskins was in a relationship with a drug dealer's sister. He needed to get her details. That could wait until the morning He looked at his watch, coming up to four o'clock, the late shift were coming in. Their sergeant came into the office. She congratulated Pegg on his new appointment Pegged thanked her and went onto explain the day sergeant's absence. She gave Pegg a look as if to say, "There but for the Grace of God....". Pegg bade her farewell and made his way out of the Station and back to his Landrover. Fifteen minutes later he was back home.

He decided to do some housework, starting with the upstairs. He smiled to himself as he went into the spare bedroom. The bed was still made, it had not been slept in. Pat had not left anything behind, except an envelope on one of the pillows.

Pegg went over and opened it. There was a card inside; on the front of the card was a cartoon of a black poodle with a grin on its face. The inside contained a written message:

> *Dearest Archie & Fred! Thank you so much for having us. Pat is looking forward to seeing you again on Friday. Zena will be staying with Pat's Mum and Dad this time.*
>
> *Take care of yourselves*
> *With all our love*
> *Pat & Zena*

Pegg put the card back in the envelope and put it on the dressing table. He continued with cleaning the upstairs, finishing off with the vacuum cleaner. He repeated the operation downstairs. After putting the cleaning stuff away, he sat down. He thought about tomorrow, he would have his own shift now; himself and five constables. At least that's what he thought there would be, unless someone phones in sick. He had checked the roster, and none of them was on leave or on a course. The responsibility of being a shift supervisor did not bother him, after all he had managed a troop of nearly forty sappers when he was a staff sergeant in the Royal Engineers. No, what concerned him was his ability to motivate his constables. Three of them had just finished their two-year probationary period. Pegg regarded this as an advantage, as these officers were at the beginning of their careers, and therefore they would be keen to demonstrate what they were made of. The other two were four and five years respectively into their service. Sometimes officers with more service under their belts could be set in their ways, and therefore not willing to take new ideas on board. Pegg could empathise with this line of thinking, as he himself had taken the same attitude. But he had come to the conclusion that policing was an occupation which was continually evolving. In the end Pegg had taken the position there was a lot of good in the old ways and a lot of bad as well, so it was common sense to retain the best of the old and integrate it with the best of the new. In other words, one can't beat the system, but one can adopt the system to one's own way of thinking. He decided he was going to throw his heart and soul into his new post.

The telephone rang. It was Pat informing him that she was home. They talked for another 20 minutes, going over the weekend, and confirming the arrangements for Pat's arrival on Friday. When he had finished he put the receiver back on its base unit.

Later he made himself some supper and after getting his uniform ready for the morning, decided to have an early night. He'd arranged for a neighbour to have Fred in the morning. She did a dog sitting service, which Pegg used when Angie could not have him, or when it was not feasible for Pegg to take him into work. After letting Fred out, and settling him down for the night, he went upstairs, and after a shower, went to bed. He slept well that night.

CHAPTER 34

P egg got into work at seven-thirty. He went to the sergeants'
office and got briefed by the night shift sergeant. It had
been a quiet night. There had been a couple of road traffic
collisions (RTCs) early that morning. Each incident had involved
a single vehicle, apart from damage to the vehicles involved, there
were no injuries to the drivers or passengers. There were a couple
of vehicles broken into, the thefts took place in Dereham. One of
the night cars had arrested a suspect, who was currently at the
Wymondham Police Investigation Centre. The officers involved had
submitted their paperwork, and the suspect would be seen by the
interviewing team later this morning. There was nothing to hand on.
Pegg then read through the briefing notes on the Intranet System.
He printed them off and added them to his millboard.

He went to the briefing room. All the 5 officers were waiting for
him. He looked at his watch, it was nearly eight o'clock. He thought
to himself that this was a good start, they are here, there was even
a mug of tea for him. As everyone knew each other there was no
need for introductions. He proceeded with the briefing, starting with
what had occurred overnight. He then went through the contents of
the briefing notes. By half an hour later Pegg had finished and the
officers left. Pegg went back into the sergeants office.

He did some research on the intelligence system. He was
looking for the name of the drug dealer whose sister, it was alleged
had been a girlfriend of Richard Hoskins. He found her details.
She was Lorraine Sharp, and she lived in Sporle, this was the

only address in the system. The whereabouts of Hoskins was not currently known. The address needed checking out. He Googled the address and brought up a Google Earth image of the property and its immediate surrounding area. The property was a detached house located at North End, which was near the junction with Southacre Road. It was set back from the road, and there was what appeared to be a hedge and trees to its front. Pegg printed the Google Earth image off, next he viewed it on Street View. There was indeed a quite high hedge and a couple of beech trees as well. He moved the image further and got a reasonable view of the driveway and entrance to the house. He printed off two Street View images of the property as viewed from the road.

He decided it was time to check the property out. He asked if he could borrow a plain car. The DS in CID was amenable to letting one of the cars go for an hour or so. Pegg got the key to the vehicle and went into the constables' report room. There was one of the newly qualified former probationers working on a file.

"Terri, I would like you to come and help me to check out an address in Sporle. You okay with that?"

"Yes sarge, just catching up with a file", she said.

"Great, grab your gear, can you put on a civvy jacket, we're using an unmarked car."

Terri Wilder was 25, and had joined the Norfolk Constabulary, 3 years previously. She had worked in retail, her last job being in a clothes shop in Norwich. She was about five feet seven inches tall, slim and of an athletic build. She had earned a reputation of being a good thief taker, and she was certainly no shrinking violet. They walked out to where the CID car was parked, both donned civilian tops, Wilder wore a fleece, and Pegg wore his Barbour. Pegg gave her the keys to the car. They drove out of the station and onto the A47. Twenty minutes later they turned off and headed north into Sporle village. The main road was called the Street, and their destination was at the other end of the village. As they approached the address, Wilder slowed the vehicle down. Pegg glanced into the entrance. There were two cars parked on the driveway. One was a blue Renault and parked behind it nearest to the road was a nearly new Silver BMW 3 Series. Pegg noted the registration numbers of both vehicles. He told Wilder to drive to the junction with North End and Southacre Road. When she got there, she pulled over and Pegg checked the car numbers through the dashboard mounted computer.

The blue Renault was registered to Lorraine Sharp at her Sporle address. The BMW was a hire car, registered to a hire company in Salford, Greater Manchester. This information immediately sent alarm bells ringing. Manchester was Hoskins' home turf.

"Right Terri I think it's game on. There is a strong possibility that our man, Hoskins, who is wanted on warrant by the MoD Police, is at this address. I am going to get one of our cars to back us up."

He called up one of the remaining four officers on the shift. The officer was about five minutes away in Swaffham. Pegg gave the officer, Pc Greg Knight, directions where to join them. He also told the officer to approach along the Southacre Road and not to drive up through the village. Too many marked police cars could spook their quarry.

When Knight arrived Pegg briefed the two of them as to how he wanted the visit to the address carried out. He wanted Knight to go to the front door and Wilder to go around the back of the house, he used the pictures he had previously printed off to assist him in the short briefing.

"I am going to hang back as I want you guys to do the arresting if Hoskins is there. But I will be able to ID Hoskins for you. Now there is not much intel about this suspect, as far as I know he has no markers for violence, he has not even got a CRO Number. He is I'm ashamed to say a former Norfolk police officer. He knows the system, so we have got to make the arrest completely by the book. Any questions?"

Wilder and Knight shook their heads and said nothing

"Right guys, let's do it."

They returned to the address, Wilder parked their vehicle on the road adjacent to the hedge, they both got out, and removed their civilian tops, meanwhile Knight parked his car immediately behind the silver BMW completely blocking off access onto the road. Knight went to the front door whilst Wilder went around the back. Pegg waited by the nearside of the blue Renault.

Knight knocked and waited. Nothing happened. He knocked harder. After a couple of minutes, the door was opened by a dark-haired woman. She was wearing a dressing gown and looked as if she had just got up. She was about thirty-five and was of a slight build. She looked disheveled, Knight 's knocking had obviously got her out of bed.

"We're looking for Richard Hoskins, is he here?" he said.

She looked startled but said nothing.

"I am informing you that he is wanted, and there is a warrant for his arrest. So, I'm asking you again is he here?"

She said nothing but tried to shut the door. Knight had his hand against it, preventing her from doing so. There was a shout from the rear of the house. Pegg ran around the side of the house, followed by Knight. They greeted by the sight of Hoskins wearing bath towel around his middle. The scene would have been comical, had it not been for the fact he had an arm round Wilder's shoulders, and was holding a kitchen knife to her throat. He was behind Wilder holding as if she was some kind of shield.

"Back off you bastards or I'll do her."

Pegg was about to say something, when Wilder went limp and slumped down as if feigning a faint. The next thing, she slipped out one of her arms and shoved her hand beneath the bath towel and up between Hoskins legs. The next thing Hoskins gasped and dropped the knife. Wilder had twisted and squeezed Hoskins' genitalia. He howled with the pain of having his testicles crushed. Wilder withdrew her hand and jumped on top of the moaning Hoskins, she turned him over and sitting astride him, took out her handcuffs and snapped them around Hoskins wrists. She leaned forward and shouted into Hoskins ear:

"Richard Hoskins you are under arrest for offences contrary to the Official Secrets Act, Misconduct in Public Office, assaulting a Police Officer with a deadly weapon, and resisting arrest. You do not have to say anything, but it may harm your defence if you fail to mention when questioned something you may rely on in court. Anything you do say will be taken down and used in evidence. Did you understand the caution?"

Hoskins moaned, "you vicious little mare."

They dragged Hoskins to his feet, to add to his woes the towel had fallen off.

"Right," Pegg said, "let's get some clothes on Mr Hoskins."

They went through the back of the house through the kitchen and into the living room. They sat Lorraine on the sofa next to the handcuffed and much subdued Hoskins. Knight retrieved some clothing for Hoskins. He was temporarily released from the 'cuffs in order to get dressed, after which the 'cuffs were put back on.

Hoskins remained silent. Pegg explained to Lorraine Sharp and Hoskins, that as Hoskins was now under arrest, the police were entitled to search the place where he had been arrested.

Sharp said, "You bastard Ritchie, you never said anything about this, you said you just wanted to stay for a couple nights before you went...."

"Shut up, you dumb bitch," shouted Hoskins.

"Don't call..."

"Enough", Pegg said.

Things went quiet. Pegg instructed Wilder and Knight to take the restrained Hoskins with them whilst they searched the house for any property belonging to Hoskins which may be evidential to the case. They had already retrieved the knife Hoskins had used. Pegg remained with Sharp, who was sobbing. Pegg found and gave her a couple of tissues.

"Ritchie never told me he was in any trouble he said he had some work problems and wanted to chill a bit with me, before going to Belgium for a break to get his head together. I really did not know anything about this other stuff. Am I in any trouble?"

"I can't tell you yet Lorraine, there are no warrants for you to be nicked. We may ask you for a statement at some stage, but apart from that, you may have been an unwilling stooge."

A while later the others returned to the living room. Wilder sat Hoskins down next to Sharp. She immediately got up and sat in one of the armchairs well away from Hoskins. She said nothing further to him or the others.

Knight was carrying a messenger bag.

"We found a number of items all of which are contained in the bag."

"Such as?"

"Passport, phones, debit and credit cards, a large wodge of cash, dollars, euros and sterling, as well as a tablet and Apple Book."

"Right you two take all that and Mr Hoskins to Wymondham and get him booked in. I'll speak to the custody officer and let them know you're on your way. Now go."

Hoskins said," I know you, you're the arsehole who interfered with the interview with that fucking Irish ex-squaddie. You never said you were the filth."

"Sticks and stones and all that Mr Hoskins; right guys get him out of my sight."

Knight and Wilder led Hoskins out of the house and placed him in the back of Knight's car, Wilder sat beside Hoskins in the back. Pegg watched them drive off. He went back to the house and spoke briefly to Sharp. He gave her his card and left. When he got to the CID car, he phoned by secure means the Custody Officer at the Wymondham Police Investigation Centre.

"Two officers are in-bound to you with one arrested on a Warrant issued by the Mod Police. They have with them property belonging to the suspect which is of evidential value. He is a flight risk. He also used a knife on the arresting officer, she is fine. The suspect came off worse. I think she will want additional charges of assault with a deadly weapon and resisting arrest adding to the suspect's rap sheet. If you have a medic on site, can you get her checked out?"

"No problem. Leave it to us."

Pegg returned to Dereham and gave the vehicle's keys to the DS. He typed a statement regarding the incidents surrounding Hoskins arrest. After saving it, printed off a copy and after signing it, faxed a copy to the Custody Office at Wymondham. He carried on reading and signing off crime files submitted by his officers. By three o'clock his tray was clear.

Wilder and Knight had got back from Wymondham. They had completed the paperwork, including their statements. Hoskins had played up the Custody Officer and tried to assault one of the Custody Assistants. He was shoved in a cell before the booking in was completed. Mod Police officers are traveling from Braintree in

Essex to interview him. Pegg asked if Wilder was okay. She said that she was fine. She went back to the crime file she was working on. She said that Hoskins may make a complaint against her. Pegg made sure that both she and Knight completed their notebooks regarding the incident, he gave them both copies of his statement. He looked at his watch it was coming up for four o'clock. The remaining members of the shift were already in. Pegg said:

"Right guys off you go I'll see you in the morning."

He went to the sergeant's office where he managed to speak to the late turn sergeant before he went to brief the late turn officers. Pegg brought him up to date with the day's events, and he handed over some notes. Pegg gathered his stuff together and made his way out to the Landover. He reflected on what had been achieved today. He was pleased with the way things had gone. The officers who assisted in the apprehension and arrest were brilliant. He was still a bit shaken by the way Hoskins had attempted to use a knife on Wilder. He should have planned for that. Still Hoskins came off worse. He drove out of the station and headed home. He was looking forward to tomorrow.

EPILOGUE

Pegg attended the Constable to Sergeants Promotion Board. He was successful and was appointed substantive sergeant taking the place of Mark Styles, who because of the seriousness of his illness was forced to take ill health retirement. Pegg continues as a Patrol Sergeant based at Dereham.

Pat Warrington spent ten days in Norfolk, living at Pegg's house and commuting daily to the UEA in Norwich. Her teams designs and working model of the cylindrical wind turbine were enthusiastically received by the UEA. However so far there have not been any request for details of the design to be implemented on a commercial basis. Her relationship with Pegg continues to develop. They visit each other on a regular basis.

Angie, Ross and Catherine Rose, continue to thrive. Angie has become close friends with Pat.

The poodle Fred continues to be Pegg's loyal companion, and is often with Pegg at work, especially night shifts. The senior management either do not know this, or if they do, they are turning a blind eye.

Richard Hoskins was found guilty of offences contrary to the Official Secrets Act, Misconduct in Public Office, Perverting the Course of Justice, Assault with a Deadly Weapon, and false accounting. He was sentenced to ten years imprisonment.

Mehmet Ali was convicted of a string of offences, including Perverting the Course of Justice, Supplying Drugs and Extortion. He is currently serving ten years in prison.

Afrim Babic now owns three car washes, he is also the owner of a small convenience store. He continues to grow his businesses. He maintains his contact with Pegg. He assists in running a drop-in centre for asylum seekers and refugees.

Tony Spratt continues with his kitchen fitting business. He has also set up a Veterans Self-Help Group, which advises serving and former Service personnel regarding potential court action regarding so-called war crimes. Rachel Gluckstein gives him support regarding legal issues.

Gavin Henderson was convicted of Misconduct in Public Office, and under the Official Secrets Act, he was sentenced to four years imprisonment

Unfortunately, there seems to be no shortage of work for Rachel and her firm. She continues to take on cases of persecuted veterans. She is currently working on Northern Ireland veterans' cases.

James Smithson was cleared of any wrongdoing. He has renamed the firm of solicitors Smithson's Law. He continues to practice in Nottingham, but not at Coronation Buildings. His firm is doing well.

Lightning Source UK Ltd.
Milton Keynes UK
UKHW040729310320
361115UK00002B/24